THE MAN WIT'   A

REDEM.

THE MAN WITH THE SILVER BERETTA

or

REDEMPTION

PAUL KELLY

NORTH
OAK

First published in Great Britain in 2023 by
North Oak

NORTH
OAK

A CIP catalogue record of this book
is available from the British Library.

ISBN
978 1 7398376 17

Typeset by Hewer Text UK Ltd, Edinburgh
Printed and bound in Great Britain by CPI Group (UK) Ltd, Croydon, CR0 4YY

Inspired by Jhon 'Popeye' Velásquez
(1962 – 2020)

AFTERMATH

Bolivia 1992

CHAPTER ONE

It was a bright, hot morning in July. Ramón wiped some sweat from his forehead and looked around in disbelief. He was under the shade of a huge kapok tree and a refreshing breeze was drifting over from a nearby river. Normally it was an idyllic setting and he managed to stay cool. Not today. It was a battle zone and he was boiling hot. Groaning men were sprawled across a large clearing and a lifeless anaconda was stretched over a bamboo pole. The whole place was a heaving mess of bodies and cartridge shells, and a piercing cry was only making matters worse.

Ramón was still in shock and trying to make sense of it all. The camp had been decimated by a couple of gringos with Uzis and he had no idea how it had happened. And it got worse. The anaconda was supposed to have swallowed the DEA agent whole; instead, a lunatic with a bowie-knife had plunged a blade through her neck.

The shrieking was growing steadily louder and breaking his concentration. It was as though a man were being tortured, and the noise finally made Ramón snap. He looked around for a suitable object to put an end to it and caught sight of a clump of bushes swaying violently; another shake and a caiman appeared, dragging a man by his leg. He was desperately kicking out with his other foot, yet despite the fight left in him, there was nothing he could do to stop his inexorable demise as each clump of grass he seized came out in his hands and every root slipped through his fingers. Eventually he disappeared down the riverbank and his shrieking came to an abrupt end. Ramón nodded and picked his way through the other bodies.

In one corner, a table was covered in starched white linen. It was relatively unscathed, other than a small line of blood dotted down the front of its tablecloth. The remains of his breakfast were still laid out and Ramón was determined to finish it. He lowered his enormous frame onto a stool and pulled over a plate of *salteñas*. It had been a disaster and he needed to find a way out of it. He still could not believe that the DEA agent had been rescued. It spelt trouble, and he knew there would be repercussions.

Ramón finished his *salteña* and threw its crust at one of the bodies. It just missed a man's head, and he reached for a *pomelo*. With a sharp knife, he slowly peeled its tough green skin into a contiguous conical sphere and placed it carefully on the table. He would have a use for it later, but first he needed to contemplate his next move. Pulling it apart, he popped a segment of the citrus fruit into his mouth and began to formulate a plan to extricate himself from the mess he was in.

An hour later he was gripping the tiller of an outboard motor, guiding his boat down a small tributary on his way to the Rio Beni. As he turned a corner, a partly submerged bamboo cage appeared and he let the engine idle as he steered the boat slowly past. Inside, the skeletal remains of a man were hanging, stripped of flesh by a shoal of red-bellied piranhas. He nodded in approval, gave a mock salute to his victim and popped open a small box. Inside, the lush green *pomelo* rind had been carefully placed, almost reverently, coiled like a spring ready to jump. Gently lifting it, he unwound the brilliant-white pith of the rind and pulled out the bottom half, taking care not to let it bounce. The top half was placed carefully on his head, the strip wound delicately around his neck, and the bottom half was arranged on his collarbone.

Only then did Ramón Emilio Escobar Sanchez power the boat out of the forest and into the muddy brown Rio Beni, resplendent in his native crown and brimming with confidence. At his back lay the bloody remains of the battle, ahead the glorious opportunities that awaited the cousin of the world's most famous cocaine trafficker – Pablo Escobar.

CHAPTER TWO

A round the same time that Ramón was powering up the Beni, Ernesto Serrudo was sitting in a wicker armchair on the veranda of a large hall. He was glaring down over his compound from his vantage point, and a pair of secateurs was gently tapping on his lap.

In front of him a modest hacienda was surrounded by rainforest, and behind him a row of flowers stretched across the veranda, neatly arranged in ascending size and graduating colour. Everyone knew the significance of the flowers: dark to light when Ernesto was brooding and the reverse when he was on an upper. The plants never lied. He was most certainly brooding; in fact, he was furious. The compound was empty. All of his hit-men were either dead or dying. One of the DEA agents was still alive, and he had no men to finish off the job.

Ernesto got up and paced around. He was surrounded by incompetence. It was one of his runners, a man called Martín, who had wreaked havoc on the camp. He had a simple task – deliver his precursors and collect some tools, not show up with armed Israelis and a lunatic with a bowie-knife. Apparently the men in the camp were wearing fatigues and Martín had confused them with DEA agents and law-enforcement officers! Ernesto had no idea what Martín was even doing with some gringos in the first place, and when he suggested bringing the injured DEA agent back to the compound, Ernesto had exploded.

Ernesto reached down and flicked an insect from one of his orchids. Martín would regret his actions, though right now he

5

needed to bring the situation under control. He had given him strict instructions to take the agent to Rurrenabaque, where Horqueta would be waiting with Pala. Horqueta was his top hit-man and would take care of the agent. Ramón was lucky that Ernesto was there to clear up his mess. If the agent survived to tell the tale, the Colombian would soon realise that the wrath of the DEA was far more deadly than the constriction of a green anaconda.

Ernesto opened his secateurs and turned to his flowers for some light distraction. Horticulture was his passion, and he was pleased to be able to combine it with cartel business. Horqueta, or 'pitchfork', was named after the sicario's weapon of choice, and Pala, or 'spade', was a common tool used for solid graft, which described him perfectly. He found the magic of the garden transcended everything, and nature's beauty was a crucial guide when making difficult decisions. Opening his secateurs, he turned to an angel wing begonia, and he was just about to deadhead a withered flower when he heard the rumble of an outboard motor.

'You *are* joking!' he murmured, and swung round to face the compound.

It had to be Martín; everyone else was either dead or injured. Martín had disobeyed him and was returning to the camp. Ernesto turned a slight plum colour and thought about the best way for him to suffer. His mind turned to his centrefire, bolt-action harpoon gun, but that was back in La Paz; he had lent his M2 flamethrower to Mauricio and his STIHL FS 86 strimmer was still being serviced . . .

'*Puta!*' he swore.

Before he had time to consider other tools to use on Martín, a thought occurred. *Maybe Martín's floating in the Beni and a gringo's driving the boat?* Then the engine cut out and there was no time to hesitate. The thought of that *puta* knife pushed him back into the hall, and he found a dark corner in which to hide.

The hall had no windows and its solid walls kept the burning heat at bay. It should keep him hidden from that vicious blade, although his grip still tightened on the secateurs as he peered through a small crack. There was no movement in the compound and he started to relax. Then he realised it was Monday and it had to be his team of gardeners that were arriving. His grip relaxed and he emerged from the shadows.

Stepping through the doorway, his eyes wandered down to the riverbank. He needed the men to start weeding around the hall, and he would wave them over before they got stuck into the beds by the hacienda. As he waited for them to appear, only the sound of wind rustling through the trees and a bird screeching overhead broke the silence. Then he saw it. A man was creeping through the trees. His upper half was smeared in mud, his face was covered in camo cream and something green snaked around his neck and over his shoulders. Springing back through the doorway, Ernesto knew he had been spotted. He rushed into a far corner, pressed himself against the wall and grasped the secateurs, which no longer felt in the least bit threatening.

It was not long before his worst fear was confirmed – there was an unmistakable snap of a twig and then the creak of a veranda step. He did not know for sure, but it was easy to imagine that the assassin was creeping up with a knife in one hand and a rudimentary club in the other. He cursed Ramón again for his lack of men and rued his habit of not carrying a firearm.

Another creak, then the silhouette of a man appeared in the doorway, edged in tiny particles of dried mud that sparkled as they fell from his shoulders. A long shadow stretched across the floor and the man turned his head slowly . . . scanning the hall for his prey. Ernesto held his breath, hidden in the corner. The man cursed and returned to the veranda. Ernesto knew he had to strike before he returned. He crept out of the shadows and peered through the doorway. The man was leaning over the handrail, scouring the compound for his target. The secateurs glinted briefly in Ernesto's hand, then he lunged forward. The blade swept towards the man, and it was about to plunge through his neck when the sight of the ridiculous *pomelo* crown made Ernesto hesitate for just a split second, and the creak of a floorboard was enough to give him away.

The *pomelo* crown spun round and the man lurched back in alarm.

CHAPTER THREE

It was early evening and Ernesto and Ramón were drinking *aguardiente* in the hacienda. Nearly five hours had passed since their encounter, long enough for Ramón to freshen up, although too short for Ernesto to have forgotten crouching in the shadows with a pair of secateurs. Outside, the last streaks of sunlight were outlining the treetops and turning the river red, yet the men were lost in thought and paid no attention to the glorious rays that streamed through the shutters.

Ernesto swirled a chunk of ice around his glass and contemplated the speed with which things had changed. The cartel had been transformed by Decree no. 22881, the so-called *Decreto de Arrepentimiento*, or Decree of Repentance. The leadership had surrendered in return for immunity from extradition proceedings, and although he was now the de facto head, the Colombians had exploited their weakness and muscled in on the coca paste business. He glanced at Ramón and took a slug of his drink. Puta *Colombians!* Puta *Pablo Escobar! As for his fat, useless cousin . . .*

Everyone knew that Ramón was talentless and slow-witted, although he was well connected and that was what counted. His father had bankrolled Pablo's early contraband activities and secured him a position in the expanding cocaine business. *His father was probably relieved to get him off his hands . . . He should be a delivery boy, at least then all he could fuck up would be a consignment of bananas or a shipment of* chicharrones *. . .* Ernesto huffed, but just a little too loudly, and Ramón picked up on it. 'What's up, *hermano*? Still sulking about earlier?'

Ernesto turned to the much younger representative of the Medellín cartel and bit his tongue. Rather than share his thoughts, he waved a hand and smiled.

'Of course not. I was thinking how close you came to being impaled. If you hadn't turned round, you'd have a pair of secateurs in your neck and I'd be worrying how I was going to explain it to your cousin.' The words were delivered confidently and in a condescending tone. He objected to being referred to as 'brother' by the younger man, and he was in no mood to hide his disapproval.

Ramón raised his glass. Ernesto noticed a hint of irritation that was quickly replaced by a broad grin.

'You might have been saving him a job, *güevón*. If the DEA find out what happened, my cousin will be top of their hit list, and you know what that will mean for us?' He raised a hand and fired off a round with his thumb and forefinger.

'What—' But the words stuck in Ernesto's mouth. His temper rose at the brazen attempt to tie him into Ramón's fuck-up and at being referred to as 'dude'. He managed to control himself and replied, almost casually:

'He won't know unless the DEA find their agent, but as I had no men to finish off what *you* half started . . .' He let his words linger for an apology. Ramón waved him on impatiently.

Ernesto's fingers drummed on the armrest and he scowled. Not only was the motherfucker incompetent, unaccountable and short on contrition, he also lacked respect. After a long pause, his temper finally boiled over and he blurted out:

'Instead, *I* cleared up your mess. Martín took the agent to Rurrenabaque and my sicarios finished off the job—'

'What?' Ramón gasped. 'That *hijo de puta* with the gringos? That arsehole—' He was lost for words. Sweeping some hair from his forehead, he gripped the arms of his chair. 'That *hijo de puta* works for you?' he spluttered. 'He's one of your men!'

Ernesto knew he had blown it. His association with Martín implicated him in the attack on Ramón. His temper was to blame, yet he had only lost it because the *malparido* refused to take responsibility. A simple bullet would have finished off the DEA

9

agents, but no, the upstart was determined that one of them be eaten alive by flesh-eating piranhas and the other swallowed whole by an enormous reptile. It was obvious that the plan was idiotic. *As for Martín, well, his day of reckoning is coming.* He was, again, imagining Horqueta inflicting pain on Martín, ideally with a power tool, when Ramón grabbed his arm.

'What was your plan, *hermano*? Send mercenaries to try and assassinate me, then finish off the job with a pair of rusty secateurs?'

Ernesto dragged his arm free and jumped up, furious at being manhandled.

'Get your fucking hands off me!' he bellowed, wiping his sleeve in disgust. 'What were you doing skulking around painted in camouflage in the first place? What did you expect me to think?'

'Camouflage!' Ramón roared. 'That was mud, arsehole! When does mud look like camouflage?'

Levering himself from his seat, he squared up to the taller man.

'I told you already. I slipped on the riverbank and got covered in shit. The only way to find a grip up that *puta* bank was through the undergrowth, and I tripped on a root. What is it you don't get?'

He had also explained that the camo cream was the only sunblock he could find, and that he had ripped his shirt off when it got soaked in a rough section of river. But Ernesto was no longer listening. His mind had wandered off again as reality hit – instinct told him that his future was now inextricably tied to the fat, ranting Colombian, and he fell back into his armchair, let out a small sigh and gazed at the sunset glowing on the tin roof of his hall. It was a perfect match for the brilliant pink of his begonias.

'Yes, yes . . . I must finish deadheading them tomorrow, otherwise they'll be disappointing this year . . .' he mumbled in a deep baritone as his eyes locked on to a pair of toucans that were screeching over the distant treeline. Then he watched them dip and turn into the sinking sun and disappear as his eyes glazed over and his fingers tapped on the armrest.

CHAPTER FOUR

L uis cursed as a small trickle of diesel dribbled down the tanks and over the fuel line. Wiping it away with a grubby cloth, he grabbed a knife, fashioned a funnel from a plastic bottle and finished topping up the fuel. Only then could he get to the most important part: replacing the ignition cartridge on the barrel fixed to the fuel line. He was taking no chances. That little mother was the difference between standing there all powerful and standing there with his pants down. He had absolutely no intention of exposing himself to anything other than a terrified man scrambling for cover, and with that in mind, and a wry smile, he attached a new cartridge, swung the tanks onto his back and approached a scarecrow-like figure hanging from a metal frame.

Standing with his legs apart, he turned a small dial on the side of the tanks, waited for the pressurised fuel to reach the big squeeze trigger and then swung towards the scarecrow. There was a loud click as he pulled hard on the trigger. The ignition cartridge spun furiously, a puff of smoke burst out and a small flame shot from the barrel. The stream of liquid fuel that followed it blasted across the camp and turned the figure into a fireball, sending black smoke spiralling into the forest. Seconds later, monkeys leapt for cover across the treeline and birds fled in panic, but they went unnoticed, for the man had already turned on his heels and was heading back to the camp. His M2 flamethrower was in perfect working order.

Horqueta was busy in his workshop in Rurrenabaque. Pala was organising the smaller details of the ambush, but Horqueta was concentrating on the coup de grâce, an important part of which lay in his hand. He was bent over a long bench and his tools were laid out neatly in front. A half-finished cup of coffee had been pushed to one side and a small calendar was out of the way, balanced on a box of chisels. This month Zappa was being promoted by the calendar, and a scantily clad woman was posing with one of the small, cockroach-zapping gizmos in her hand. Her mouth was wide open in surprise and an exploding message over her read: 'Zappa Kills All Known Cockroaches . . . DEAD!'

It was a small gadget, not unlike a potato peeler, with a wire running between two prongs and a handle that could be gripped or fitted to the end of a broom. A small battery slotted into its side, and Horqueta wondered if its electric shock could be boosted – if so, it might come in handy in his line of work.

In the background, his favourite track had just started. As the *thud, thud, thud* of the bass grew louder his foot started tapping and his head began nodding; by the time Tina Turner had launched into the chorus, his foot was thumping and his head was banging. With a deft movement, his hand shot down a whetstone and the sharp edge of a knife rang out. Tina sang that he was simply the best . . . better than all the rest . . . and the message was repeated over and over as his scraping became more insistent and his sharpening more intense. The *clank, clank, clank* of the ceiling fan was out of time, the tape cassette crackled and the air in the room was sticky, but it made no difference. Horqueta was totally focussed on the blade whizzing across the whetstone.

The track finally petered out and Horqueta put the whetstone to one side. Then he raised the blade and ran his finger across the hooks on its spine. He nodded in approval. When the time came, its two barbs would grip the gringo's flesh like a grappling iron and tear his intestines out like a butcher's knife. For now, though, it was just a wonderful thing to admire. After a final check, he swivelled round in his chair, held the blade up to the light and reflected a beam of sunlight across the room.

It came to rest on a large painting on the wall opposite. It was a portrait of a sea captain with a beard turning grey and piercing eyes that were focussed on some distant point, as though it held a special fascination for him alone. In days gone by he might have been looking at an exotic shoreline shimmering in the distance; now it was simply a small toilet tucked away in a corner of the workshop. Attached to the frame, a small brass plate read 'In memory of Captain Muñoz'. It was a simple message, written when men were taciturn and emotions were restrained, yet Horqueta knew the legacy his grandfather had left. He had worked tirelessly to build up the shipping business that was left to his father on his untimely death, churned up one day in the propeller of his own ship.

The speakers crackled once more as the cassette tape moved on to the next track. Now it was Barry Gibb's falsetto that filled the room, and Horqueta knew exactly what was coming. A sharp tingle rose up his spine as Barry got his teeth into 'Stayin' Alive', and Horqueta stood up for the ritual he carried out before each assignment.

Directly below the portrait, twelve gilded wooden frames were hanging in a neat row. His eyes wandered across them and he nodded in approval. They were the 'School of 1992', his victims for the year to date, staring back with blank expressions as though in an identity parade. His narrow hips and broad shoulders swung slightly to the beat; he raised his knife to his chest and turned to the first victim.

'Informer.'

(screech!) Ah, ha, ha, ha . . .

A beam of sunlight hit the man's forehead and Horqueta marked it with a sign of the cross.

(sing!) Stayin' alive, stayin' alive . . .

'Double-crosser.'

(screech!) Ah, ha, ha, ha . . .

And the next victim received another sign of the cross.

Each of them received a blessing in turn as though they were a line of penitents awaiting benediction, and Horqueta looked from one face to another, yet none of them returned his smile. Finally, he reached the last frame and lowered his blade. The photograph that had arrived that morning was grainy, indistinct and totally unsuitable for the gallery. It had been taken in a bar and the guy looked drunk. When he'd found out it was a DEA agent, he was determined to mark the occasion with a special performance.

The thought of a drink reminded Horqueta that he could do with a top-up, and he spun round for his coffee mug. In doing so, his foot caught the leg of the workbench and the calendar flew off. Lying on the floor, the image of Zappa stared back, and its deadly message sparked an idea. As he walked across to the kitchen, the idea grew into a firm option, and by the time his powdered milk had dissolved in a small whirlpool of instant Nescafé, it was a definite plan. He sauntered back to the workbench, chuckling. Don Ernesto had left the manner of Martín's punishment to Horqueta's discretion. It had to be painful, not debilitating, and a Zappa would be perfect. Then he picked up his blade and tested out some stabbing moves.

It was razor sharp, just like the other blades that formed the prongs of his pitchfork. Technically, it was closer to a trident than a pitchfork, and Horqueta's first moniker had been Neptune on account of him representing the cartel astride the bow of a boat, a trident in one hand and a Colt. 45 in the other. He had been surprised, not to say pained, by Don Ernesto's reference to it as a pitchfork, but when Don Ernesto assumed control of the Beni Cartel, he was aghast at being ascribed the persona of a farm tool, which in terms of kudos was several steps down from being the Roman god of fresh water.

Placing the blade into a long black case with velvet-lined compartments, he slotted the others alongside and ran a finger down the carbon fibre head to which they would be attached. It was fitted to a stainless-steel shaft with a slender handle that slotted into a cushioned recess. The original model lacked a handle and became slippery to hold; the current model did a better job by avoiding the tugging and pulling that went with a weak grip. The last piece of the weapon was a heavy bottom tube that screwed into the shaft and provided the momentum needed to deliver a solid thrust.

There was a chiselled-out space for the bottom tube, yet it was nowhere to be seen.

'*Puta*,' he muttered. Horqueta knew exactly where it was: screwed to the end of a pool cue down at Ramudo's. It was only there because he had arrived late to an unscheduled match, straight from work without time to drop off his tools. The tube provided a perfect cue end, and it would have been a shame not to use the heavy cylinder to smash his opponent's pool balls around the table. Nevertheless, it was now needed for the job in hand, and he would have to collect it before meeting Pala.

The thought of a visit to Ramudo's perked him up – *Plenty of time for a quick game and a chilled beer* – and with that in mind and the prospect of a new addition to his gallery, he spun on his heels, leaving his victims staring blankly at his back and his grandfather still mesmerised by the small toilet.

CHAPTER FIVE

It was only a short walk down to the river. Horqueta stopped by the timber decking alongside Ramudo's General Store and gazed down at the old jetty. Once there had been a grand cast-iron wharf for the boats plying their trade up and down the Rio Beni. However, the rapids at Esperanza made river transport difficult and the advent of railways and air travel uneconomic; now all that remained was a small jetty that had seen better days.

Turning away, he shook his head. Not only was it a shadow of its former self, it was also totally unsuitable for the upcoming assignment. Don Ernesto in his wisdom had chosen it for the rendezvous, but Horqueta could not think of a worse place. Martín also happened to have two Israeli soldiers with Uzis on his boat. How Don Ernesto thought standing in plain sight with a Colt .45 and a pitchfork would overpower a couple of submachine guns was beyond him. Luckily, he had another plan.

Pushing open the door to Ramudo's, he strode towards a display of agricultural tools, down an aisle stacked with fertiliser and plastic buckets, past a counter with a man reading a newspaper and finally into a small area with several tables and chairs arranged in a haphazard fashion. In one corner, a nervous-looking girl was standing next to a large serving counter with an array of sauce bottles clustered at one end and a pile of utensils at the other. But it was not her nervous smile that caught his attention, nor the sound of crashing pans and sizzling food coming from the kitchen; rather, it was the man sitting at one of the tables with his zip undone for coolness and a beer opened for refreshment. It was an unexpected yet pleasant surprise, for it was none other than his partner, Pala.

'*Hermano!*' he shouted, walking over. 'You read my mind,' he added, waving at the waitress and pointing at Pala's bottle.

Pala looked up, equally surprised – they had arranged to meet at the boat, not in the bar.

'*Güevón!*' he replied, raising his bottle.

Horqueta pulled up a chair as the beer arrived.

'All good?' he asked.

'Yeah. Luis can help out.' Pala acknowledged Horqueta's plan with a slight nod. 'Nice touch,' he continued with a hint of admiration. 'Creative,' he added, then paused for a drink. 'The boat's loaded and Emilio brought over the armoured shield.'

Horqueta nodded.

The shield had got them into the heart of the battle with the Colombians, bullets pinging off it as they stormed the coca paste laboratory close to Don Ernesto's compound. It was only a few months ago, yet so much seemed to have changed since then.

'We'll need it if the Uzis open fire,' Horqueta said, and took a large slug of his Pilsner. 'But that won't be happening. They'll light up like Chinese crackers once Luis' fireball hits them.'

He laughed and waved for another beer. The news that his territory had been invaded by a couple of gun-toting gringos had first shocked him, then steeled his resolve. *They'll be paying for it in a few hours*, he promised himself, and checked his watch. *Still plenty of time for a game.*

'Come on. Quick game. Best of three.'

Pala agreed and they headed to the pool room. It was only recently built and still had a smell of drying paint and fresh floor varnish. Horqueta walked up to a prominent photograph on one of its walls and raised his bottle to it. A man was opening a new school, surrounded by smiling dignitaries and excited schoolchildren, and a shorter, stocky man was grinning by his side. It was the stocky man Horqueta was toasting – Jhon 'Popeye' Velásquez – not his boss. Popeye was the muscle behind the Medellín cartel and Horqueta had made it known that he would soon be replacing him.

The sound of balls being racked brought him back to the task in hand, and he strode over to a row of maple wood cues. They were all identical, other than the small nametags added by their owners; that was, except for the one with a large black base. Horqueta grabbed it, lined up the white ball and smashed it into a rack of spots and stripes. Two stripes dropped in a pocket and he nodded in approval.

The first game went to Horqueta, the second to Pala, and the third was the decider. Pala started well, Horqueta recovered with some good positioning, and soon only a few balls remained. Horqueta bent down to line up his shot. It was his last striped ball and it would need a fine cut to drop it into the middle pocket. He was still unsure whether to take the shot or play safe when the door opened and María appeared with their kit bag. Pala turned round and flashed her a smile and Horqueta seized the opportunity. Rolling the white ball into a better position, he slammed the stripe into the pocket and the black soon followed.

'Ooh yeess!' he crowed 'Look and learn, *hermano*, look and learn . . .' Then he strode off waving his cue, leaving Pala to pay for the beer as he paid a visit to the bathroom.

On his way back he slipped a couple of Zappas into his pocket. The man at the counter was now fast asleep and snoring lightly but Horqueta did not feel remotely bad about cheating him; after all, he was on cartel business, and what's more, it would be free advertising for Ramudo's. Martín would soon be explaining the nasty burn it was going to leave on his forehead and its branding would be clear evidence of Zappa's effectiveness.

A few minutes later the men were making their way down to the river as the town around them slipped into a collective siesta of half-drawn curtains and closed shops – one of them struggling with a heavy kit bag and the other swaggering with a large ego in the midday heat that had silenced even the barking dogs.

CHAPTER SIX

The jetty was more than just a shadow of its former self – it was a painful reminder of the faded glory of Rurrenabaque. Where white buoys once floated, slime-covered tyres now hung on rusty chains dangling from timber posts; the decking was a patchwork of repairs and a few indistinct letters were all that remained of a name board where the shipping companies had once been listed in alphabetical order. The 'M' of Muñoz could just be made out; the other letters were long gone, blasted away by the blazing sun and torrential rain. Three fuel pumps with brand-new casings stood out amidst the decay, yet beneath their shiny exteriors even they were as ancient and crumbling as the name board. The diesel dispensed through their rusty pipework was awash with iron filings that damaged even the most robust engines and their tanks dripped diesel that pooled in an iridescent film below the jetty.

Pala let their boat drift up to the jetty before starting the engine. It pulled into the current, the engine roared, and soon they were racing past a line of plastic baskets and brightly coloured washing that marked the edge of the town. Before long they reached the place chosen by Horqueta. It was a small inlet hidden away on a broad curve of the river and it brought back fond memories for Horqueta. Only a few weeks earlier he had rammed Miguel from that very same spot and been forced to listen to the usual pleading, the insistence that Miguel had not cheated the cartel, the begging for a last chance to speak to Don Ernesto . . . Horqueta had put an end to it with a bullet in his chest.

It was only later, when he was laying out Miguel's intestines over the gunwale, that he was reminded of the rolls of paper that used to cascade from the Muñoz counting machines as he watched the clerks close their ledgers for the day. And it seemed a fitting end for the accountant who had been siphoning off funds; his debt had been totalled by the cartel and found wanting.

The double-crossing accountant was victim number ten on the wall, staring down from a rosewood frame with attractive corner mouldings.

'Horqueta!' Pala shouted, and a low branch appeared. Horqueta dipped his head to avoid it and stretched out an arm to cushion the boat from the approaching riverbank. Once it was tied up, he told Pala to unload their equipment.

'No, no, sort the radio out first,' he snapped. 'I want to speak to Luis.' Pala brought over the high-frequency ground-to-ground radio and Horqueta dialled out. No one picked up.

'*Puta.* He knows to have his radio on.'

'Try checking the signal.'

Horqueta got a *ping* return signal from the base station.

'The signal's fine. He's got his radio off!'

'Relax. He'll call when Martín appears. He's probably checking his flamethrower.'

Horqueta scowled, looked at his watch and turned to the kit bag.

'Okay. We've got about an hour. Sort the stuff out,' he ordered. And with that he sauntered over to the scrub and the dense forest that lay beyond. He was excited, yet also nervous, and he always peed a lot before assignments. Today was no exception, and the fact that this performance was about to surpass all others was marked by a prodigious spraying of the scrub.

'No. Pass the mirror and lay out the aprons,' he barked on his return, 'then unpack my pitchfork. Leave the blades to me.' Pala was no longer allowed to fit them. They had come loose during a particularly challenging extraction last year and Horqueta had not forgotten.

'Careful with the video camera, *hermano*!'

Pala was placing it next to the overalls and Horqueta noticed his back stiffen.

'Relax. It's fine,' Pala replied.

'Don't "relax" me. It's on loan from Ramudo's. Any damage and you'll be paying.'

Pala bit his tongue. Horqueta would soon be working in Colombia and it was simpler not to argue.

'No!' shouted Horqueta. 'The shield stays in the boat. Who told you to get it out? What's the point in that?'

Pala bristled and Horqueta picked up on it.

'*Hermano*, stop sulking about losing at pool. Act professional. Get this shit organised. Your time will come to beat me, but right now you need to focus on the job in hand.' Then he threw his apron over his shoulder, picked up the large mirror and walked off to find a good spot to get ready.

Horqueta was prone to seizing any opportunity that presented itself and today was no exception. It offered the perfect stage to show off his talent and the camcorder was going to record it for promotional purposes. He was still undecided whether to request an audience with Don Escobar and talk him through the execution himself or send him the tape with a detailed explanation. Whichever it was, he needed to look his best, and with that in mind he fastened his apron and rolled up the sleeves of his T-shirt to reveal his biceps. With one hand he mimicked holding his pitchfork and with the other he pulled out his Colt .45 and let it drop to his side. Only then did he take a long hard look in the mirror, and he was pleased with what he saw. Don Ernesto had insisted that they wear brown overalls with 'H' and 'P' monograms. Horqueta had stubbornly refused. The compromise was matching black aprons in moisture-repelling fabric that was easy to clean, and deep front pockets that were handy for the small essentials. The monogram idea was quietly dropped.

When he returned, Pala had organised their kit and fitted the shield to the front of the boat. Horqueta pointed at it and barked, 'Make sure it's fixed securely! I'm going to be attached to it, so it had better not fall off. And go get the mirror. Put it by the shield so I can reach it easily.'

'*Hermano*, there won't be time to check yourself out on the boat!' Pala replied. 'Do whatever you need to do now, not then . . .' Horqueta stared hard at his partner. 'I'm just saying, with bullets flying around . . .'

'*Malparido!* he exploded. 'What the fuck are you on? You *know* what the mirror is for. Don't lay your fancy-boy stuff on me.'

'Relax, *hermano*,' said Pala, backing away. 'I'm just messing with you.'

It did nothing to alleviate the pressure building up in Horqueta's forehead. Were Pala not needed to drive the boat then Horqueta would have given him a solid beating, courtesy of the heavy end of his pitchfork. As it was, he had to tolerate Pala's weak sense of humour. Bending down, he slowly picked up his heavy leather belt, and Pala took another step back, but Horqueta simply fastened the belt under his apron and clipped an enormous carabiner to a large brass ring dangling from its side. Without another word, he picked up the camcorder and boarded the boat.

A small shelf had been fitted to its stern and Horqueta attached the camcorder to it. Once he had checked its angle of view, he sat down and shouted to Pala:

'Fetch me the radio. I want to know what Luis is up to.'

Channel One . . . *hiss.*

'*Puta.*'

Channel Two . . . *hiss.*

'*Hijo de puta.*'

Channel Three . . . *hiss.*

'Fuck me!' Horqueta thundered. 'He'll regret it when I see him.' He pulled out a Zappa as if to emphasise the point. Pala also failed to reach Luis, and they were forced to keep an eye out for Martín's boat.

It was a simple plan.

According to Martín, the Israelis were at the front of the boat and the injured DEA agent was laid over some barrels. Whilst there was another gringo with them, his exact whereabouts were unimportant as he was unarmed. Once their boat had gone past, Luis would contact the sicarios and they would wait for Martín to reach the curved section of the river; it should take him no more than five or six minutes. Pala would then power the boat out with Horqueta astride its bow – one foot on the gunwale and a hand on his thigh. Horqueta's plan was to recreate the pose struck by George Washington when crossing the Delaware River in 1776. Not only would it be a powerful theatrical effect, but it would also emphasise his dominion of the territory (at least for those who got the reference); he also imagined it would be an impressive spectacle for Don Escobar.

With the extra-long carabiner hanging from his belt, Horqueta would attach himself to the post at the bow, leaving his hands free to grip the pitchfork and hold up the mirror. The pitchfork would attract the Israelis' attention and the mirror would dazzle them. Half blinded by sunlight, they would be too distracted to notice Luis sneaking up from behind. The flamethrower would blast them, Horqueta would board their vessel and the other gringo would be killed. After that he would get to the best part . . . disembowelling the DEA agent.

And if things did not go exactly to plan, he knew he would always beat the Israelis in a shoot-out; they would be out in the open whereas he would be behind his impenetrable shield.

Horqueta was irritated. He was getting hotter and hotter in his apron and a mosquito had bitten his neck. Also, the hard wooden bench was uncomfortable and he was growing impatient for Martín to appear. He should have reached them by now. Luis would regret not keeping them informed.

Horqueta turned round and told Pala to try him one last time. Pala bent down and was about to reach for the radio when Horqueta picked up a faint sound. He knocked Pala's arm to one side and raised a finger to his lips. It was coming from downriver, growing louder and louder and approaching fast. Horqueta gave the signal and Pala paddled their boat to the edge of the inlet. Horqueta recognised the distinctive rumble of an outboard motor, and it had to be Martín. Sure enough, seconds later, they caught the glint of an aluminium hull, and it was heading straight for them.

Horqueta stood up calmly, rehearsed his blessing one last time and locked his carabiner to the post. Pala yanked hard on the starter motor; the engine roared into life and Horqueta emerged from the inlet in full majesty.

The Israelis jumped to their feet and Martín slowed down. For a moment it seemed as though he was going make a run for it, then he brought the boat to a complete stop. Horqueta gave a small bow, pointed his pitchfork at them and raised it high. The first sign of the cross was a little hurried, the second one was an improvement, and the third one was delivered with panache. With a nod of approval he reached for his mirror, held it aloft as though in a solstice ritual and sent a ray of sunlight flashing across the Israelis.

Standing proud with his pitchfork and makeshift ray gun, he felt indomitable. Best of all, the camcorder was capturing the very moment his career was about to take off. Martín was frozen to the spot and the Israelis were at first confused, then began shouting and waving their guns. Yet Horqueta was supremely confident behind his armoured shield, and he waited patiently for Luis' arrival.

He did not have to wait long. Luis' boat was gliding silently towards them, though not as Horqueta imagined. His flamethrower was charged with fuel and its ignition cartridge was in place, yet its barrel was pointing not at the Israelis but straight at the sicario. It was as though fate had waited for the perfect moment to shatter Horqueta's sense of invincibility, and as the boat approached, Luis took full advantage.

There was a small puff of smoke. A jet of blazing napalm flew out and the moisture-repelling fabric of Horqueta's apron burst into flames. Horqueta lunged at the carabiner and fiddled frantically with its lock. It was over-tightened and impossible to open. He quickly gave up and turned to his apron. His hands ripped at its ties and tore it off, then flew up to the flames that were catching light in his hair. His head was smoking like a damp bonfire and his hands beat furiously to put the fire out. It was pointless. The next blast turned him into a human fireball.

His body shook and he crashed repeatedly against the post, shrieking in agony. No amount of effort would move it and the flames swirled and roared around his body as he struggled in vain. Eventually his screams turned into a low moan, and as the flames died down, his smoking body appeared and the stench of roasted flesh and gasoline drifted across the river.

A few seconds later, the boat drifted past. Martín realised that Pala was nowhere to be seen. All that remained was a burnt figurehead and a red light, flashing like a warning beacon. As the boat reached the bend, Horqueta's back and shoulder muscles started to contract and his left arm rose slowly above his head . . . then, a moment later, he simply disappeared around the corner.

CHAPTER SEVEN

The following morning Ernesto and Ramón were having break-fast in silence. News of the DEA agent's escape had coincided with the arrival of a plate of scrambled eggs and Ramón had been too distracted to pay sufficient attention to Ernesto's ranting. Ernesto's irritation had grown as a consequence.

'You worry too much, *güevón*,' Ramón said, breaking the silence. 'The DEA got their man back. So what? They know Medellín runs the Beni. They'll be after my cousin, not us. *Tranquilo*,' he added, 'I've got a plan.' He pointed his fork at Ernesto. 'The gringos will take revenge and they'll do what *we* can't do. They'll get rid of Don Pablo and close down Medellín.' He nodded, as though it was an indisputable fact, and grabbed a cup. 'Fail to plan, plan to fail,' he declared confidently, and raised it in celebration of their good fortune.

Ernesto had no intention of acknowledging the gesture. Instead, he watched Ramón put down his cup and grab some toast. '*Hermano*, all problems create opportunities,' Ramón continued. 'We step in. We take over. We get rich,' he said, smearing some butter on the toast and slapping on some marmalade. 'I'll run sales and distribution and you can organise production.' He paused for confirmation and got none in return. 'I've got contacts in Mexico who'll get the product stateside for us. At the start there'll be a large tax to pay – it'll come down once the business grows.'

Ramón tore into his toast and a blob of marmalade dropped on the table. Ernesto remained silent, his hand tapping impatiently on his thigh. It was a reflex that came with a rising temper and a growing irritation from listening to someone spouting nonsense. 'Coca from the Chapare and Yungas is superior to the crop in Colombia,' Ramón continued, chewing loudly, 'but we'll need more labs to process the coca paste into cocaine hydrochloride.'

By now Ernesto had stopped listening. His mind had veered off along lines determined more by self-preservation than profit generation. He could not believe the DEA had somehow tracked down and eliminated his sicarios before they had even got to the agent. And what were his sicarios even doing on the Beni in the first place? His instructions were to deal with the matter on the jetty, not carry out some river-borne attack with the added risks it entailed. And when did the gringos start using flamethrowers? They must have brought in some mercenaries, as it was not their modus operandi, and he was certain that it would not have received official approval. It made him nervous. If the DEA were acting outside normal channels, then they were either intent on a devastating response or they had a rogue group operating independently. He would see what Martín had to say about it when he arrived later.

'Can you get the precursors we need to set up more labs? It'll be a large outlay and we'll need our reserves.' Ramón was still talking and eating. Waving a new slice of toast, he added, 'There's the funds from Medellín, and of course you have your emeralds—' He stopped dead. 'Ernesto!' he shouted. 'You're not listening. This is serious shit I'm explaining. Pay attention, *güevón*.'

Ernesto stared at him incredulously. Not only was he deluded if he thought the DEA would forget he tortured their agents, but he must be mentally impaired if he was planning to double-cross his own cousin.

'Can you organise the ammonium hydroxide and ethanol we need through Ramudo's or—'

'I know what's needed for a *puta* lab, *cabrón*!' Ernesto shouted, interrupting him. He could no longer contain himself. 'You pin two targets on our backs – one from the DEA and one from Medellín – and you're worried about how we get new labs up and running?'

'*Hermano . . .*'

'Don't "*hermano*" me.'

'*Tranquilo* . . .'

Ernesto jumped to his feet. 'Say that again! Go on, say it again, I dare you. Tell me to chill once more and I swear I'll stick you with this knife just like the fat pig you are.'

Ernesto stood facing Ramón with a steak knife in his hand and a wild look in his eyes. Ramón shrank into his chair and kept a careful watch on the blade. Finally, he stretched out a hand, which Ernesto refused to take. 'Please, sit down. I apologise,' he said. 'I know this sounds crazy and I know you're angry. When the idea first came to me, I thought it was crazy as well,' he added, and tried to coax Ernesto back into his chair. Ernesto was having none of it. After a long sigh, he continued, 'I came to realise that if we carry on as normal and pretend it'll be okay, we're dead men . . .' He went quiet for a moment, and when he spoke again it was with a slight smirk. 'We crossed the line, Don Ernesto, and there's no coming back.'

Ernesto stood with a ramrod spine and white knuckles. The suggestion, again, that he was somehow accountable for the mess stung him hard. It was only by pacing around the room that he managed to avoid scalping Ramón with the steak knife and wiping that smirk off his face. Instead, he simmered and deliberated over his options, one of which was to remain with the *hijo de puta*, the other to hand him over to his cousin. He was sorely tempted to hand him over, but Ramón was family and Colombians put family above everything else. Even if Don Pablo believed Ernesto's version of events, the fact remained that he was inextricably linked to this disaster by virtue of his position as de facto head of the Beni cartel. It followed that he would receive a punishment equally harsh as that reserved for the man who was sitting at the breakfast table, whom he circled with a loathing.

'Please, sit down, Don Ernesto,' Ramón repeated, swivelling his head as he tried to keep track of Ernesto's movements. 'I accept I am young and impetuous. I act on instinct and perhaps make mistakes. But I have good ideas, and with your guidance and experience we could achieve great things.'

Ernesto noted the use of 'Don' again, and the contrition in Ramón's voice. He made one last circuit of the table then dropped into his chair.

'All I'm saying is—'

Ernesto cut him off.

'Shut the fuck up! Let me think.' He waved for more coffee. Placing a napkin over his lap, he spread some butter over a slice of toast and took a bite.

There's got to be another way out . . . there's always another way.

REPERCUSSION

Colombia – two weeks later.

CHAPTER EIGHT

Popeye wasn't inherently bad, he just enjoyed killing. Yet despite that, he knew it didn't suit everyone, and he was curious to find out how the young guy had got on.

Sitting at a table outside a sunlit café, he caught two men staring at him from the counter. They were locals, clearly curious at what the cartel's top hit-man looked like in person. Not wishing to disappoint them, he flashed one of his engaging smiles and raised a cup; the men beamed back. He returned to his coffee and nodded his head imperceptibly to the salsa coming from inside.

Around him the day was starting just like any other in his hometown. Shops were opening with a clatter, dogs were barking incessantly and scores of men were drinking coffee and contemplating the traffic circling the plaza. In front, the church of San Pio X dominated the square, a great, hulking place with a sharp, angular roof, a Star of David flowerbed outside and a peculiar white tower bolted to its wall that looked more like a ventilation shaft than a bell tower. Although Popeye had made his first communion in that church, he only paid it the occasional visit now that he neither lived locally nor attended Mass regularly.

Nowhere was he as safe as in Itagüí; nevertheless, he was always at risk of capture by the national police or, even worse, Los Pepes, the paramilitary group that had assassinated dozens of his friends. For that reason, if nothing else, he had told the young guy to be discrete. He didn't need any unnecessary attention and he certainly did not need him making a conspicuous entrance, swaggering with adrenaline after his first kill.

The target for his initiation was the son of a wealthy businessman living with his family in the affluent district of La Florida. Felipe had attacked and hospitalised a local girl one night, yet despite her injuries, no charges were brought on account of his father's contacts. La Florida was only a thirty-minute drive away, so he would not have much longer to wait.

Instinct told him that the rumble of an approaching motorbike was his guy. Without exception, all of the new sicarios were poor, and Popeye had been no different. A stint in the navy, and even the national police, had not offered any respite, yet once he had passed his own initiation, he never looked back. All the same, he had told the guy to be discreet, and turning up on a motorbike that sounded like a Moto Guzzi was anything but that.

Popeye's instinct was right. A Kawasaki KZ250 turned into the plaza, ridden by a man wearing a red helmet with a bright blue knapsack on his back. Popeye stood up and watched him make a beeline for the café.

'*Puta*,' he muttered.

The motorbike parked and a couple of locals beat away its exhaust fumes with their newspapers. Popeye stepped inside before the plaza's collective focus turned to him. Shortly afterwards, the door swung open and the man stood there with his helmet in one hand and a freshly lit cigarette in the other. He spotted Popeye sitting in the corner, raised his cigarette in acknowledgement and sauntered over.

'*Señor*, it's a pleasure to meet you. Thank you for giving me the opportunity to work for Don Escobar.' Popeye nodded, but said nothing. 'I'm sorry if I'm late,' he added, glancing at his watch. 'I got tied up this morning . . .' he continued with a nervous laugh, awaiting a response. There was none. The young man hurriedly stuck the cigarette in his mouth, took a deep drag and blew the smoke to one side. Popeye noticed the cigarette tremble and watched him shift awkwardly in the silence. 'I wanted to say how much I appreciate—' Popeye cut him off with a wave of his hand.

'Take a seat, *joven*.'

Whilst he was irritated by the man's lack of discretion, he was prepared to make allowances. After all, it was his first kill and he was new to the game. He called over the waitress.

'*Aguardiente*. One glass.'

Popeye did not smoke or drink, but he made each prospective hit-man take a shot after their initiation. He was undecided whether the tremble was adrenaline or nerves, and he watched closely; he needed to know which it was before the man joined his team of sicarios.

'So, tell me how it went.'

The man stubbed out his cigarette and Popeye watched carefully. There were definite signs of a tremble, then his hands slid under the table, out of sight.

'Amazing. Really easy. I didn't—' The *aguardiente* appeared and stopped him mid-sentence. Throwing the drink back, he slammed the glass down and gasped. 'No. It went really well. I didn't feel—'

Popeye cut him off before his voice recovered from the bite of the alcohol. 'No, *hermano*, I don't want to hear how you felt . . .' He glanced at the hand shaking by the glass. The man quickly slipped it under the table again. 'I want to hear how the hit *went*. Start at the beginning, slowly, and take your time. Tell me what went according to plan and what didn't. It's how you react to the unexpected that's important. Don't sit there pretending it worked out exactly as you planned. That's bullshit. It never works out exactly as you plan.'

The man squirmed slightly, as though caught out, before starting again.

'I'm glad you said that, Don Velásquez. You're right, I had to improvise along the way.'

'Go on.'

'It started fine. My brother was driving and I was riding pillion.'

'On a stolen bike?'

'Yeah, from Belén. We waited on Calle 14 and picked up his silver Land Cruiser as it joined Avenida Los Industriales. He was punctual, as you said.'

'Was anyone else inside?'

'We couldn't tell. The windows were tinted.'

'Okay.'

'We were about to come alongside him at some lights when a *puta* school bus drove up our inside. It was the bus to Collegio de la Virgen, which my brother used to go to . . .' He paused, looking a little nervous. 'Some of the students recognised him – well, one in particular he had beef with – and he and his *muchachos* started baiting Carlos—'

'That's your brother?' Popeye asked, interrupting him.

The man nodded.

'The next minute a fire extinguisher appeared and Carlos was being sprayed down by the *hijo de puta*. So I whipped out my piece and the extinguisher vanished, but Felipe must have seen me and he jumped the lights.' He paused and shrugged. 'It was now or never, and we chased after him.'

Popeye shook his head. The guy wasn't wearing a jacket, probably because it was covered in extinguisher solvent, although his knapsack had managed to avoid it. 'When he turned down Calle 27,' the man continued, 'he got stuck behind a refuse cart, and that was where I dispatched him.'

'What? You *dispatched* him. Don't give me that, tell me what happened,' Popeye said with irritation. He could tell that the guy was starting to relax and his confidence was returning, probably because he had confessed to the fire extinguisher incident.

'Well, as we pulled up, his passenger door burst open and a huge guy jumped out with a piece. But I got lucky – he slipped on something from the cart and fell on his back. My first shot missed him and exploded the car windscreen, the next one hit his shoulder and his gun flew across the road.' He paused for encouragement, but got none. 'Then out of nowhere,' he said, 'a dog jumped out of the car and seized Carlos by the leg. They were rolling on the ground and it was too risky to take a shot, so I stabbed the dog a couple of times.'

Popeye's eyes narrowed.

'Then I went over to Felipe and pumped three bullets into him.'

'Where?'

'Where? Into him.'

'No, where did you hit him?'

'I'm not sure, all over, I didn't have time to look. Carlos was still struggling with that *puta* dog and I had to use my knife again. Felipe was dead when I went back to check.'

Popeye stared at him incredulously.

'You did what?'

'I went back to check—'

'No, you did *what* to the dog?'

'I gutted it. It was still attacking Carlos!'

'And a bullet wouldn't do?' An awkward silence returned.

Popeye stared hard at the young guy for a second, then whipped out his silver Beretta and started tapping its grip on the table, out of time with the three-two rhythm of the salsa but in sync with the options pinging around his head. His lips barely moved as he whispered, '*Sí . . . no . . . sí*,' and flicked the safety on and off, all the while glaring at the young guy. Then in a swift movement he pulled back the hammer and the guy leapt to his feet and lunged for his knapsack. Popeye was renowned for his quick reactions, and with a bang of irritation, he slammed the pistol grip on the table and grabbed the man's arm and dragged him down. Once more the gun was pointed at him. This time he was smiling.

'Relax, *hermano*. This is reserved for informers, double-crossers and the cartel's enemies, not dog-killers.' He dropped the magazine into his palm and placed it on the table, and a bullet flew from the chamber as he pulled back the slide. Putting the gun down, he reached into his pocket, pulled out a wad of notes and handed over fifty thousand pesos. 'Here, take this. Get your exhaust fixed, buy a new jacket . . .'

The guy looked puzzled and was not sure if he was dismissed or not. He was, which Popeye confirmed with a perfunctory wave and a nod towards the door.

'Don Velásquez, I—'

Popeye interrupted him. 'And stop calling me "Don". There's only one don in the organisation and you're lucky he wasn't here to hear about your fuck-up.'

The guy looked crestfallen and began to justify himself. 'If it wasn't for the fire extinguisher . . .' Then he gave up. With a sigh, he pushed back his chair, picked up his helmet and swung the knapsack over his shoulder. Popeye once more grabbed his arm, this time more gently, and stuffed another fifty thousand pesos into his hand.

'Go in peace, *hermano*. Live a good life. Love your fellow creatures.'

The guy wandered off, and Popeye watched him drop his knapsack by the café's payphone and slot some coins into the bright blue metal box. The blue of his knapsack was a perfect match for the payphone, and it caught Popeye's attention. *Unusual . . .*

'Another espresso, *señor?*'

The waitress was standing by his shoulder. Turning round, he smiled and nodded.

CHAPTER NINE

One hour and three espressos later, Popeye was still waiting for a call on that payphone. The ubiquitous bright blue boxes were the conduit through which the head of the Medellín cartel ran his empire from La Catedral, the prison he had built for his incarceration. He was over a year into the five-year sentence he had agreed to serve once the government had banned extraditions. Popeye knew he had decided to serve no more than twenty-four months of the sentence and regular face-to-face meetings would resume soon.

The meeting with the young guy was still on Popeye's mind, and it got him thinking about his own initiation. It was almost four years earlier, though it felt longer. Back then he was the one showing up, trying to hide his nerves and still buzzing from the kill – *Just not on a busted motorbike* – and checking the tables at Carlos V for his recruiter, Piña. The restaurant had once stood prominently on Plaza Central, a proud colonial building with delicious pastries served on cane tables with crisp white tablecloths. It was the first time Popeye had mixed with the elite of Medellín, and it had left a lasting impression.

When Carlos V was blown up a few years later, he had some regrets, not least as he had grown to like some of its waiters. However, it was owned by the Sastre family, and they had been stubbornly blocking attempts in the Senate to ban extraditions. After their eldest son was kidnapped, their position changed significantly and the legislation was passed within a few months. Strangely enough, Popeye preferred killing to kidnapping. The rush of adrenaline from a kill was what drove the sicarios, that and the buzz that came with avoiding capture or assassination. Kidnapping was all about psychological torture, not physical retribution, and he had not taken to it.

Unlike the young guy, he had arrived on time, ready and prepared for his debrief. The target for his initiation had been a bus driver called Alfonso or Alonso (he could not remember the exact name) who lived in Comuna 13 and went drinking every Friday evening in La Plancha, a local bar.

In his eulogy he was described as a considerate driver – and perhaps it was an aberration, yet on the night in question he was anything but considerate. He had pulled away as an elderly lady was getting off his bus and she had fallen under its wheels. Rather than stop, his foot hit the accelerator and spun her into the gutter like a rag doll. It was only the shouts of the passengers that finally made him pull over.

It was never clear why he had driven off in the first place. His defence was that he had not seen her 'stumble off the bus' and he thought he had run over a dead dog. After a short inquest, he was cleared of any wrongdoing and was back driving his bus. It later transpired that he had been running late and was not prepared to put his Friday evening at risk. At least that was what he was overheard bragging in a bar one night.

Popeye had clear memories of his first kill. It was a warm Friday evening and he was tracking the man and his friends after one of their drinking sessions. The streets were full of people, spilling out of the bars and restaurants that were closing. Eventually they reached the dimly lit residential streets beyond the centre, and one by one they peeled off and Popeye was left alone with his target.

He was still slightly embarrassed about the gun he was carrying that evening. It was a clunky old Walther PPK that he thought made him a proper gangster. It was only later he found out that the Beretta 92 was the choice of a true professional, and it had reliably executed one hundred and ninety-three people since. He distinctly remembered checking the Walther PPK was properly hidden under his jacket and worrying if he would know when to strike.

It proved a distraction, and he almost bumped into the man as he turned a corner. The man had stopped outside a shop and was fumbling with his lighter. He gave up after a few sparks of its wheel and went inside for a box of matches (it was funny how he remembered the smallest details), and when he came out, his cigarette was lit and he strolled off with its end glowing regularly in the night. By now there was only the occasional car passing, and as the streetlights became less frequent, Popeye decided to attack. The man was only a short distance away and Popeye quickened his step. The man must have heard him, and he darted down a dark alley. Popeye raced after him and stopped dead.

The man was simply taking a pee, yet Popeye had other plans in mind. Pulling out his gun, he spun him round and was about to press it against his forehead when a warm, wet sensation spread down his legs. As he let go, the man stumbled back, fumbling with his zip. He probably thought that the worst thing coming was a mugging. He was wrong. Popeye put him right with a solid pistol whip that sent him to the ground. He thought it would relieve his anger. It didn't. He was still furious and scanned the alleyway for something to deliver further retribution. A dustbin would have to do, and he emptied its contents over the man splayed out.

Leaning over him, he pushed the barrel against the man's temple and distinctly remembered it trembling. Not from nerves, but from the rush of power and excitement. The man was mumbling something about his wallet being in his jacket (as though Popeye was some cheap mugger) and Popeye's temper boiled over at the insult. The man's voice soon trailed away when Popeye mentioned the old lady's name, and he waited silently for what was coming.

Popeye did not disappoint. Kneeling on the man's legs and pushing his head into the ground, he pulled back the hammer and delivered the first bullet of his career. And it felt good. The crack of the gun and the miniature sonic shockwave that followed hit his sinuses and chest like the bass from a subwoofer, and the adrenaline that accompanied it left him in no doubt that this was his calling. Getting up and rolling the man on his back, he leant over and pumped another bullet into his chest. Afterwards, Piña

41

recommended that he always look a victim in the face and watch their pupils dilate before the kill. It was some sort of reflex, an instinct for survival, and Popeye always made sure to follow his advice thereafter. *Mind you, it was probably too dark that evening*, he reflected.

He also reflected on his recent failure to tolerate youthful inexperience. After all, he was stupid enough to have run blindly into an alley (where the man might have been waiting for him with a gun), and what was he doing interrupting him whilst he was taking a pee! He had not mentioned any of this to Piña. Had he done so, maybe his recruiter would have reacted less favourably. It made him realise that perhaps he had been a little hasty, and he decided to see if the young guy was still around. Maybe give him another chance?

Casting his eyes around the café, something started to feel slightly off, and he had a growing sense of being at risk. The café looked perfectly normal and he struggled to put his finger on it, yet something was telling him to leave . . . and fast. Then the payphone jumped into life, breaking his concentration.

He knew it would be a message from El Patrón. Tucking the Beretta into his belt, he turned towards the bright blue steel box and froze. The matching knapsack was still there, rammed on a narrow shelf used for directories, but with two wires running up to the receiver cradle. They were well hidden against the dark tiles, yet their intention was clear. Popeye lunged for the door and burst through it.

The last thing he heard was the ring cutting out as the phone was answered. The explosion that followed blasted out the café windows and sent a pressure wave that lifted Popeye from his feet and threw him across the bonnet of a car. The swarm of broken glass that accompanied it tore across his arms, legs and torso, and his mouth began to fill with blood. A man across the street started waving frantically, then everything went blank.

CHAPTER TEN

Three weeks later Popeye was in a ditch with Pablo Escobar, up to his neck in water and crouching as quietly as possible in a freezing-cold stream. The forest around them was pitch black and a thick fog was swirling through the trees. It would keep them safe from the soldiers hunting them, unless a sound gave them away.

A faint glow appeared from where they had just come, growing brighter and brighter by the minute. Popeye tapped Pablo on the shoulder and put a finger to his lips. The soldiers were on the path above and they would soon reach them. A column of men emerged from the mist with rifles slung over their shoulders and flashlights pointing straight ahead. Trying to peer through the gloom and not fall over, never once taking their eyes off the man in front in case they stopped suddenly. The line of combat boots passed slowly and the night swallowed them up.

The sharp crackle of a radio in the distance was Popeye's cue to leave the ditch. He climbed out and checked that the coast was clear before waving at Pablo to join him. They walked for a few minutes then stopped by a white cross painted on a large tree. It was the marker for a steep trail that went down to a small gully. A shallow stream running down its centre led to a small village no more than half an hour away, and a car was waiting there with its engine running.

Popeye picked up a set of walking poles and two head torches from behind the tree, and they made their way down the trail. The gully was shallow, and they entered the stream with hardly a sound. Above them a spotlight swept over the treetops, but the fog was impenetrable and it cut out the beam and muffled all sound other than the gentle trickle of water over their feet. They reached the car sooner than expected and Popeye climbed in the back with Pablo.

As they bounced towards a safe house, Popeye sat back and reflected on his achievement. He had organised the escape of Colombia's most famous prisoner and he had done it right under the nose of the army. He was still sore from his injuries and would have liked more time to recover, but the government had ordered troops in to remove El Patrón sooner than expected and his recuperation had been put on hold; the buzz of the escape had made it more than worth it.

The cartel had known about the government's plan for months, although it was a surprise when the army arrived out of the blue. Popeye had been rushed up to the prison, hidden in the back of a laundry vehicle, and spent the afternoon checking their preparations. Everything was in order: the kill switch to the electric fence was still connected (hidden away in a corner of Pablo's cell), the hollow bricks in the perimeter wall had been left untouched and the guard roster for the twenty-second of July had been agreed in advance. Everyone knew what was expected, it was a straightforward plan and it had worked like a dream.

He always knew it would work. It had been meticulously planned from the start, even down to the location chosen for the prison. Planning for an escape had always been the most important consideration and Envigado was the perfect spot. The prison loomed over the surrounding countryside like a defensive tower and its access road had been cleared of trees so that any approaching vehicles were easy to spot. The remainder of the forest had been left intact and its thick cover was ideal for an escape. The evening fogs that rolled in made it doubly difficult to track anyone, and the streams and rivers hid any scent that might be picked up by a dog.

Popeye's job was now to protect El Patrón, not carry out assassinations.

Several hours later they were surrounded by potatoes, onions and rudimentary tools in a small cellar lit by a paraffin lamp. Dawn was just breaking and a gentle breeze and a sliver of light were coming through a small grill set in the wall. The smell of onions permeated everything, even the coffee on the table, and the air was cool, almost cold on account of the stone walls. Popeye watched Pablo lean back on the legs of his chair and grin.

'My family are farmers, *hermano*. This is like coming home.'

No mention was made of their escape nor of the search party that had passed the safe house a few hours earlier.

'Enjoy a taste of the countryside, Popeye – you'll be getting used to it.'

'No. I like the countryside, Patrón, even the dirt floors and the stink of onions.'

Both men laughed.

Popeye then turned to the arrangements he had made for Pablo's safety.

'We'll stay in La Ceja a few more days until things have settled down. After that I've made arrangements for us to be taken to Rionegro—'

Pablo cut him off. 'You won't be joining me, *hermano*,' he said, and leant forward. 'You're going to Bolivia.'

CHAPTER ELEVEN

The thrill of the escape was nothing compared to the shock of the bombshell delivered by El Patrón. Popeye was responsible for his security, and now he was being sent three thousand miles away to a remote corner of a remote country whose only saving grace was its coca crop. He had heard the food was atrocious and the women ugly.

He was in a foul mood as he drove down Calle 55 and rued the day that Ramón Escobar had joined the cartel. He was fat and useless and he stank, yet his disgust for Ramón was surpassed by the contempt he now felt. Not only had he managed to single-handedly strip away El Patrón's protection from extradition by torturing some DEA agents, now he was intent on double-crossing the cartel by setting up his own operation in Bolivia. Popeye was amazed that he had thought he could get away with it. Of course, the first thing the Mexicans did after Ramón made contact was speak to Piña. When the news reached El Patrón, he exploded. At least, that was what he had heard.

Once in Bolivia he would kill Ramón and then turn to Ernesto Serrudo. After he had discovered where Ernesto kept his emeralds, he too would be dispatched. The cartel had organised the trade that was worth several million dollars and the profit coming out of the Beni had aroused their interest and indirectly led to the takeover. Ironically, the task of delivering the emeralds had been given to Ramón as it was something that even he could not fuck up. The idea then developed into packing him off to Bolivia more permanently, away from the real business, a sort of sleepy backwater where he would be forgotten about and 'couldn't do any real harm'.

An old man standing by the road tried to flag Popeye down, and he rammed his foot on the accelerator. He was driving one of the hundreds of bright yellow taxis in Medellín that provided him with perfect cover; a four-wheel drive with tinted windows was reserved for pseudo-gangsters with political protection – he had neither and his taxi was both unmistakable and inconspicuous in the traffic. When he turned down Avenida 80 it was jammed with cars, and he came to a shuddering stop.

Popeye leant back in his seat and resigned himself to a slow journey. A large billboard dominated the road (maybe two hundred metres away) and he used it as a marker for his slow progress and counted down the minutes. Fifteen minutes later he was underneath it and two children were beaming down at him from the shoulders of their parents. They were clearly excited at being up there and their parents were delighted to be living in an apartment that was 'cheaper than renting'. The developer promised Popeye that he too could share in their good fortune, and the Municipality of Medellín had added a slogan to the billboard that read 'Tolerance Makes Us All Winners'.

Popeye ignored both messages and his taxi lumbered past them. Gradually the traffic became lighter and the brick and concrete less frequent, and as the outskirts of the city approached, Popeye turned off the highway. The road carried on for a few miles then turned into a narrow, winding street that ended at a steep flight of steps. Above him, rows of brick houses towered down from angular concrete slabs, and heavy black electricity cables hung between them like a spider's web. If it were not for the cables the whole place might have slipped down the hillside, and the paths that ran between the houses looked more like escape routes than means of access. It was the barrio above Robledo, and Popeye was in the heart of the cartel.

It was out of the barrios that Pablo Escobar recruited his foot soldiers, sicarios and runners. Rather than promoting a future based on tolerance, he offered a safety net for thousands of the

Medellín poor. Popeye knew he would always find support in their communities; today he would be relying upon that support.

The steps carved a route into the heart of the barrio, across narrow roads and broken pavements and through rows of tenements. As Popeye climbed, he found himself thinking about Ramón, if not fondly at least with a renewed interest. *Why would someone who has everything want even more?* He was in the heart of the cartel, admittedly not from ability but from the fortune of birthright, yet he had bitten the hand that fed him. *Strange.* It would be a challenge to track him down in the Beni region, but Popeye knew he would succeed. Then, out of nowhere, a cascade of soapy water shot down and splashed heavily on the steps, just missing him. It broke his concentration and made him jump to the side. As he looked up, shouting, the head of a young girl poked out from a row of shirts, giggling, with a hand over her mouth. She leant over the balcony railing, waved a hand in apology and disappeared. Popeye shook his head and carried on.

Finally the stairs came out in a dusty square surrounded on three sides by brick tenements and dominated by a large building in one corner. It was painted a deep blue with a large sign hanging over its door and some furniture was stacked up against its wall, as though it had been cleared away in a hurry. The other side of the square was undeveloped; only a small wall stood between it and a steep drop. Popeye strode up to the wall, gazed out for a moment, then spun round. The tenement windows were full of expectant faces and their roofs were packed with young men. Nobody moved. It was like an audience waiting for the curtain to rise; the only sound in the square was a low hum of distant traffic.

Three men emerged from the blue building and stood by its door. They were dressed in white with black armbands and the tallest also wore a purple, orange and green sash that marked him out as the community leader. He was holding a small black box, raised up like a votive offering. The men paused for a moment, then walked slowly into the middle of the square and stopped. The community leader approached Popeye and held out the box. There was no point in the men trying to bargain. Popeye was not prepared to accept the pesos as reparation. He pulled out his Beretta and the men knew what was expected. Bowing, the community leader returned to the blue building, and the others followed.

A new man emerged. This one was dressed plainly and he was holding coarse rope. He took a few steps into the square, then yanked it violently, and a figure stumbled out. His hands were tied in front and his head was bowed. He was led to the same spot where the other men had stood and the rope was dropped. Popeye approached him. The man did not look up and kept his eyes firmly on the ground.

'Raise your head, *hermano*.'

The man shook his head.

Popeye pulled back the slide of his Beretta.

'Don't make me pull your head back. If I have to then your family will also suffer.'

A pair of blinking eyelids and dilated pupils looked up.

'You know why it's come to this. Choose a good death in front of your community. Don't resist.'

Still the young man did not respond.

Popeye took hold of the rope and led him over to the small wall and the precipice that lay beyond. Holding his chin in one hand, he looked at the terror in his eyes for a moment then shot him twice in the chest. The crack of the gun ricocheted around the square, the traffic still hummed below and the community continued to watch, yet Popeye knew somewhere a mother would be weeping for the son who had double-crossed the cartel.

Three men dressed from head to foot in black strode across to the lifeless body. Blood was seeping into the concrete and beginning to pool, but they took no notice and grabbed his legs and arms whilst a fourth placed a stepladder against a lamppost. One end of a rope was tied under his arms, the other end was flung over the lamppost and the body was hauled up. A woman then came out from one of the tenements with a wooden board. It had two holes at either end, through which another rope had been threaded and knotted to form a loop. She handed it to the man by the stepladder, who hung it around the neck of the body. In bold red letters it read 'Here hangs an enemy of Pablo Escobar'.

Popeye nodded in approval, took one final look at the assembled crowd and left the square.

Walking down the steps, the execution got him thinking again about human failings – *Or was it human weakness?* Ramón had no excuse. He was wealthy and connected, yet despite that he had still betrayed the cartel.

The guy hanging from the lamppost was just weak and the offer of money from the Cali cartel had been too much for him to resist. He huffed when thinking that he had only received the equivalent of three hundred dollars for trying to blow him up. Surely he was worth more than that? What the guy forgot was that the cartel was an essential part of his community's welfare. Not only did it provide rudimentary healthcare and basic education, it had also built the football pitch on which its youngsters dreamt of becoming professional players. Of course, when the guy eventually returned to visit his mother under the cover of darkness, the community leaders pounced on him. Popeye had been told it was the roar of his motorbike that had alerted the neighbours; he doubted it. He knew the guy had plenty of money to mend his exhaust.

Getting into his car, Popeye also knew that El Patrón would have expected him to kill the guy *and* take the pesos offered as reparation, yet he could not bring himself to do it. *Best tell him the money from Cali had already been spent.* Digging out a small black book from the glove compartment, he flipped it open and ran a finger down a list of items for the day:

Pay electric bill
Pasta sheets
Gym
Drop off library book

He turned round to check that *The Count of Monte Cristo* was on the back seat.

Visit Juan D
Fresh clips – Bolivia

That reminded him to reload his Beretta. He never travelled without a full clip. Only an amateur would forget to reload, and he slotted another two bullets into the magazine. Fifteen in all, more than double the number of a Walther PPK. Another good reason to choose it over the latter.

P.A.X.

Not peace, rather a cross against the initials of Pedro Álvarez. Pedro was a local official, relatively low level but determined to make life awkward for the cartel. Recently promoted to Head of Vehicle Registration, he was insistent that their fleet of trucks be properly registered. Of course, he had received an offer of *plata o plomo* – a bullet or a bribe – and given a couple of weeks to mull it over. Two weeks were up and there had been no reply. Popeye would be delivering his bullet later that afternoon.

The list in his book was neatly split between domestic and work items. One of the advantages of being a sicario was the flexibility of his hours, and he managed to slot daily chores around his working day. He would drop the book off at the library before dealing with Pedro. It was, after all, on the way to City Hall.

By now his mood had improved immeasurably, and even though it was the same five hundred dollars for each hit, he would have executed the young guy for free. It was an absolute pleasure to kill for revenge. It was not only that the man had tried to kill him; he had also betrayed the trust of the cartel, the very same people who had offered him an escape from poverty and who supported his community. Popeye shrugged, put his Beretta in the glove compartment, checked his side mirror and took off down the street.

The traffic soon turned heavy, and he slotted a salsa tape into the cassette player to relieve the monotony.

'*En Barranquilla me quedo . . .*' Joe Arroyo sang.

The traffic was now lumbering down Avenida Castro.

Stop – Start – Stop – Start.

Popeye's fingers tapped on the steering wheel, exhaust fumes swirled around and a line of cars trundled along at a snail's pace. The traffic lights turned red again, brake lights came on and horns blasted. Popeye slowed down and turned up the air conditioning. A few seconds later his rear door flew open and he lunged for his Beretta. Spinning round, he was caught completely by surprise.

An elderly lady was getting in, clutching a large material bag. It was purple with gold-coloured motifs and sparkling beads . . . gaudy, like some cheap pantomime prop. She dropped the bag on his library book and took a seat.

'No, don't close the door, *señora*.'

She slammed it anyway and reached for a seat belt that wasn't there.

'*Señora*, this isn't a taxi,' Popeye said, turning round fully to face the old lady.

'Yes, it is, young man. You've got a taxi sign on top.'

'Okay, but I'm not working today.'

'You are. Your light is on.'

Popeye eyed the dashboard and flicked the light off.

'There, I'm not working now.'

What followed was a short battle of wills, and the old lady matched the stare of the cartel's top sicario. 'Young man,' she repeated, 'I need to get to the hospital by twelve' – she pointed a bony finger – 'before visiting hours finish. I'm not waiting until three o'clock.'

By now the traffic lights had turned green and a cacophony of impatient horns gave Popeye little choice. He swung round, shook his head, put Joe Arroyo on full blast and pressed hard on the accelerator.

'Young man – *turn that racket down!*' she shouted. 'How do you expect me to talk with that blaring out? You don't even know where we're going.'

'To the hospital – I know.'

'You don't know which one.'

Robledo was called the hospital district as it had three hospitals. Popeye turned the music down.

'Pablo Tobón Uribe,' she barked, and repeated, 'U-ri-be,' syllable by syllable. 'And don't race there either, you haven't got any seat belts.'

By now Popeye had decided to have some fun with her. It was not out of the way, and besides, she reminded him of his grandmother and the scolding he used to get whenever she caught him at the biscuit tin.

'Ah, that's a nice hospital, Grandma. You must have a wealthy friend there?' he asked, painfully aware that no one from the barrio could afford a visit.

'It's my nephew. He's artistic and it makes him anxious. His mother checked him in. What he needs is something to keep him occupied, not some treatment from a so-called specialist.'

The gaudy bag began to take on more significance.

'So, what's in the bag? Something to keep him occupied?'

'You're nosey, aren't you?'

Popeye tried not to laugh.

'If you must know . . . his mother goes on about his mood swings and his *obsession*,' she said, emphasising the word, 'with finding things exactly as he left them.' She paused and gave a loud sigh. 'It's because he's *artistic*. You tell me why people need to be diagnosed as artistic nowadays like it's an illness?' Lifting up the bag, she shook it roughly. 'I'm bringing him paint, brushes and a sketchpad. He can sketch me whilst I'm there and paint me in oils once I've left.'

'Wouldn't he do a better job in watercolours, Grandma?' Popeye asked, unable to control his laughter.

'You *are* a rude young man, aren't you?' she snapped. 'I've had eight children, what do you expect? One of *them* was exactly the same, moody and obsessive, but he couldn't draw *or* paint. Angelo wasn't diagnosed as *artistic*, he was just awkward . . .' And her voice drifted off as a bright road sign approached.

It was not long before they swung into the hospital, a magnificent ten-storey private facility with nearly four hundred beds and almost two thousand employees, glistening white with a façade that would not be out of place in downtown New York. Popeye pulled up and turned round to see the old lady fiddling with her bag.

'No, Grandma, this ride's for free. It's for humanitarian purposes,' he said, laughing and expecting her to produce a purse; instead his copy of *The Count of Monte Cristo* was in her hand.

'Hey, get your fucking hands off my book,' he shouted, snatching it from her. *What is it with the rich – always stealing from the poor?* Annoyed that he had tolerated the abrasive old lady, he was about to tell her to get out when she barked once more:

'Young man, that isn't your book. It's owned by the Municipal Library of Medellín. Don't lie to me, I've seen the label . . .' She paused, as though struggling with a decision.

'No! It's checked out to me,' Popeye snapped.

She cut him off before he could explain further. 'As you haven't charged me, I won't report you for stealing.'

Popeye told the old lady to get out.

'Well, you are the rudest of young men,' she said, standing by the door. 'And take my advice.' She had her hand on the doorhandle. 'Beware his casino.'

She closed the door at once, as though she had delivered some profound advice that Popeye should heed. Before he had time to reply, she had stormed off. Popeye leant out of the window at her disappearing back. 'What casino?'

She turned and shouted, 'The Count of Monte Carlo. He's a crook. His casino's rigged.'

Popeye could not get her dismissive wave out of his mind, certain now of the source of her nephew's mental illness.

CHAPTER TWELVE

Popeye dipped his finger into a bowl of holy water, made the sign of the cross and slid across a pew. At the front of the church a group of parishioners were fiddling with their rosary beads as they waited for confession. Morning Mass had just ended and the smoke from a strong-smelling incense was still hanging around the altar. Above it, a large crucifix loomed down on the parishioners, and he knew they looked to it, along with regular confession, for their salvation. For Popeye its bloodied figure was more a warning of the retribution that awaited unrepentant sinners, and he was not there for confession; he needed a quiet place to reflect on the task ahead, and where better than the church of San Pio X?

It was almost three weeks since he had organised El Patrón's escape and so much had changed since then, not least his appearance. His fingers absentmindedly stroked and twisted the hair on his chin that itched when it got hot, and his hand ran over his close-cropped hair which was sharp to the touch. He did not suppose for one moment that his new appearance would protect him for long, though it might give him a small head start. Besides, it had taken a couple of weeks to organise his fake ID and find a trustworthy pilot, and he might as well use the time to do everything he could to stay one step ahead of his enemies.

Finding a suitable pilot had been a challenge. All of the regular crew were contractors with an allegiance to the highest bidder, and Popeye needed someone different: a person whose integrity was beyond question, someone he could trust with his life. In the end, it was El Patrón himself who found the pilot, and he was flying out at dawn tomorrow.

Popeye watched the first parishioner genuflect, then disappear into an ornate wooden box pushed against the wall. A painting of Jesus hung alongside it. He was in the arms of his supporters and they were carrying him to the tomb. It was the last Station of the Cross: the sign of redemption, of a death that brought life.

A figure limping across the apse caught his eye. He had his back turned slightly, as though trying to avoid attention, and his black cassock and white surplice were a poor fit. He disappeared into the sacristy and Popeye was certain that he was not from around Itagüí. The shock of blond hair and his pale skin marked him out as a foreigner.

Strange. Maybe a missionary is helping out Father Santiago?

It got him thinking about foreigners and the difficulties they had caused him. No more than a week after the breakout, the US Justice Department had issued an indictment for El Patrón's arrest. Not only was he a 'notorious drug trafficker', but he was also 'engaged in international terrorism to further his trafficking enterprise'. At least that was what Robert C. Bonner, the chief of the Drug Enforcement Administration, had assured the American public when accusing him of blowing up Avianca Flight HK-1803.

What it confirmed to Popeye was that the Colombian government never had any intention of moving El Patrón to a different jail. He would have been handed over to the gringos, despite their ban on extraditions. The arrest warrant was a sham. It was the cocaine trade that the gringos wanted to shut down, not President Gavíria's enemies brought to justice. Popeye shrugged. Gavíria had only avoided the assassination attempt by a very last-minute change to his travel plans. Had he been on that plane then he would no longer be president and the cartel would have a more sympathetic ear in government. Maybe it was more collusion than luck. Gavíria was Cali's man, and perhaps they had learnt of the plot and alerted him? Nobody knew, but they had their suspicions.

Although the indictment was expected, the government's announcement that the Americans were hunting for El Patrón came as a shock. Right now, Hercules C-130 spy planes were scouring the airwaves for the slightest clue to his whereabouts and all electronic communication had been shut down. The old system of delivering messages using runners and multiple drop points had been reinstated. It was a failsafe way to communicate, as none of the runners knew the end destination of a message, and by the time the authorities got further up the chain, it would be broken, typically by a bullet. It meant things were taking longer to organise, another reason why Popeye was still in Itagüí.

It did have one small benefit. Popeye was still in Medellín when the cartel's response shook the city . . . a one-hundred-and-fifty-pound car bomb detonated outside Los Molinos shopping centre. Seventy-nine people were killed and the response from the government had been predictable . . . a combined army, navy and air force initiative to track down 'the fugitive terrorist'. *And so things ratchet and a war begins*, he thought. It would follow the usual path of recrimination, escalation and destruction before a stalemate would be reached and peace agreed. Just like last time.

Popeye had no idea why the government had decided to break the peace in the first place, although he guessed the gringos were behind it. He also knew that he would be away in Bolivia for at least six weeks and would miss some of the opening shots. El Gordo would be co-ordinating the bombing campaign, so he would not be needed for the initial phase, yet he was determined to get approval for Gavíria's assassination when he returned. *A bomb's a blunt tool; a bullet has a sharp focus*, he assured himself.

Whilst there was no open competition between him and El Gordo, it was common knowledge that both were vying for El Patrón's approval, and he was irritated to be away when the war really started. He planned to return as soon as possible.

El Gordo's success reminded him that he still needed to make a shopping trip. Top of the list was a pair of thick socks for the colder nights, and his supply of paracetamol was running low. He whipped out his notebook to check whether he needed anything else and was pleased to see a line through the other items.

By now the row of penitents was shrinking fast. Popeye glanced up from his notebook as another emerged from the confession box and knelt down for their penance. *Probably three Hail Marys and one Our Father.* He wondered what penance he would receive if he popped in, and more from curiosity than desire, he contemplated paying Father Santiago a visit. The idea was quickly dismissed. Whilst the parishioners took solace in the physical sacrament, for him it was a metaphysical construct that allowed him to do his job with a clear conscience.

Somewhere a set of scales measured his good deeds against his bad deeds. The trick for Popeye was to make sure they tipped in his favour. His assassination of Pedro Álvarez would have tipped them slightly against him, although the Robledo killing would have made good the transgression. His actions had saved the community from losing all welfare and forcing some of their girls onto the street. He knew that the priest in the confessional would never see it that way. Sin was black and white and 'thou shalt not kill' was perfectly clear, yet Popeye had confidence in the supreme being, whose omnipotence outweighed even Father Santiago's long experience in His service.

One of the elderly ladies awaiting confession caught his attention. She was struggling to get out of her pew, and Popeye came to the rescue.

'*Señora*, take my arm,' he said, gently supporting her back. She clung to his arm and pointed a stick at the box. It was clear what was expected. He led her slowly towards the gloomy innards that smelt of polish and hid the dark grill that awaited her supplication. It was only when they reached the door that her grip became firmer, her posture more steady, and she gently but firmly pushed Popeye inside. He laughed and shook his head. He was not going to make a scene like a truculent child; instead he sat down and leant against the wall. Opposite him, a dim light shone over a small sign.

Popeye shrugged.

'Bless me, Father, for I have sinned. It has been . . . quite a while . . . since I last made a confession, and I seek forgiveness for my transgressions.' Popeye read the words directly from the sign. It was obvious that infrequent visits were common and the experience was made more accommodating by providing a prompt. There was a blank space between 'It has been' and 'since I last made' to allow the repentant to tailor their confession to their own individual circumstances.

'I await your confession, my son.'

Popeye leant towards the grill. It was hard to see through its dark wire mesh. The voice did not sound familiar. Father Santiago was an old man with a smoker's rattle; this was a younger man with an unusual accent.

'I am tempted by venal pleasures.' He remembered that one. It was the first item on the list learnt by rote at first communion lessons. The second one was about not respecting his parents. Try as he might, he could not remember the third. 'Er . . . I don't always attend Mass on Sunday and I am impatient.'

'Bless you, my son. These are sins from which we must all turn.' Popeye wondered if the priest also skipped Mass but assumed he was referring to his impatience. 'I wish to return to your venal sins, my son,' the priest added. Normally, the 'venal' wrapper covered a multitude of vices, none of which needed to be divulged in detail, and Popeye was taken by surprise.

'Okay.'

'Tell me what temptation you have succumbed to, my son.'

'Nothing special. Just the usual . . . venal pleasures.'

'Do you consume pornography, my son?'

'What!'

'Do you consume pornography?'

Popeye struck the metal grill with the palm of his hand and bent it slightly. The priest ignored him. 'Does my question offend you, my son?' he asked. 'If so, let me ask you another. How did it feel when you killed Pedro Álvarez?'

Popeye pressed his head against the grill to get a look at the priest. He was sitting with his back to the wall. All he could make out in the half-light were his hands, placed calmly on his lap. 'Motherfucker – you're no priest,' he growled, furious that the sanctum of confession had been desecrated by some *hijo de puta* with a sense of humour.

He regretted leaving his Beretta in the car. Its grip was perfect for delivering a solid pistol whip, yet it would have been sacrilegious to bring a gun into church. He would have to administer the punishment with his bare hands. Springing up, he pushed the door. It didn't move. He pushed his shoulder against it. It was definitely locked. The confession box was built of solid teak with large hinges. By the time he kicked it open the imposter would be long gone.

'My son, calm yourself. Aggression and profanities have no place in the confessional.'

Popeye returned to his seat and quickly assessed the situation. The light in the box was poor, and the wood too dense for an accurate shot. There was no risk of an assassination, yet he was acutely embarrassed about being trapped in a confession box. He did not want to draw any more attention to his predicament than was necessary and he knew kicking the door open would not go unnoticed. Instead, he leant forward and chose his words carefully.

'I don't know who you are or where you live, but I'm going to find out.' The words were delivered slowly and with a menace that came from experience. 'Say your prayers, Father, you'll need them. When I catch you, my Beretta's going to wipe that smile off your face.'

The answer he received came like a thunderbolt.

'Will that be after you return from Bolivia, or do you have time this afternoon . . . my son?'

CHAPTER THIRTEEN

Just after one o'clock the following morning Popeye's car joined the highway. Ignoring signs for the city centre and international airport, the driver carried on for a few miles then swung off in the direction of Envigado and the Andes. Popeye sat in the back and watched the lights of Medellín disappear as the car plunged into the darkness of the mountainside. He was now finally on his way, although less certain of where it would take him. His encounter with the fake priest had suggested the real possibility that Bolivia would be *his* grave, not that of the double-crossers. Yet it had not deterred him. Quite the opposite. He was more determined than ever to make sure they got a bullet first.

Pablo Escobar's escape had changed everything. The airstrips surrounding Medellín were now strictly monitored and checkpoints had sprung up on all major routes out of the city. It was only once a suitable airstrip had been found, and safe passage organised, that 'Señor Juan Arroyo Fernández' could travel with the confidence that came from a network of military and civilian supporters.

The road down to Puerto Perales Nuevo was a bright strip of tarmac that stood out in the moonlight and cut a path through the forest below. Dogs chased their car through each small settlement they passed and the checkpoints they approached were bathed in an artificial light that glowed yellow in the winter gloom. They passed three in total, each one as identical as the last, with a barricade of army lorries, soldiers brandishing semi-automatic rifles and a smartly uniformed officer checking papers.

It gave Popeye plenty of time to reflect, and his thoughts kept turning back to the fake priest and the warning he had received. He had been right. There had been no physical threat and his promise of retribution had hung awkwardly, something that would have prevented further discourse were it not for his foe's serenity. Thankfully the man had quickly dropped all pretence at being a priest along with the term 'my son'. If he were to be believed, then his interest was aligned with the cartel and he wished to see Ramón and Ernesto dead just as much as Popeye did. He had come to warn Popeye of a threat he faced before even leaving Colombia; however, the warning made no sense:

'Beware the pilot.'

Yet it was none other than El Patrón who had chosen him! Popeye had received his written note just the other day, and his impenetrable scrawl was unmistakable. Of course, Popeye had asked for more information from the fake priest. Who was he? How had he come by this information? Why was he helping him? The vague answers he received went no further in allaying the suspicion that he was being set up, that it was a crude plan either to delay his flight or raise doubts about the very man who had selected the pilot. Whilst he hadn't *actually* heard the words from El Patrón's mouth, his signature and the message looked authentic.

The suggestion of betrayal was at first incredulous, then credible, and his thoughts had swung from disbelief to anger and back again. Had it not been for the fake priest's knowledge of the Pedro Álvarez assassination, he would have immediately put it down to a fishing exercise from the Cali cartel, or even Los Pepes, yet neither of them had the resources to monitor the hourly movements of the cartel and none of them would have been interested in such a low-level hit job. It must have been someone who was either on the inside or had a powerful surveillance network. It pointed to the DEA and their C-130 Hercules spy planes, and the blond hair of the limping priest further pointed a finger that way, for he was certain that the *hijo de puta* on the other side of the screen must have been a gringo.

By now a heavy rain had arrived in great, sudden swathes across the treetops, hitting the windscreen and making its wipers swish frantically. It was a summer storm that Popeye knew would pass shortly, and he pressed his face against the window to savour its power. For some sicarios it would be a bad omen; for him it was simply a natural phenomenon. He was not in the least bit superstitious, and he knew that planning and preparation were more important to a kill than carrying a talisman or kissing a cross. With this in mind, and as the rain drummed on the roof and poured down his window, he began to formulate a plan on how best to deal with a potentially rogue pilot.

An hour later the car turned off the highway and followed a dirt road where an occasional shack sprang up in the glare of their headlights then disappeared just as suddenly in the total darkness. Eventually the first streaks of dawn outlined the treetops and a fine mist rose to reveal a landscape of small farms and ragged livestock. The airstrip was nearby, down a single-track road with a battered white sign and the words 'Airstrip traffic ONLY' painted in faded red letters.

A strip of silver-coloured lamps sparkled across a field and a gap in a long hedgerow marked the entrance to the airstrip. The car swung in and followed a bumpy track along the perimeter, then turned towards the runway. A Piper PA-18 was waiting there with its engine running and passenger door open. The car slowed to a walking pace and Popeye half opened his door. As they approached the plane he rolled out of the car and crouched behind it, then sprinted to the side before it drew up.

The car stopped and the driver got out. He was short and stocky like Popeye. A baseball cap was pulled over his eyes and he wore a heavy leather jacket. Taking a bag out of the boot, he reached the passenger door of the plane at the exact moment Popeye tore open the pilot's door. Popeye rammed his Beretta into the crisp white shirt of the pilot and a scream rang out.

The ponytail that swung round stopped him in his tracks. He had expected to see a sicario reaching for his weapon, not a female pilot with a flight checklist in her hand. He was speechless, totally thrown by the sight of her. The message from El Patrón had been perfectly clear: '*He* will be waiting for you at the airstrip', not '*she*'.

Or was it that specific? It could have read 'the pilot' and maybe he assumed it was a man. After all, every single drug courier between Bolivia and Colombia was a man.

'Please don't shoot, *señor*!' she said timidly.

The request broke Popeye from his thoughts and he pulled the gun away.

'My apologies, *señorita*, you were . . .' He hesitated. 'Not what I was expecting.'

She gave a weak smile, gestured at the passenger seat and did her best to compose herself. Popeye took his bag from the driver and climbed into the passenger seat, and within a few minutes they were flying high over the Magdalena River, following riverbanks dotted with small settlements and miniature boats.

Once they had reached three thousand feet she switched to autopilot, turned to Popeye and pointed at his headset. He flicked it on. Would he like some breakfast? It was like the offer of manna from heaven. He was starving.

'That was all I could think of. Thank you, *señorita*.'

She nodded, took off the headset and unclipped herself. As she squeezed past, she brushed against his arm. It had not escaped Popeye's attention that she was slim and attractive, with long, luxurious dark hair. She was a typical *morena* that the likes of Joe Arroyo sang about – stunning, bewitching creatures that made a man's heart melt after they had cast their spell – at least that was Joe's take on it.

The small hamper she returned with was full of pastries, fruit and a flask of fresh coffee; she was about to pass it over when Popeye stopped her.

'No, *señorita*. Take some food. There's too much for me and you have an important job ahead.'

She hesitated, put her headset back on and replied, '*Señor*, my name is Dolores. "*Señorita*" is a bit formal.' She had a slightly husky tone and a dazzling smile that made Popeye grateful for El Patrón's choice. Selecting a handful of grapes, she passed back the hamper and popped one into her mouth.

'How was your journey, *señor*? Did you pass many checkpoints?' she asked.

'The name's Popeye . . . just Popeye . . . as in Popeye the Sailor Man. It's a long story. If I must call you Dolores, then you must call me Popeye.' His suggestion was met with a nod and another smile. 'We passed three in total. There weren't many cars, so we got through quickly.' Another grape disappeared and he was sure that she was teasing him, maybe even leading him on. It was not what he had been expecting, and it certainly was like nothing he had ever experienced in the cartel's light aircraft.

'So, Popeye' – she said his name as if savouring the 'P' – 'of course I know who you are. Everyone does. You feed the poor and clothe the vulnerable of Medellín. Even in Bogotá we talk about your good works.'

Popeye flashed one of his charismatic smiles and opened the flask of coffee.

'I have the good fortune to work for a genius, Dolores,' he said, pouring a cup and offering it to her. She shook her head and Popeye raised it to his lips. 'You're sure? There's only one cup . . .' he added, before taking a sip.

'You have the sweetest smile, Popeye. I don't think I'm going to catch anything sharing a cup with such a smile!'

Popeye felt the thrill of an invitation to get to know Dolores better and counted his blessings.

The coffee was hot and soothing like a warm blanket in the cold morning and the scenery around him dazzled in the brilliant sun. *Just like the* morena's *smile*, he thought as his eyes closed and his head nodded. He woke with a start and tried to resume the conversation. The words echoed around the cockpit, sounding like someone else's voice. A hand on his shoulder . . . a stare, or was it a sneer? Then his head bounced and he was falling into a dark pit.

His hands shot out and he tried to grasp the stone blocks that were racing past. They were covered in slime and impossible to grip. He plunged into a pool of freezing-cold water, and when he came to the surface, Dolores was waving down from a stone parapet. Popeye was in a well and there was no escape. Dolores disappeared and his body began to swirl round a hole that had appeared in its centre. It was a small whirlpool and he was getting closer and closer. Suddenly his body was sucked down a watery column that grew brighter with each turn and he was spat out into a dazzling light that signalled its end.

His eyes sprang open in a cold wind. He was back in the plane, though not for long. The passenger door was open and he was being launched through it. Then he was half out of the plane with one leg trapped in the seat belt. Someone, or something, was frantically trying to free it, and he twisted his foot further into the belt and lashed out with the other. There was a sharp gasp and his leg was released. Popeye managed to grab the seat belt as a blade flashed past and sliced the material above his hand. Another cut and the belt was torn in half, but Popeye had a grip on the door and he pulled himself up. His other hand parried the next blow then he was back inside. He launched himself into Dolores, and after a brief struggle the knife was in his hands. She aimed a punch at his head. Popeye ducked and plunged the knife through the top of her boot. She screamed in pain and Popeye slammed the passenger door shut.

'Beware the pilot.'

The warning rang loudly in his head as he pressed his Beretta into her ribs. It made him question the true intentions of the man behind the operation, and a doubt about El Patrón's loyalty grew that was difficult to dispel. The *morena* had said he was behind the attack, yet she was not able to give any reason for Popeye's sudden loss of favour and she was too insistent to be convincing.

Popeye needed her to land the plane, so he had accepted her story and gave an implicit promise that she would come to no harm if she landed them safely in Bolivia. Meanwhile, his senses were in turmoil. The coffee must have been drugged and he felt sluggish, not the best time to try and unravel what it all meant. Instead he had to focus on staying awake. He knew if he dropped off again she would seize her chance and he would not be so lucky the next time. With that in mind, and spurred on by an irritation born out of his entrapment, he leant over and delivered a crack across her head that not only told her he was still very much awake but reminded her that he was not wholly susceptible to her particular method of bewitchment.

An airstrip appeared, carved through a dense forest at the foot of a small mountain range. They descended quickly and taxied to a stop. Popeye gestured for Dolores to get out and followed her through the pilot's door. Her eyes burned with hatred yet she made no sound, despite her painful injury. Popeye matched her defiant stare, and admired her courage and confidence to take on the cartel's top sicario. As he pushed her to the front of the plane, he could think of only a handful of men who would have accepted the challenge. When her shoulder was carved open by the propeller he knew she would have made a good member of his team.

After Popeye had put a couple of bullets into her body, he returned to the plane, climbed into the passenger seat and promptly fell asleep.

He awoke to find a stray dog tucking into the remains of his breakfast, and he was about to stroke it when he saw specks of dried blood around its mouth. With a curse, he booted it out of the cabin and looked for something to cover the woman's body. A dark green tarpaulin at the back of the plane drew his attention, and when he went to retrieve it, he found the body of a man whose uniform marked him out as one of the regular pilots. His throat had been slit.

There was no time to try and make sense of it. Two cones of light were speeding towards him in a cloud of dust and the roar of an engine was growing louder and louder. Grabbing his bag, he jumped down from the plane and ran for cover. Two men got out, one straining to control a black Doberman, the other with a radio in his hand. They crouched down by the pilot's body for a moment, then the man with the Doberman strode to the plane and the dog jumped inside.

Popeye knew what was coming. He tore off his jacket and yanked a knife from his bag. Running nimbly through the trees, he bound the jacket tightly around his left arm and listened out for his pursuers. Before long the Doberman could be heard crashing through the undergrowth, louder and louder, as it bounded full pelt towards the scent of a prey twice its weight and a third as fast. Popeye burst into a small clearing covered in a spongy moss and stopped dead. He raised his left arm, unsheathed the knife and waited.

A few seconds later the dog leapt out of the trees and ran full pelt towards Popeye. It launched itself at his outstretched arm and slammed him to the ground, but the moss cushioned Popeye's fall and the knife in his other hand flashed in and out of the Doberman like the needle on a sewing machine. Eventually the dog released its grip and rolled away. Popeye stumbled to his feet, plunged the blade through its neck and watched the bright green moss turn red. The dog was panting heavily and the handle of the blade jerked as it struggled to breathe. Popeye sorely wished to put it out of its misery, yet the report of a bullet would give him away and he knew the two men would not be far behind. Unravelling his jacket, he smeared some blood across his face then pulled out his gun, dropped to the floor and dragged his jacket over the weapon. With his other arm stretched out, he played dead.

Soon the men appeared and one of them broke into a desperate run. It was the dog handler, sprinting towards the body of his Doberman. As he bent over to pull out the knife, Popeye put a bullet through his leg. When he hit the floor, the next shot caught him square in the chest. Rolling away, Popeye saw the other man quickly retreat into the forest, and he leapt to his feet and sprinted after him. He was a big man but in bad shape; with Popeye it was a full-time job, and he reached the man in no time. He forced him to his knees, and the man started gibbering about being innocent, a family man, just a driver for the Huallaga Valley cartel.

Popeye's ears pricked up at the mention of the Peruvian cartel.

'What are you doing in Bolivia then, *güevón?*'

'Bolivia, *señor?*' the man replied. 'We're in Tambopata, not Bolivia.'

Popeye pressed his Beretta into the man's temple. 'Don't get smart. Tambopata is in Bolivia.'

The man looked puzzled.

'Tambopata is in Peru, *señor*. Please put down your gun. If you need to get to Bolivia I can drive you, but—'

Popeye snatched the radio from the man's shaking hand and turned it off. He was in Peru and in danger. Ramón had persuaded the Huallaga Valley cartel to join him, and they controlled the area down to the Bolivian border. The advantage of being driven in one of their cars did not escape him and he pulled the gun away. What's more, if Ramón hadn't known that he was gunning for him, he did now – unless it was Ramón all along who had ordered the hit? But then, how could he have known about his mission unless someone in the Medellín cartel had betrayed him? Once more his head spun with unanswered questions and instinct told him the fake priest would be somewhere behind it all.

CHAPTER FOURTEEN

Popeye was driving the pickup. The driver's shirt on his back reeked, like it hadn't been washed for days, and his head still ached from the drugged coffee, *but*, if it was a confident Popeye that had left Itagüí, it was a determined one now tearing up the switchbacks into the *altiplano*.

The man in the passenger seat was wearing Popeye's bloodstained shirt. His left arm was tied underneath as though in a sling and his legs were fastened to the seat. Popeye was not taking any chances, although his other arm was free so that he could point directions, open the window, smoke cigarettes . . . *After all, there's no need to make the journey more uncomfortable than necessary.* If they were stopped, the bloody shirt would draw attention away from Popeye and give him precious seconds to react.

'A smoke?' he asked, pointing at a cigarette packet sliding across the dashboard.

The man nodded. Popeye threw him the packet of Manzanas Rojas.

'Are we in danger, *güevón*?'

Popeye knew the answer. Once the cartel, or whoever it was behind the attack, failed to reach him, they would know something was up. He was just curious to see if he could trust the man. His answer would not change his plan: get to the *altiplano* as soon as possible and disappear amongst the roads up there. Until then he was at risk on the only route in and out of the lowlands, stuck behind lumbering lorries and hemmed in by precipitous drops.

'*Sí*,' the man replied.

Popeye glanced at him. His shirt was a tight fit, almost bursting at the buttons, and the streaks of blood gave him a ghoulish appearance. He was still struggling to retrieve a lighter from his pocket, although a cigarette was in his mouth.

'Do you love your family?'

The man nodded as he finally reached his lighter.

'Me too, and if we work together, we'll get to see them again. If not, then my Beretta will protect me.' The car dropped down a gear as a corner approached. 'Do you have any protection?' Popeye asked as the car turned the bend and the steering wheel slid through his fingers.

A small flame shot out of the man's hand and he shook his head.

'So, here's what we are going to do,' Popeye continued, winding down his window and gesturing at the man to do the same. 'If we are stopped by the police, by the cartel, or by anyone else come to think of it, you do the talking. You were injured in a shoot-out at the airstrip. Some *hijo de puta* from Colombia shot your partner and you put a bullet in his head. Point at the shirt, wave your arm at the sling, whatever you need to do to get us out of it, understood?'

The man hesitated. 'But your face, *señor*?'

'What?'

'Your face is covered in blood.'

Popeye twisted the rear-view mirror. It was a mess of blood and dried sweat, and he laughed loudly.

'You think I look suspicious?'

The man chuckled. Popeye poured some bottled water over his head and rubbed it around his face. When they got stuck behind a lorry he finished off the job properly, then swung the car into the opposite lane. Tearing past, he handed the man the radio and pulled out his Beretta.

'Call your boss. Keep it short. Tell him you've got the pilot. She's injured and you're taking her to a hospital – somewhere, anywhere, so long as it's in the opposite direction. Your partner didn't make it, and neither did Popeye. And remember,' he said with no attempt to hide the threat, 'a bullet from my Beretta will split your liver long before you've given me away.'

The man did as he was told, and Popeye listened carefully for any unusual words that might have been code for a warning. Satisfied that there were none, he replaced his gun, took the radio back and turned it off.

An hour later the verdant slopes had been replaced with a row of jagged peaks and the pickup was passing through a narrow valley and onto a wide plain. Power cables stretched as far as the eye could see, and as Popeye started to relax, his mind turned to his running total of kills. He was now five short of reaching two hundred. Ramón and Ernesto would take it closer to the line and there would be other bodies before then, he was sure of it.

As usual, his latest kills were weighed on the scales of judgement and he was pleased not to come up wanting. The dog handler was simply an act of self-preservation that kept them level. The pilot had initially swung them against him as he had broken the promise to release her if she landed them safely. However, he had been very specific that the landing was to be in Bolivia, not Peru, and her back-sliding had invalidated their agreement. Once again it made the kill one of self-preservation, not indulgence, and with it the scales were balanced out. When he added his humane treatment of the man next to him, they swung in his favour – after all, he could have put a bullet in him. He shrugged. *That would have been indulgence, and besides, he's a useful decoy and knows the roads into Bolivia.* With that in mind, and now that they were on the *altiplano*, he decided to tip the scales further in his favour by buying provisions for them at an approaching village.

Pulling up alongside a row of rundown shops, he grabbed his gun, checked the man was tied securely and locked the car. The shop was pitiful. Small plastic baskets full of onions, potatoes and dried llama lay on the floor surrounded by mounds of toilet rolls in large plastic sacks and crates of beer. Turning to the counter, nowhere were the warm *salteñas*, a small savoury pastry crammed full of vegetables, nor the spicy chicken legs that he had hoped to see. Instead, what greeted him was an uninspiring collection of dry biscuits and a woman with her hand over her mouth, doing her very best to suppress a laugh.

Popeye stared hard at her, and she rushed into the storeroom to let it out. Eventually she reappeared, more in control.

'*Niña*, do you sell—'

She cut him off.

'Yes, I have soap and shampoo,' she said, and disappeared again before he had time to ask for bottled water.

'Here, use the soap first,' she said, thrusting a packet and a shampoo bottle over the counter, laughing.

'What?'

'Llama blood won't come out with just shampoo.'

The penny dropped. Popeye realised his hasty clean-up was less effective than he had thought. Out of nowhere a small mirror appeared in the woman's hand, and she encouraged him to use it. Dotted around his beard were small pieces of dog flesh hanging like baubles on a Christmas tree, and on his head a streak of dried blood stood out like a bright red Mohican.

'Was it a sacrifice?'

Popeye just grimaced and decided that the man would no longer be enjoying whatever meagre provisions he managed to find. It was only then that he realised he had left the radio behind and dashed back to the car, cursing his rare lapse of concentration. Luckily, the radio had not been moved. Snatching it from the console, he returned to the shop, indulged the woman selling the soap and shampoo and added some water and biscuits to the order.

Shortly afterwards, when he was bending over a sink picking out small pieces of flesh, he sighed. The Doberman was just following its natural instincts, unlike its handler, who deserved the bullets he got. His tally of rights and wrongs did not extend to animals, and the image of the Doberman, quivering and suffering on the moss, weighed on his mind. Walking back to the car, he resolved to put it right with an act of kindness at the next opportunity.

Ten minutes later Popeye was enjoying a biscuit and a drink of water.

'So, *güevón*, you didn't think to mention the *puta* Doberman in my beard?' he asked, taking another glug of water from the bottle. It had not been offered to the man; neither had the packet of biscuits. Popeye realised he was not listening and was peering intently at the road racing past. The hand that slammed onto his thigh made him jump and got his attention.

Popeye shouted, 'Doberman' – and pointed – 'beard.'

'My apologies, *señor*, I didn't notice,' he replied with a slight chuckle. Popeye's irritation grew, and he had a sense of the man being somehow less on edge – not exactly relaxed, but more confident. It put Popeye on alert. When returning to the pickup he had tied both his arms together as a punishment; now it seemed like a sensible precaution. With his rising temper there came the temptation to deliver further physical retribution, yet he knew it would undo the credit gained from his recent magnanimity. The packet of Manzanas Rojas flew out the window instead.

The road carried on for another hour or so, alongside a fast-flowing river and through a wide valley lined with mountains that trapped the clouds and turned the scenery grey and lifeless. Only the swirling eddies of the lively river gave the scenery any life. It was as though the altitude had stripped it of everything other than coarse tussock grass. The back of Popeye's eyes had begun to ache from the thinner air and his head was pounding from the altitude, yet that was the least of his concerns; he noticed his passenger repeatedly glancing in the wing mirror, and when Popeye checked in the rear-view, he spotted a vehicle far off in the distance.

'You think those men will rescue you? You're wrong, *hermano*,' Popeye said calmly, and pushed his foot to the floor. The man's head was thrown back as the car hit sixty miles an hour . . . seventy miles an hour . . . then eighty miles an hour. Popeye slammed on the brakes and the man's head catapulted into the dashboard. Were it not for the straps around his legs he would have gone straight through the windscreen. Instead, he fell back, semi-conscious, against the door.

Popeye swung the car round and faced the oncoming vehicle. It was fast approaching with a motorbike alongside. Popeye saw its pillion rider was armed and he quickly looked around for something to jam on the accelerator. Spotting a fire extinguisher, he shoved it on the pedal, cut the leg ties of his passenger and pushed hard on the top of its cylinder.

The pickup leapt forward and raced towards the motorbike. Bullets started pinging off its body, but Popeye's timing was impeccable. He opened the passenger door and yanked on the steering wheel just as the motorbike closed in for the kill. The pickup swerved to the side, its passenger tumbled out and the motorbike cartwheeled over the man as he rolled across the tarmac. Popeye removed the fire extinguisher, strapped himself in and floored it. Both cars were now speeding towards each other in a deadly game of chicken. Popeye stayed cool, wound his window down and took aim at the driver's front wheel. His first shot missed and hit the wheel arch. The second bullet caught the bumper. Finally, the third one hit home just as a submachine gun opened up. Popeye ducked.

The next thing he knew, the roof was swirling, spinning, crashing and throwing glass everywhere as a glancing blow from the other vehicle sent the pickup rolling faster and faster down a precipice. A small bounce, another tumble, then a large rock in the river brought it to a shuddering halt and tore a large gash in its roof.

Popeye was upside down, strapped into the driver's seat, dazed by a head wound but otherwise protected by the roll bars. The freezing water rushing in through the roof and windscreen quickly brought him to his senses. He had no idea if his assailants were at large, yet he needed to escape from the car, which was quickly filling with water. He yanked at the seat belt; the catch was trapped between the seat frames. He needed a knife. It was out of reach. Then gunshots echoed round the valley and he realised danger was close at hand.

CHAPTER FIFTEEN

It was the white makeup and dazzling orange shirt that drew the passengers' attention, more like a blouse than a shirt, with a turquoise cravat and black tiepin. A broad-brimmed hat was balanced on the man's head and he wore bright red lipstick that was turned up into a hideous smile. Two large men were holding him up as they passed down the aisle and his feet were dragging on the floor. He was clearly unconscious.

'Drunk!' said the man supporting his waist.

'The last fling before marriage,' his partner added, patting his hat as they helped him to the back of the bus.

Other than a few passengers who stared, the drunkard in the Joker outfit was accepted as a wayward fiancé, and by the time he had been propped up in his seat, no one was paying him any more attention and he was left to sleep it off.

Popeye blinked.

It was dark and he was moving. His head was aching and something was pulled over his eyes. He went to move it, but his arm was tied to a heavy object. Was he underwater? Was he trapped? Was he dead . . .? A large pothole reminded him that he was moving and the pain in his head suggested he was very much alive. He tentatively moved his other arm, knocked the hat to one side and was promptly blinded by a streetlamp flashing past.

'*Puta*,' he cursed, and looked around. *What the fuck am I doing on a bus?* Then he looked down. His legs were covered in a gaudy plaid material more suited to a golf course, and he was wearing a purple jacket. With his free hand he ripped off the cravat and undid the rope that was tied to the bag. Only then did he reach into it for his gun. It was still there, and he let out a sigh of relief. Pulling it out to check the magazine, he noticed a long stick in its barrel. It was wrapped in a small strip of red material, and when he tore it out, a flag unravelled with the word 'BANG!' written on it in bright white letters.

Hijo de puta. *You don't mess with a man's tools.* It was the ultimate disrespect, and it made the humiliation of being dressed up as the Joker seem insignificant. The sick sense of humour immediately reminded him of his experience in the confession box, and it had to be the work of the fake priest. Yet instinct told him he was rescued for a reason, and it was not just to ridicule him.

Slowly the events of the past few days came back: the double-crossing *morena* . . . the suffering dog . . . the devious Peruvian driver. The image of the vehicle speeding towards him was still fresh in his mind, as was the sensation of crashing helplessly down the side of a bank. Other than a brief memory of being upside down in the pickup, he had no recollection of what happened after he blacked out. How he ended up on the bus was a mystery.

Sitting back, he wondered if he was being played. Why not simply kill him? Why save him only to humiliate him?

He also had a growing sense that the scales of justice were no longer working quite as he expected. He knew that without good deeds to balance out the bad ones, he faced an eternity of pain, suffering and red-hot pokers; yet for some reason each of his good deeds had recently delivered a great deal of pain and plenty of suffering. And it had not escaped him that the payback had been very much in the present, and not some far-off Judgement Day. At least he had avoided a red-hot poker, but that missed the point; his good works were supposed to be a benign offset, not a catalyst for divine retribution.

For the compassion shown to the prospective sicario, he was almost blown up. For the patience shown to the crazy woman, he nearly got his book stolen. And his reward for helping an old lady in church was a ritual humiliation. Yet it was the cartel driver who really got under his skin. Although he'd had every opportunity to punish this man, his restraint had shone through. *I mean, I even let him smoke in the car, and I can't stand smoking.* His payback for that one was a near-drowning in freezing water, having his gun desecrated and now waking up on a bus dressed as the Joker. And he didn't even know where the *puta* bus was going!

With that in mind, he fished around in his pocket for a ticket. *I must have one, otherwise I wouldn't have been allowed on the bus.*

'*Puta!*' An electric charge surged through his middle finger and he whipped out his hand. A mousetrap was hanging from it and a playing card was dangling from the mousetrap on a purple string. The card had an angel rising from hell on one side and a man wearing an orange shirt and a turquoise cravat on the other. Popeye immediately recognised it as the Joker costume he was wearing. The inference was clear, and the slur on his reputation did not go unnoticed.

Releasing the trap, he snatched the card and vowed to stuff it down the throat of the fraudulent priest once he caught him. He was certain it was the gringo's work. It wasn't the Cali cartel as their style was more severed-finger-wrapped-in-a-message, not finger-caught-in-a-toy-mousetrap.

Turning to the window, there was no clue as to his whereabouts. Only a dry landscape stared back at him in the morning mist. He was still on the *altiplano*, and it could be anywhere. He wobbled to his feet, staggered along the aisle, gripping headrests, and bent over to speak to the driver.

'*Hermano*, where's the bus going?'

If the sight of his reflection in the driver's mirror was a shock, then the answer he received nearly poleaxed him. Shaking his head, he returned to his seat and collapsed into it.

Cochabamba.

Not only were they in Bolivia, they were also on their way to the very town where he had chosen to launch his mission. Not anyone else. *Him.* Nobody else knew. His plan was to befriend the *cocaleros* that supplied coca leaf to the cartel and discover where Ramón and Ernesto were hiding. Even El Patrón did not know the destination; he had only chosen it on his way to the airstrip.

Popeye did not believe in coincidences. Whenever a coincidence was offered up by a sicario as an excuse for an unsuccessful hit – 'it was just a coincidence that the bodyguard had changed his night off' – he instantly knew the job had been poorly prepared. However, unless this *was* a coincidence, then someone must have known. He knew the sedative they gave him must have contained an amnesiac, for all memories were missing between freezing water lapping at his body and waking up on the bus. *Could it also have contained a truth serum?*

Get a grip. This isn't a Jed Lawson thriller. Start thinking straight, he told himself. The first thing he did was tear off the Joker outfit. His window shot open and the jacket, shirt and trousers flew into the road, followed by the mousetrap wrapped in the 'BANG!' flag. Once the makeup was removed with some water and a towel, he pulled on his own clothes and sat back to think. There were times when acting on instinct worked, yet this was not one of them; planning his revenge would only blind him to the real threat, which was more serious than being the object of a joke.

Although he did not want to admit it, he had a grudging respect for the men who had put him on the bus. Not only had they rescued him, but they must also have finished off his assailants. He had a vague recollection of gunshots going off before he was pulled from the car. Dressing him in the Joker outfit was no more than a ploy to wind him up and distract him from the real game.

But what is the real game?

Someone wanted him killed and someone wanted him kept alive. As far as he could tell, his guardian angel was one step ahead of his enemies, yet it did not fill him with confidence. It could only be the fake priest; he had admitted as much in the church. Their interests were aligned, at least for the time being. What happened once Ramón and Ernesto were killed was another matter.

It still left the question of who was trying to kill him. The attempt by the Huallaga cartel pointed to Ramón, but it was hard to believe that he was behind the failed attempt by the Colombian pilot. There was no way he would have the information or the means to organise it whilst hiding in the Bolivian rainforest. As to the question of how his guardian angel knew about Cochabamba, that remained a mystery.

He returned to the most obvious explanation, that somehow Ramón knew he was coming and the gringos had a vested interest in him delivering that bullet. Doing their dirty work made him feel uncomfortable and plenty of questions remained unanswered, the first of which was how they knew he was going to Cochabamba. By returning to the topic, he realised he was going round in circles and decided to let the facts sink in before jumping to a hasty conclusion.

All he could say was that for the first time in his life he felt manipulated . . . like he was dancing to the beat of someone else's drum. His belief in self-determination was also shaken. It was as though someone or something was in charge and he had lost control over the direction his life was taking. What's more, the scales of judgement were starting to feel rigged, or perhaps his bad deeds had grown to such a point that no amount of good deeds would right them?

Then it came to him. He tore open his bag and dug around for his black book. Luckily it was still there, and scribbled inside was a list of locations in Bolivia – one of which was marked with a large cross, and it was none other than Cochabamba. Popeye smiled at the simple explanation and sat back in his seat.

Twenty minutes later the bus turned off the highway and took a winding road down to Cochabamba. Whereas only a few days earlier Popeye had been racing up to the *altiplano* full of confidence, now he was trundling into the sprawling city of the *cocaleros* with a distinct sense of trepidation.

CHAPTER SIXTEEN

A whiff of carbon dioxide slipped through a gap in the shutters and a speckled mosquito sprang from one of the slats. It followed the scent back into the room and searched for the source. It was coming from an untidy bedroom that was dominated by a large bed, and the bed was filled by an enormous man. He was sweating profusely, and the room smelt of body odour. Darting around, it searched hungrily for a way through the net that protected him. Once a small tear was found, a sharp proboscis sank into his skin and the mosquito filled its stomach with warm blood. Then, with a final bite, it jumped off his lip and disappeared out the window on a warm breeze.

Morning arrived, and with it the sound of screeching birds and buzzing insects. Ramón had not slept well; he never did during full moon. It was one of the downsides of his creative days, that and an increased appetite. He had long since stopped worrying about the latter, yet the lack of sleep irritated him, and it was made worse by the mosquitoes in the Beni. From the moment he had set foot in the rainforest he had been plagued by them, despite the cavernous net that covered his bed; last night was no different. Sitting up, he counted the bites dotting his belly. There had to be a hole somewhere, even though the maid had checked and told him the net was fine. Determined to double-check it himself, he ran a finger lightly around its hoop, then down and around the net that spread to the very edge of his mattress. And there it was! A small cut, not a tear, hidden away in a corner. '*Chucha madre*,' he whispered. Whether it was coincidence or a reaction to his discovery, suddenly his bites began to itch like mad and he fell back on the bed, scratching wildly.

People who acted against him were enemies, and Ramón had no time for enemies. It could only have been Helena, the maid, who had made the incision – probably out of spite for the criticism he made of her cooking. Either that or she was complicit in a sick joke designed to make his stay in the rainforest as short and as unpleasant as possible. '*Hijo de putas*,' he muttered. *If they think a few mosquito bites and bad food will get rid of me, they're sorely mistaken.* And it was at that precise moment that the idea of avenging the attack came to him; he knew exactly how to punish Helena.

It was always like that at full moon: sometimes crazy thoughts came in the middle of the mundane; more often than not he was hit by a flash of inspiration. She would receive a practical punishment, not overly creative, just fitting. And he knew the very man to do it, none other than the disgraced sicario, Pala.

Ramón counted his blessings. Pala's recent loss of favour had left him no choice – either align with Ramón or face ignominy. Whilst he had taken some nurturing, an inventive spark was finally coming through. And he would need it. Popeye would soon be in Bolivia, and unless the next attempt at stopping him succeeded, it was only a matter of time before he would have to face him.

Rolling out from under the net, his belly dropped over his boxers and he waddled over to a mirror. Tired eyes looked back, and three new bites gave his upper lip a slight squashed banana look. Ramón was annoyed. Whilst the maid was a charmless, asexual creature, he did not want to disappoint the handful of other ladies in the camp. Admittedly his physique needed some work, but he liked to think of his face as a handsome beacon that signalled his availability.

Not this morning. He looked more like a cartoon character.

Once more cursing the maid, he stepped back, gripped his belly and turned sideways. With his chest pushed out, he flexed one bicep, then the other, and headed over to the washbasin. *It's liposuction I need, not plastic surgery*, he assured himself. His muscles were fine. It was the fatty deposits over them that were the issue. *Ernesto's emeralds should cover it,* he thought as he whisked a toothbrush around his teeth, *especially now I'm not going to be making as much money,* and a jet of foamy spit hit the basin. *Besides, they're wasted on an old man like Ernesto.*

Once he had finished rinsing his mouth, he got dressed and made his way to the dining room. Ernesto was sitting at one end of the table and Helena was lurking in a corner. As he pulled up a stool, she emerged from the shadows gripping a coffee pot in one hand and a milk jug in the other.

'*Café, señor?*'

Ramón looked up at her expressionless face and there was not the faintest hint of a smile. The roar of laughter that came from Ernesto's end of the table left him in no doubt that he had spotted his swollen lip.

'Herpes?' he asked loudly.

Ramón glared back.

'Mosquitoes,' he replied, waving at Helena to pour him a coffee. '*Puta,*' he added as she turned away. Watching her slip back into the shadows gave him another full moon idea, and he turned to the food with a smile. He was about to reach for a pastry when Ernesto shouted over his shoulder:

'Helena, do we have a blender? Don Ramón is going to struggle with his food this morning.'

She emerged once more and nodded.

Ramón waved her away impatiently. 'No need. It tastes like sludge already.' And she retreated with a short bow.

In the ensuing silence, Ramón knew that Ernesto was observing him. Calculating, if not exactly scheming, yet always deliberating. Despite his relaxed posture, his eyes gave him away. Ramón decided to disturb his composure.

'So, remind me . . . your man, Martín, the one who nearly killed me. He's gone AWOL and you still haven't found him?' The question was asked with an indifference that belied its sharp focus. A raw nerve had been struck and Ernesto glared back.

'No, we haven't.'

83

'And?' Ramón prodded again.

'And what?'

'And what are you doing about it?'

After a short sigh and a long pause, Ernesto leant forward.

'*Hermano*,' his baritone rumbled, 'you don't need to worry yourself about Martín. Your job is to secure a route into the North American market now that your *connections*' – he underlined the word in a tone of deep irony – 'are unable to help us whilst your cousin is still in business.' Ramón bristled, but did not rise to the bait.

'*Hermano*, you don't need to worry yourself about the Mexicans,' he replied, repeating Ernesto's riposte. 'The Huallaga cartel are working on a sea route out of Matarani. It'll bypass the *hijo de putas* in Tijuana.' And he got straight back to the point: 'Rumours are your guy is lying low with the *cocaleros*.'

Ernesto was having none of it. 'How long before it's open?'

'Just waiting for the port authority to be bought off. Are your men out there looking for Martín?'

'We'll find him. Maybe he isn't to blame. We'll see.' A short pause. 'Each week's delay costs us fifty thousand dollars, *hermano*. Focus on that, not Martín.'

After ten minutes the conversation dried up and the men retreated to the comfort of a deadly silence and some finely sliced fruit.

Yet despite Ernesto's confidence and his condescending manner, it was Ramón who knew what was going on, not the de facto head of the Beni cartel. Martín was hiding out with the *cocaleros* in Cochabamba and his family had moved to Guanay. Pala was not the sharpest tool in the box, but he had an extensive network of contacts and Ramón had made full use of them. As far as he was concerned, Ernesto did not need to know. He was stupid to have punished Pala for his role in the incident and deserved to be kept in the dark. After all, without Pala, there would have been no account of what took place and the bizarre video would not have come to light.

Ernesto missed the point. Their enemy was not the man jumping into the river to save his life, it was the one with the flamethrower. Pala's instinct for survival was perfectly understandable. They would all have done the same. Yet Ernesto was determined to make an example of him. Not only was Pala 'a coward and a disgrace to the cartel', he had also failed to identify the man with the deadly weapon. What Ernesto forgot was that Pala was also fiercely loyal, and that loyalty was rewarded by him being dragged around the compound with his ankles tied to the back of Ernesto's Massey Ferguson tractor.

Ramón had watched that loyalty fade with each new lap of the compound Pala had been forced to endure. If his ankles were still sore from the rope tied around them, it was nothing compared to the agony of his back, which had bounced and scraped along the scrub. The thought of it made Ramón wince, and it reminded him that he needed to catch up with Pala. He got up to leave.

'*Hermano*,' Ernesto shouted, 'remember we're meeting Carlos later this morning.'

Ramón gave him a dismissive wave as he left the room and strolled out onto the veranda. It was a large area covered in dazzling flowers and hanging plants, and at one end a row of small banana trees were just coming into fruit. A small monkey was munching one of the bananas, and Ramón's hand swiped thin air as it jumped away with a rattle of its chain and a loud screech. It was Ernesto's monkey, and Ramón baited it at every opportunity. And his animosity was returned in full measure. Whenever he got close to its tree, it shot up and threw objects down with bared teeth. Only occasionally did Ramón catch it asleep and deliver a solid blow.

Cursing the monkey, he went down the steps and crossed a dusty path in the middle of the compound. Now that there was a real risk of reprisal from the DEA and Medellín, the whole place was turning into a fortress. New lookouts stretched for several miles along the riverbank and a huge searchlight had been placed at the compound entrance. Its sweeping beam could pick out a boat at five hundred metres and it bathed the compound in a searing light that captured the slightest movement. Further accommodation was being provided for the extra men, and some women had been brought in to help with the additional laundry and catering.

It should have been Pala organising the new security measures, yet he was no longer Horqueta's right-hand man and his fall from grace had been spectacular. His new role was now as a shift worker on guard duty, and Ramón knew yesterday's shift had been a particularly long one. He walked up to Pala's hut and took full advantage.

'*Hermano*,' he shouted. 'Rise and shine.'

Pala emerged and stood stiffly against the door jamb. Ramón looked him up and down and pronounced:

'Standing on guard doesn't help your back.'

The man shrugged, as though it was nothing, yet Ramón knew his pride was hurting along with his spine. Ramón planned on cementing the loyalty of the sicario by reminding him of his concern for his welfare and the confidence he had in his discretion.

'I've got you off guard duty for the rest of the week, *hermano*. I need to visit one of our new labs and you're the only one I can trust.'

A nod and subtle smile confirmed the offer was appreciated. Ramón told him he had something to discuss in private and they made their way across to the hall, where he collapsed into a large chair. Pala pulled up a seat.

'Popeye escaped again,' he said. 'Once is good luck, twice is more than coincidence. Someone is warning him, which means we have an informant at large.'

Pala stared back.

'Maybe it was someone in the Huallaga cartel?'

Ramón shook his head.

'No, it's not them. They're going to make a lot of money from us.'

'The Cali cartel?'

'No. They want Popeye dead as much as we do.'

'Only you and I knew Huallaga Valley were on to him . . . so it was *you*, Don Ramón?' he exclaimed.

Ramón struggled to remain calm.

'*Only* you and I . . .?' he replied.

Pala hesitated for a moment, then a light came on.

'Don Ernesto! It has to be him,' he said confidently. 'He's been kept informed at every stage.'

'My thoughts exactly,' Ramón said with relief.

Pala needed time to consider the ramifications.

'We need to confront him,' he concluded, and Ramón's patience nearly snapped.

'Well, we *could* do that . . . but he'll be more careful once he knows we're on to him.'

'We need to catch him in the act?' Pala suggested.

Ramón nodded.

'I need to sneak under his bedroom window with a tape recorder.'

Ramón shook his head.

'I need to hide under his bed . . .?'

'*Chucha madre!*' Ramón shouted. 'No, *hermano*. We need to have some witnesses . . . *witnesses*,' he repeated. 'Your word alone is not enough.'

Ramón then described his plan for Ernesto's downfall. Even if Ernesto were not the rat, it suited him to have suspicions raised; if he was an informant then that would be the end of him. His protection would melt away if he were known to be colluding with the deadly assassin. Popeye's reputation was fearsome, and all the sicarios knew their lives were at risk if he arrived in their midst.

Pala's admiration for his new boss increased further when Ramón described his plan for Helena. He had drawn on his experience of her serving in the dining room, and with a slight tweak here and there, it was shaping up to be one of his more inspired punishments. Nowhere near as grandiose as the piranha flesh-strippers, and less deadly, yet he had a good feeling about it. It was simple, cost-effective and an entirely appropriate response to the amount of discomfort she had put him through.

The memory of it made him delicately touch his lip. It was beginning to throb in the midday heat and he wondered if the

87

punishment should be more deadly, but a flashback to the failed anaconda procedure hit him hard and he shuddered. Deep down, for his own mental well-being if nothing else, he knew this one needed to be a success. *Best leave it as planned*, he decided, and left Pala to make the arrangements.

CHAPTER SEVENTEEN

It was approaching midday. Ernesto had started without Ramón and was going through numbers with Carlos.

'You're late,' he said, pointing at his watch.

Ramón ignored him, nodded at the accountant and picked up a sheet of paper covered in figures.

'Sit down, *hermano*, you're disturbing us.'

Ramón shook his head and said nothing.

'Now you're here,' Ernesto chided him, 'you can see how much money we're losing from your fuck-up.' He waved a sea of red digits at Ramón. Carlos was about to start explaining the profit and loss when Ramón interrupted him.

'All new ventures run at a loss, *hermano*,' he replied dismissively, and turned to Carlos. 'Surely you've explained this to Don Ernesto?'

Ernesto snapped back before Carlos had time to answer.

'Don't lecture me on setting up a business, *güevón*. You of all people—'

'*Me* of all people?' Ramón's temper rose. 'What are you saying, *hermano*?'

'*Señores*, please,' Carlos interjected, 'we need to focus on the profit and loss. We're running a fifty-thousand-dollar deficit each week and accruing expensive inventory. Unless revenue starts flowing by the end of the month, you'll need another injection of capital, as . . .' He hesitated, as though not wishing to share the information. 'Don Yayo has decided to stop funding the operation after August.'

'What!' Ramón shouted. '*Hijo de puta.* Funding was agreed to the end of November. That's three months away, *cabrón.*'

'I understand Don Yayo has recently incurred a large personal debt,' Carlos replied, 'and he has been forced to make some difficult decisions.' There was an awkward silence, and Ernesto could see that Carlos was uncomfortable. He was about to see if anything could be done to change Yayo's mind when Ramón turned to him.

'Don Ernesto, this means we'll have to use your emeralds as collateral, or sell some of them to plug the gap in funding.'

'Fuck off!' Ernesto snapped. 'This means you get off your fat arse and start distributing, or we go under.'

'*Señores*, please,' said Carlos. 'We have a healthy inventory of more than fifty kilos of cocaine base and twenty-five kilos of cocaine hydrochloride. Why not sell this to the Peruvians until the supply route has opened?'

Ramón shook his head, but Ernesto nodded.

'I'll be at the warehouse later this week,' Ernesto said, 'and will send you up-to-date numbers. In the meantime, Don Ramón will arrange the trade with the Huallaga Valley cartel.'

Ramón was still shaking his head.

'No. It makes no sense,' he replied. 'We'll make maybe twenty to thirty per cent on the sale. We're giving it away. You're bankrupting us, *hermano.*'

Ernesto turned to the younger man.

'Don Ramón,' he said, as though addressing a child, 'our cashflow problems are entirely down to a failure in distribution. The last time I looked at the business plan, sales and distribution were your responsibility. Unless your *papa* is prepared to fund your fuck-up, I suggest you listen and learn, take notes and come back a stronger man. For now, we are going to shift the inventory and buy some time.' And as if to ram the point home, he continued before Ramón had a chance to reply. 'And why are you wasting your time visiting every last one of our facilities? Production is my responsibility. There's no need for you to visit the lab in Guanay tomorrow. Concentrate on your job, *hermano*, and I'll concentrate on mine.'

Ramón detested this man who reminded him of his father, quick to criticise and slow to encourage. He stared back with burning eyes and an inner reckoner that added Ernesto's insult to his growing tally of wrongs. *Ernesto's time will come.* It made him determined to expose what he suspected. After that, he would dispose of the man, but first there was the small issue of the maid.

CHAPTER EIGHTEEN

There was heavy cloud cover that evening and the camp was pitch black. The only light came from two small lamps hanging on poles by the riverbank, but Pala had had no need for any light and his sights were set in the opposite direction. He picked his way carefully across the camp towards six cabins that were neatly arranged in a semicircle with a large fire pit in front. It was where the women whiled away their evenings on old deck chairs, and he took care not to bump into any of their rusty furniture. A wind chime masked the sound of him lifting the catch of a door and darting across to the bed. A woman was lying on her back and he clamped a hand over her mouth.

'Keep quiet and you'll come to no harm,' he whispered. He felt her eyes bore into him. 'Understood?' he asked, pressing his blade against her neck. She nodded, and he lifted his hand slightly so she could breathe. 'You know what's against your throat, *niña*. One scream and it'll be your last.' She nodded once more, and Pala knew she was compliant. 'Get dressed, we're going for a short walk,' he said, releasing his grip. 'No. Not leggings,' he hissed as she started pulling on a pair. 'Put on a dress.'

A moment later they were on their way to a remote area recently cleared for the new huts. Pala needed a flashlight to find a path through its sawn stumps and felled trees, and he used a lantern sparkling in the distance as a marker. It spread a beam of light across the torn-up ground like a miniature lighthouse, guiding them towards the building from which it hung. They climbed the steps of its veranda and Helena was pushed inside.

The room was bare, apart from two chairs with a pair of waders draped over them – hefty rubber garments with clunky boots and long straps, sinister-looking in the half-light. Above them a large paraffin lamp hung from a broad wooden beam and a collection of coloured lanterns had been strung along it, bathing the floorboards in a carnival glow. It was only the paraffin lamp that gave out any proper light; the corners of the room were dark and hidden.

Helena started to whimper and look for an escape. Pala caught hold of her and bound her hands tightly together, then slung the rope over the beam and hauled her up as she screamed in pain and her legs kicked viciously. He ignored her screams and forced her legs into a pair of waders, then tightened their straps over her shoulders. Once a gag was fastened across her mouth, he took a step back and watched her wriggling like a newly caught fish on the end of a line. *You won't have long to wait*, he promised himself, and checked he had not forgotten anything.

'*Puta!*'

She was facing the wrong way and he swivelled her round. Now that she was facing the door, everything was in place and he could relax. A moment later, the door swung open, seemingly of its own accord, and something made Helena jolt violently.

A terrifying figure appeared.

Suddenly and silently in the doorway, dimly lit by the lantern outside: a spirit of darkness with the head of an enormous ant. Its grotesqueness was magnified many times over, and Pala could see fear spreading through the woman as it imposed its presence on her. Giant, black and chilling as the darkest night, it emerged awkwardly from the shadows and stood in the light. It was a man holding a blue jug in one hand and a red one in the other one, yet the ant head gave him the appearance of a demon from hell. The woman started to whimper as he approached, then the point of an antenna caught her cheek and he stopped, as though equally surprised by the contact, and retreated into the shadows.

Pala shut the door and turned to the woman.

'*Café, señora?*' he asked. Despite her head shaking frantically, he gestured at the figure, and it came out of the shadows. 'Milk and sugar?' he added. There was the same frantic shaking. Pala ignored it and turned to the man. 'I think she prefers honey to milk and sugar.' The large red jug was raised in acknowledgement and the man slowly approached, this time taking care with his protruding antennae. The spout was balanced on the edge of the waders and a jet of amber-coloured liquid was poured inside.

Tears streamed down Helena's face and her eyes implored him to stop. Every last drop was poured out before he disappeared into the corner. Pala shouted, 'No, *niña*, you've forgotten the coffee!' And he emerged with the blue jug held high and almost bounded up to Helena in his bid to make good the omission. She shook violently to try and avoid the scalding liquid that was coming, but instead of a stream of boiling-hot coffee, a line of black insects tumbled out. The bullet ants that dropped into her waders made her shake violently and her muffled screams forced their way through the gag.

The inch-long insects swarmed around the tough skin of her calves and ankles, ripping, tearing and biting with their sharp fangs, and she began to convulse as their toxic venom seeped into her central nervous system and stimulated the receptors associated with acute pain. Spasms racked her body and Ramón savoured her torment through his compound eyes. He knew that no amount of scalding coffee could ever match the pain she was experiencing. It was like having flaming charcoal dropped over her legs, and it would last for several hours.

It was not long before the pain was too much and she fainted. Her head dropped to her chest and Ramón's arm flew up in exasperation. He had expected the torture to last longer, and he regretted pouring all the ants down the waders at the same time. With a wave he gestured at Pala to get her out.

Nodding, Pala whipped out a camera.

'No, take her out,' Ramón shouted, but his words were muffled by the insect mask. Then the burst of a flash lit up the room.

'Take her out!' he roared, and lurched towards the man, who was trying out a new angle of view. However, his peripheral vision was limited, and his mask swivelled when an antenna snagged on a post. With his compound eyes twisted to one side he floundered across the room and crashed into Pala. Both of them tumbled to the floor. A large rip appeared in the papier mâché mask and Ramón bellowed:

'*Chucha madre, güevón* . . . GET HER OUT!'

Pala was crushed under the weight of the enormous man, and it took an effort to push him off. Finally he rolled free and removed the waders. In his hurry, some of the ants fell to the floor, and he wiped the others off with an old towel; he was about to sling it out of the window when Ramón's roar shook the room.

'Fuck me!' Ramón yelled with a violence that almost woke the camp.

Pala spun round.

Ramón was rolling around the floor and his hands were smashing the mask on his head. A bullet ant must have crawled inside and papier mâché was flying around the room. Pala went to his aid – slowly – and helped him to his feet, trying not to laugh.

'Wake her up and stick her in the other pair,' Ramón snapped, panting heavily. 'Be sure she's awake,' he repeated, ripping off his apron. Then, snatching the lamp, he held it up to her face and emitted a high-pitched whine like a mosquito. 'Don't worry about preparing breakfast, have a lie-in this morning,' he said, then turned towards the door. Pala pulled the new waders over her raw legs and fastened their straps. A bucket of water was tipped into them, and Helena quickly came round.

Her fresh screams warmed Ramón's soul and he paused for a moment on the veranda. If her punishment had not exactly gone to plan then at least he was rubbing salt into her wounds. The legs of the waders were full of a fine rock salt that would cleanse the woman of her deceit and cure her conniving. A moment later he strolled off into the night.

CHAPTER NINETEEN

The following morning both men were flying high. The glorious canopy of the rainforest stretched out below them and the previous evening was still fresh in their minds. Only the inadequate breakfast hamper was a small disappointment. *Well, that and the unexpected brevity of Helena's correction*, Ramón reflected as he watched the Rio Mapiri snake down from the Yungas and into the rainforest.

It was not long before they landed at a small airport on the edge of Guanay where a car was waiting with its engine running. It was a gleaming black Land Cruiser with a large roof rack and a silver-coloured running board, both of which Ramón used to haul himself in. The car tilted slightly, its engine roared and they took off in a cloud of dust. Ramón turned to Pala.

'Remind me of the man's name.'

'Santiago Flores.'

'And the reward's five hundred dollars?'

Pala confirmed it with a nod.

'Does his wife know he's informed on her sister and family?'

'No. It's a condition of the reward. He gets half now and the other half at the end of three months. If she escapes before then, he loses the other two-fifty.'

This time it was Ramón who nodded, and the car sped around a corner on its way out of Guanay.

'Lunch?' he asked.

'In two hours,' Pala replied, knowing that breakfast had fallen short of Ramón's expectations. 'A cook has been brought from

Guanay and she's aware of your dietary requirements. There'll be time to inspect the facilities, meet Santiago, have lunch and attend to your other request . . .' He paused slightly, as though it was a delicate subject. 'How long will you need with the girl?'

'What?' Ramón shot back. 'Are we on some sort of clock, *hermano*? Are you timing me or something?'

'No, Don Ramón, I apologise. I'm just thinking logistics. We need to return in daylight. If your exertions extend further into the afternoon then we'll need to reschedule the flight back.'

'Exertions!' Ramón spat. 'What do you mean, "exertions", *cabrón*?' And Pala visibly shrank into the upholstery of the Land Cruiser.

'I mean your meeting, Don Ramón. The private meeting you have organised with the village girl.'

'Yes. The *meeting* I have to discuss a charitable donation for her school. If you must ask, it normally takes me—' He checked himself. 'These meetings normally last around fifteen to twenty minutes.'

The cloak of charitable endeavour covered a multitude of sins. Pala had heard too many reports of Ramón's visits to the laboratories, and of the weeping girls left in his wake, to doubt their real purpose. Instead he acknowledged the correction with a small bow and added an hour to their schedule to be on the safe side. *Still time to return to the Beni in daylight*, he assured himself.

At around the same time that Ramón and Pala were landing in Guanay, a man in a pair of ripped Y-fronts was walking up to the Rio Mapiri. A large black balloon was clutched under his arm and a cigarette burned in his fingers; tossing it to one side, he gripped the balloon against his belly and launched himself into the rushing water. Before long the small town of Guanay had disappeared behind him and he was no more than a tiny dot, bobbing down the river that cut its way through the vast forest of the Yungas.

It was the very same man that Ramón and Pala's boat powered past half an hour later, spinning him into a riverbank and forcing him to reach out for a low-hanging branch. A few bends later and

97

the rusty conveyor of an old mine appeared – huge, green and decaying on the riverbank, a stark reminder of higher gold prices and the employment that had once supported the surrounding villages. It was here where Ernesto had set up his cocaine base laboratory, hidden in the large crater left by its open-cast operation. Ramón and Pala disembarked.

They were met by a man carrying a large machete and led into the camp. Three lines of heavy tarpaulin stretched below them, hanging on wooden poles that were sagging slightly. From a distance it looked more like a refugee camp than a high-tech facility, but as they descended it quickly revealed itself to be a hive of activity. The tents were full of workers, and a group of men were huddled around a toolbox and an old generator; all of them wore brightly coloured shorts.

One of the tents was filled with some large blue barrels that had been squeezed into a corner to make room for a makeshift kitchen. The other tents were full of microwaves and packaging on long benches that ran the length of the black tarpaulin. A wisp of smoke rose from a corner of the camp and the men were ushered towards a small shelter arranged there with a large canopy. It was laid out with a table and chairs, and a fresh pot of coffee awaited them. Pala instinctively knew there was going to be a problem.

'Who are these chairs meant for, *hermano*, little girls?' Ramón asked, kicking one aside. 'How do you expect a grown man to squeeze into them? Fetch a decent bench, or a stool, *güevón*.'

The man went away and returned with a long bench that Pala was forced to share. Waving at one of the seats, Ramón invited the man to join them. He was the foreman who oversaw the daily operation of the facility. Once he was seated, Ramón addressed him from the long bench.

'I'm not here to interfere with your process, and Don Ernesto is responsible for the production side of the business, but I have a suggestion you may wish to consider.' The man leant forward, his interest piqued. 'A cocaine laboratory is like a beautiful woman, *hermano*,' Ramón pronounced. 'She needs pampering to keep her looking good, and you've caked her in cheap, nasty cosmetics.'

The man stared back, puzzled.

'The roof, *hermano* . . . the roof,' he repeated, exasperated. 'It should be tin, not tarpaulin, and you need gutters to collect rainwater. That way she remains beautiful, the men take pride in their workplace, and you'll have a ready supply of drinking water.'

'Don Ramón, the cost of taking the lab out of production—'

Ramón raised a hand and stopped him.

'No, the decision has been made. This isn't a suggestion. Make it a priority.' Turning towards the facility, he added, 'And those floorboards haven't been sealed – they're bare wood. Sand them and apply two coats of quality varnish at the same time.'

'*Señor*, that will mean shutting down production for at least two weeks. Are you sure Don Ernesto—'

His concern was dismissed with a sharp wave.

'Don Ernesto appreciates beauty just as much as I do. He'll be fully supportive of the works.'

'And what about the workers?'

'What about them?'

'They'll lose two weeks' salary if the lab's closed.'

'And they'll *gain* two weeks' hard-earned rest, *hermano*. Time for them to relax and catch up with their families . . . no?'

The man simply nodded.

Their attention then turned to a figure struggling across the camp with a large balloon, but before they had time to look properly, he had disappeared inside a small hut. Ten minutes later he emerged in a pair of green board shorts, carrying a pile of brown parcels. It was the coca paste that he delivered each morning, hidden in the balloons he received at the start of each week. A pile of them were stacked against the hut, glistening black balls with large screw caps.

'That's Santiago, Don Ramón,' the foreman advised, 'the man you want to see. When do you want him to come over?'

'During his lunch break, *hermano*. Let him do some work first,' came the reply, and the men watched him offload the paste and start work. Ramón then turned to the foreman and asked, almost casually:

'The girl who wishes to see me. What school does she attend?'

'The Sacred Heart of Jesus.'

'Ah, of course,' he replied. 'Charity is a very private thing, *hermano* . . .' – he paused to find the right words – ' . . . and needs to be handled *delicately*. I'm concerned the girl will be embarrassed by my generosity. Is there a place where we can discuss the matter in private and save her blushes?'

The man nodded in appreciation.

'Yes. She *is* shy. We can put a screen around the table and nobody will hear from the lab. There's a large sheet of canvas in the stores—'

Ramón interrupted him.

'No, that won't do. We need something more substantial, *hermano*. A room . . . a door that locks. Windows aren't essential.'

This time the man was stumped.

'There's the old tool shed where Santiago changes, but it's filthy. Everything else has been built with production in mind.' He cast an arm around the camp. 'None of the buildings have doors, we don't need them.'

Ramón waved at the shed.

'Get Santiago to give it a good clean and stick a bench inside with some sacks on it. That'll have to do. He can come across and meet me once he's finished clearing up his mess.'

CHAPTER TWENTY

It was late and Ramón was dining alone in the compound. On the table a crisp sheet of notepaper read 'Gone to labs. Back in three days. Things to discuss', and the meal in front of him reeked of punishment. The table was bare other than a bowl of rice and a plate labelled 'chicken'. There was no bread. None of the sauce bottles were there and the beer normally laid out on a lacquer tray had been removed. It was only when Ramón lifted a cloche from the plate that he realised the 'chicken' was in fact a cockerel; its red plume and sharp beak stared up at him and looked about as appealing as its crowing sounded after a bad night's sleep. He pushed it away.

Fortunately, lunch had been a feast and for once he was not starving. Snatching some fruit, he went into his room, got undressed and climbed into the shower. As a warm spray of water hit his shoulders, he lathered up some Fresh Buoy shower gel and turned his mind to his next move. Ernesto's instructions had been to sell their product and Ramón knew it would be one of the first things he raised on his return. If it were not done, then there would be a reaction – there was always a reaction. Although following Ernesto's instructions went against the grain, on this occasion Ramón decided he would indulge him and make a call. He knew Ernesto would blow up about Helena's treatment and he expected a blasting when he returned. Failing to set up the deal would only make matters worse, and he wanted to have a calm conversation afterwards, not have Ernesto collapse into a chair and stare into space.

Wrapping a towel around his waist, he went into the bedroom and sat in front of his radio. It was one of three sets in the compound. Ernesto had his own, and a third was in a secure room at the end of the corridor. It was just after ten o'clock, well within the hour slot arranged with his contact. He selected that evening's frequency and picked up the transceiver.

'Pick up. This is Ramón.'

A short crackle, then a man replied.

'*Hermano!* How's the Beni?'

'Shit.'

'No *chicharrones* or girls?'

'None.'

The 'charity girls' didn't count; none of them had the experience of a Colombian *morena*. Ramón quickly turned to the subject he needed to discuss, namely the sale.

'Production is building and we've stock to sell.'

'Okay. How's Ernesto's performance?'

'Average. All the labs are up and running and I've inspected most of them. Around half needed closing down immediately and improvements made. I've got it in hand.'

'Okay. What are you selling?'

'Twenty-five kilos of cocaine hydrochloride and fifty kilos of coca base.'

'When can you get the cocaine stateside?'

Ramón paused and lowered the transceiver. It hadn't taken long to reach the difficult part of the conversation.

'*Hermano.* You still there? How long will it take?'

Ramón hesitated. He knew he had to come clean.

'Ernesto wants to sell to the Huallaga cartel. The route out of Peru isn't open and we've got some cashflow issues,' he eventually replied.

'What? Sell to Huallaga? They're mules, not customers. You need to shift our product to my contact in San Diego, not some *cabrón* in Peru.'

An awkward silence followed.

'I agree, but Ernesto is insistent.'

'*Puta.*'

'I'm setting a trap. The sale might never happen, but I need to keep him happy for a few days. Are you okay if I contact Huallaga?'

Piña was silent and Ramón could tell that he was weighing up the options. Both of them knew the sale was bad business and it made them appear weak, yet neither of them could afford to have an outright conflict with Ernesto whilst Popeye was still at large. Fighting on two fronts was an unnecessary risk, and Piña reluctantly agreed.

'Popeye needs to be stopped, then Ernesto needs to go,' Piña added. 'He got lucky with Dolores. Maybe he knew the coffee was drugged or he charmed his way out? I'm not surprised the Huallaga cartel failed. The only way to catch out Popeye is to sneak up on him. Right now he's in Cochabamba looking for some *cocaleros* to track you down. I've told him to lie low for a bit, so you've got some breathing room.'

Pasquale peered through a small window in the gable and listened intently to the conversation being held below. His acute hearing picked up the words 'cocaine' and 'Ernesto', and it seemed as though something was being organised. Pushing open the window, he climbed onto a narrow ledge and took a closer look. Below him there was a fat, partially clothed man who was soaking wet. His arms were waving as though he was agitated and there was something black in his hand that looked like it would inflict serious pain. Pasquale shrank back instinctively and watched intently. It would need to be dropped before he got any closer. Eventually the man reached for a black box and cast the weapon aside. It was then that he struck.

With a powerful spring, he landed on a beam running the length of the room, bounded across it and launched himself at the man. His feet crashed into the side of his head and the man was thrown from his chair, landing heavily and groaning. Pasquale jumped on his back and tore off a chunk of hair, then ran his sharp claws down his spine and snatched at the towel. But the man seized it in a desperate attempt to protect his modesty. It was of no use and the towel was ripped from his body, leaving him squirming on the floor as he shielded his groin from the blows that rained down. Pasquale relished the opportunity to repay the cruelty he had received and returned it in full measure. Tearing, beating and scratching at the flesh laid out before him, it was only when the man rolled on his front that his attention was drawn to his huge buttocks. Ramón roared and the room shook as Pasquale's teeth sank into them, but it was nothing compared to the high-pitched scream that issued forth when Pasquale's head snapped back and a lump of flesh was torn from Ramón's arse.

CHAPTER TWENTY-ONE

The bedroom was bathed in a glorious light and a couple of ovenbirds chattered by its window, yet Ramón was oblivious to their melody and nodded quickly to the doctor. There were times when a man needed to steel himself, and this was one of those times. With a sharp jab, the doctor sank a needle into his buttock and administered a large shot of tetanus vaccine. Ramón's nails tore into the sheet as it stung its way into his bloodstream, and his teeth ground together as a second shot of antibiotics was injected into the inflamed area. Twenty minutes later and the scratches had been treated, a large dressing had been fixed over the wound and some antibiotics had been prescribed. The doctor had not been concerned about the missing flesh and passed a flippant comment about 'ample tissue' and it being 'well hidden', but for Ramón, having a monkey attack his arse was as much an emotional trauma as it was a physical embarrassment, and he had dismissed the man with a sharp word.

Pala was summoned to his bedside.

'Who helped Ernesto?'

'What?'

'Who released his *puta* monkey?'

'He escaped. His collar was worn and it snapped off. It's still attached to the chain.'

Ramón raised his eyes to the ceiling and swore.

'*Cabrón*, please not today of all days. Stay with me. Ernesto got someone to release his monkey outside my room. It didn't escape.'

'You're sure? Sounds a bit far-fetched.'
'*Chucha madre!*'

Ramón lay on his front and waited for Pala to finish searching Ernesto's room. It was just down the corridor and he knew Pala would not be disturbed. He had given strict instructions for the other sicarios to hunt down Pasquale and roast him for dinner. Ramón knew they would never find him – the monkey was long gone – yet it allowed Pala to comb through Ernesto's belongings without interruption. And he needed Pala to be completely focussed on the task in hand as without the required information, his plan was a non-starter.

Pala had been gone for well over an hour, and Ramón was about to shout and tell him to hurry up when the sound of voices could be heard approaching the hacienda. The sicarios had finished their search and were returning to the compound earlier than expected. Pala was in danger, and if he was discovered rifling through Ernesto's papers then the consequences would be severe . . . and not just for Pala. Of course, Ramón would deny being behind the search and disown the sicario, yet without the information, his plan would undoubtedly fail and he would be back to square one.

He heard a door open and footsteps resound down the corridor. They stopped outside his door for a moment . . . there was a slight click of the lock . . . then the door flew open and crashed against the wall.

'What the fuck!' Ramón shouted.

'Sorry. My hands are full. I had to use my foot to push it open.'

Pala was in the doorway, and he had a pile of books in his arms. Ramón's heart sank.

'And the information?' he asked with a sigh.

Pala shuffled awkwardly and shook his head. He had failed. After a long pause he broke the silence. 'I had no idea Don Ernesto read so much,' he said, and his eyes lit up. 'It took a while to check his library, though what I *did* find hidden away was a book about local wildlife. Fascinating, I never knew the toucan lives longer than the Brazilian horned beak.'

He's been flipping through photographs, thought Ramón, but the words remained unspoken. Instead, he dismissed the man, this time with a sharp wave, and accepted that he would have to search the room himself another day. He was halfway through a long groan of disappointment when the door sprang open again and Pala reappeared.

'Don Ramón, I forgot. I've got some books.' He made three neat piles on the floor. 'I thought you could do with something to occupy your time. Ernesto labelled each section. There's history, Latin American literature and trash fiction to choose from.' Ramón watched Pala with a mixture of exasperation and dejection as he cast an arm over them and waited for his approval. He received a cursory nod from his mentor and disappeared once more, along with any chance of a quick fix for Ernesto.

All the same, it was good to have something take his mind off things. Ramón glanced at the first pile and noticed they were neatly arranged in date order. Simón Bolívar was at the bottom and modern history was at the top. The second pile was balanced more precariously, like a set of toy building blocks. He recognised Gabriel García Márquez and Tomás González as they were Colombian. Whilst he knew Mario Vargas Llosa and Jorge Luis Borges, Isabelle Allende was new to him. García's *Love in the Time of Cholera* looked promising, and he made a mental note to come back to it.

His attention then turned to the last pile. In some discomfort, he stretched down and picked up a handful of books. Trash fiction was all about the covers, and he needed to take a closer look. Spreading them out on the bed, they looked mostly like romance novels and cheap thrillers.

The first one that he grabbed had an illustration of a First World War nurse staring wistfully from a window. It was quickly slung towards the bin. The next one was even more clichéd. A hunky lothario was stripped to the waist with a torn letter in his hand and a red rose on the floor. This one scored a direct hit, and the bin rattled slightly but stayed upright. It left a handful of other books to choose from, most of which were thrillers. The first one had an exploding volcano as a backdrop and a solitary hero facing it in a leather jacket. The next one had a bright cover and a man throwing a grenade towards an Apache helicopter. He picked it up and took a look at the back cover.

Sleve McDichael is cruel. A master of assassination. He's the one all governments call on when the worst of the worst need stopping. Even the special services can't stop the worst of the worst. And the worst of the worst need stopping if world democracy is to survive.

'Hmm, looks promising,' Ramón mumbled. Its author was Jed Lawson, a 'Million Selling Author'. *The Player* was number forty-three in the Sleve McDichael series and a 'must read'. Ramón's interest was piqued. The initial advantage of a Nobel Prize winner over a 'Million Selling Author' began to fade and he carried on reading the blurb.

McDichael finds himself at the mercy of a woman. It's his weak spot. A gang have trafficked her only daughter. Only McDichael can rescue her. But will he reach her AND restore democracy in Iran? Has McDichael gone too far this time . . .?

The trafficking plot and hero theme hit a nerve and booted *Love in the Time of Cholera* into touch. Ramón made himself comfortable and trod the same path as a million other readers. The opening was gripping. Sleve had just bombed a Russian base in Afghanistan and was deep in negotiations to end the war there. Jed Lawson then cleverly introduced Neve McSheenamee, an Irish-Iranian Farsi translator whose daughter was in danger. By Chapter Five, the action was really building:

Sleve grabbed her by the arm and threw her across the bed. She had been teasing him for too long and there was only so much the McDichael genes could take. With a sharp slap his testosterone delivered the message that words couldn't deliver; the delivery was firm but it delivered the desired result. Neve raised herself up on one arm and SHE delivered the words that his eager ears drank in like a thirsty man lying on a desert floor.

'Come to me, Sleve,' said Neve. He lifted her powerfully and their bodies fused with a passion only Sleve could achieve.

Ramón nodded in approval. Lawson certainly had a way with words. The plot was intriguing and the language punchy. But his wound was beginning to hurt and he needed to take a break from the tension and lie on his front. Flipping through the pages for a bookmark, he got lucky. One dropped out the back, and he was about to slot it at the conclusion of McDichael's conquest when he noticed a list of figures on its reverse.

0508 – 76.3 – 2210
0608 – 63.4 – 2215
0708 – 93.4 – 2220
0808 – 87.2 – 2225
0908 – 76.7 – 2230
1008 – 92.2 – 2235
1108 – 65.7 – 2240
1208 – 91.5 – 2245
1308 – 88.4 – 2250
1408 – 98.7 – 2255
1508 – 69.1 – 2300
1608 – 82.4 – 2305
1708 – 91.2 – 2310
1808 – 86.5 – 2315

Ramón knew he had Ernesto.

CHAPTER TWENTY-TWO

'Pasquale!' Ernesto's baritone boomed across the compound, signalling his return.

Ramón shifted awkwardly in his chair and watched Ernesto stride over to Pasquale's tree. Ernesto ignored the broken collar lying there and turned and waved at the riverbank. Although Ramón could not see the person to whom he was waving, whoever it was had the attention of the whole compound, and he hobbled onto the veranda to take a look.

It was not a person, rather a whole team of men struggling with something that looked like an enormous crate. It was supported on two bamboo poles that were sagging slightly and the men were taking care not to stumble as they made their way over to Ernesto. It was covered in a dark green tarpaulin with a white emblem of a giraffe on its side, and Ramón watched the exhausted men drop the crate at Ernesto's feet, to their great relief and Ernesto's clear delight. He glanced at the veranda, ignored Ramón and strode off to the hall, where he stood with his hands on the railing. With a nod he gave an order, and four men removed the tarpaulin.

It was not a crate but an enormous cage, and inside it a large silverback gorilla lay tranquilised. The black and silver hair on its back rose and fell gently and it looked peaceful, for the time being at least; no doubt the bars of its cage would be fully tested when it woke.

'*Hermanos*,' Ernesto yelled, addressing the entire compound, 'weighing in at two hundred kilograms, I give you Freddie the

Killer Gorilla . . . Freddie the Manic Swinger . . . Freddie the Legendary Keeper Sweeper.'

Ramón had read about Freddie. He had swung a zookeeper around his enclosure and sent the man slamming into the viewing screen. And as if that was not bad enough, the screaming children on the other side had had to endure him brandishing the keeper's severed arm before he flung it in their direction. Apparently the limb just managed to clear the viewing screen before it dropped right in the middle of them and set off a stampede of screaming eight-year-olds through the primate section. 'Freddie's Lunch' had been one of the key attractions in Santa Cruz Zoo; now it was simply 'Penguin Time' and 'Gonzo the Giraffe' that were advertised.

'Freddie can keep Pasquale company,' Ernesto continued. He paused and looked around, shielding his eyes like a sailor searching a distant horizon. 'Where *is* that cheeky monkey?' Finally he turned to the veranda and looked directly at Ramón. 'Ah, Don Ramón, *there* you are. At least I've found one cheeky monkey.'

Ramón was furious. His temper boiled over and he was lost for words. Ernesto had humiliated him in front of the whole compound, and it was obvious that the gloves were now off. The threat posed by Freddie was clear. It was no coincidence that he had arranged for a heavyweight primate to replace his featherweight. Ramón had never imagined for one moment that a caged gorilla would make him shudder, but shudder he did.

He knew he had to strike before the psychopath uncaged his silverback gorilla. Wasting no time, he ignored Ernesto's offer to inspect Freddie and limped off to the riverbank. Easing himself into a boat, he reached the post where Pala was on duty, and an hour later he returned to the compound with his plan laid and a smirk on his face.

Ernesto turned to Ramón.

'What did Huallaga have to say?'

It was the first proper thing he had said since Ramón had returned to the camp; calling him a cheeky monkey had been a conversation stopper and they had spent the rest of the day avoiding each other. The sun was now setting behind the hall and they were drinking *aguardiente* on the veranda.

'They're interested,' Ramón replied. 'We just need to agree the price. I've asked for a proposal. We'll get it by the end of the week.'

Ernesto nodded in approval and Ramón continued:

'They also failed to stop Popeye.' Ernesto raised his eyebrows. 'My men say he's in Cochabamba.'

This time Ernesto leant forward.

'Doing what?' he asked.

'Lying low under the alias Juan Arroyo Fernández.' Ramón shrugged. 'Gaining the trust of the *cocaleros* and looking for a way to track us down.' He stared hard at the man sipping his *aguardiente*. 'What's the gorilla for, *hermano*?' No mention was made of Pasquale's attack, nor of Helena's treatment.

'He was going to be put down. Once they've killed, they get a taste for it. Human flesh is irresistible, and if it's bloody . . .' Ernesto paused for effect. 'It's like a line of coke to an addict. The zoo was left with no choice, and I thought Freddie might be amusing for the men. Had I known Pasquale had escaped, I would have bought one of their capuchin monkeys to replace him.'

Ramón guessed that Ernesto knew about his wound and he had chosen his words carefully. *A taste for human flesh, very smart. We'll see just how smart you are.* Ramón raised his glass.

'Good idea. The men could do with an amusement. I'm planning a little entertainment for them as well.'

'I see,' Ernesto replied. He was not interested. Topping up his own glass, he asked, almost nonchalantly, 'What are you planning to do about Popeye?' He sounded disinterested, like he was just making conversation, but Ramón was listening keenly and the question was suspicious. Ernesto was fishing for information and Ramón decided to play him.

'I don't know. He sounds superhuman. Somehow he managed to overpower the men Huallaga sent after him. Their car was rolled over on its side, each of them had a neat bullet in the head and Popeye's pickup was discovered at the bottom of a deep ditch. How he could have climbed up, avoided gunfire and put a bullet in each of their heads is a mystery . . . unless he first carried out the hit *then* rolled his pickup down the ditch to cover his tracks?'

There was no reply from Ernesto. Ramón continued.

'And there's the matter of a mangled motorbike and two riders full of bullets. He must have dealt with them around the same time? Quite a guy . . .' He paused and looked Ernesto in the eye. 'It was almost as if he had a SWAT team helping him.'

Ernesto stared back, poker-faced.

'Indeed,' he replied dismissively, 'you know as well as I do that the local police exaggerate. Their reports are pure works of fiction. They probably found a car with its driver shot, and it was a discarded bicycle that gave them the idea of a motorbike.'

'Let's hope you're right. If he's as superhuman as he appears to be, then we're dead. If he's got a team behind him, then we're also dead. If the team is the DEA, then it's worse than death: extradition.' Ramón hammed it up to get a reaction. 'But I have a practical solution for the man who refuses to die,' he continued, and was tempted to use one of Sleve McDichael's exploits for a bit of fun, but stopped himself. *Best not to draw Ernesto's attention to Jed Lawson and the incriminating bookmark.* 'We need to catch him with his guard down. Popeye doesn't drink or smoke, but his one vice is eating *chicharrones*. It's a fried pork belly dish with spices and—'

Ernesto interrupted him. 'I know what *chicharrones* are, get to the point.'

Ramón bit his tongue and described his plan.

'There's a famous *chicharrón* place called Chicharrón Alabaron in Cochabamba. One of my contacts works there. When he pays a visit, as I know he will, she'll poison him.'

Ernesto sighed.

'What, like your *morena* on the plane?'

Ramón glared back.

'No, *hermano*. Not like on the plane. That was a sedative. This will be a poison. They're different things.'

After a short pause, Ernesto took the bait.

'Remind me of her name. And the place is called . . . what, Chicharrón Alabaron or something?'

Ernesto knew what to do.

So did Ramón and Pala . . . at 22:35, to be precise. The former was sitting at his radio, the latter was standing by another radio down the corridor surrounded by sicarios; both of them were tuned in to 92.2 MHz, the frequency written next to the date on Ernesto's bookmark: '1008 – 92.2 – 2235'.

Pala heard Ernesto's deep voice crackle over the radio.

'Delta Echo Alpha, pick up.'

'Delta Echo Alpha, receiving.'

'Good evening, Angel Man. How is my American friend?'

'Roger that, Ernesto. Fine. How's Fat Toad?'

'Sore. My monkey gave him a workout and he's still recovering.'

'Roger that. Still fucking things up?'

'Totally useless.'

'Any suspicions?'

'None. My monkey's brighter than him.'

'We dealt with the Huallaga cartel and put Popeye on a bus to Cochabamba.'

'I know. Fat Toad confirmed he was lying low there. He's using the alias Juan Arroyo Fernández.'

'Confirmed. We checked his papers.'

Ernesto continued the conversation along the same lines for several minutes and never missed an opportunity to insult Ramón. The men around Pala were particularly amused by his reference to Ramón's 'sandbag physique', and Pala needed to control their laughter on more than one occasion. He did not need Ernesto to discover they were listening, and he certainly did not want Ramón to hear their enthusiastic approval of his character assassination.

Eventually Ernesto turned to the subject of Freddie.

'I have a proposal, Angel Man.'

'Roger.'

'Pablo Escobar wants us both dead. Popeye is on his way, but he'll get a bullet before he reaches me, roger?'

'Roger that, Ernesto.'

'Now he's in play it doesn't matter where he dies. What matters is that Fat Toad is eliminated and Escobar believes we're dead. He'll continue to operate as normal. You can safely use the evidence I provide. The cocaine business is compromised and you get a promotion.'

'Continue, Ernesto.'

'I now have the means to dispose of Fat Toad in the correct fashion. You have the means of eliminating Popeye. There is no need to risk him arriving in the Beni. I will continue to provide all the information you require, along with access to the financial machinery, so long as you continue to provide my new identity and West Coast apartment. The deal remains the same, the journey is slightly different.'

There was a long pause.

'Negative. There can be no change of plan. Popeye needs to arrive in the Beni. You need to keep us informed of Fat Toad's activities and we'll protect Popeye's back.'

'Why? Why does Popeye need to arrive in the Beni?'

'There can be no change of plan at this stage. The operation is in play. It can't be amended.'

This time Ernesto stayed silent. It was obvious that the DEA were determined to get Popeye into the camp, and it sounded suspicious to Pala. Ernesto was not deterred, and he repeated his request.

'There's no need to send Popeye. I recently purchased a silver-back gorilla and I would very much like to save Popeye the trouble by using him on Fat Toad.'

'What . . .! What does "use him on Fat Toad" mean?' It was obvious that Angel Man was astonished.

'I imagine Freddie would tear his limbs off.'

The DEA agent immediately reverted to a default of codenames and jargon.

'That's a negative, Deep Tongue. I repeat. That's a negative. Operation Thunder Fist continues as planned. The assassin will be procured. The target will be eliminated. The source will then be extracted.'

Ernesto started to remonstrate, but he was cut off.

'What plans does Fat Toad have for Popeye?'

There was a deep sigh, then Ernesto seemed to accept the decision and spent the next few minutes describing Ramón's plan, carefully spelling out the name of the restaurant in Cochabamba.

Meanwhile the other radios were switched off, but not before Pala had the support of the men crammed into the radio room and only after Ramón had prised his fingers from a lead paperweight. It was all he could do to stop himself from smashing it into Ernesto's head during the radio transmission, and it was only the thought of the hidden emeralds that had stopped him.

CHAPTER TWENTY-THREE

Ernesto yawned loudly and went into the dining room for breakfast.

The table was bare other than a crisp sheet of notepaper and a plate covered with a cloche. The note read 'Gone to hall. Be there all morning. Things to discuss.' He screwed it into a ball, flung it into the corner and lifted the cloche. Roses, alliums and passifloras tumbled out, along with his prized corsage orchid. With his temper fully aroused, he strode onto the veranda and stared angrily at the bare stalks of his plants. His fingers tenderly brushed their broken stems, then he marched off in the direction of the hall.

On his way he made a small detour to pick up a length of rope – *That will have to do* – and he made a couple of thick knots as his step quickened. His eyes were drawn to a pile of debris below the hall. Someone had thrown his pots over the railing, and the ground was strewn with broken terracotta and compost.

A blanket of pink and white flowers lay by his feet, and their crushed petals brought a lump to his throat. 'My prize begonias . . .' he muttered softly, before bounding up the stairs.

His silhouette appeared in the door, a rudimentary lash in one hand and the other clenched into a tight fist. A long shadow stretched across the floor and his head turned slowly, scanning the hall for his prey. And there he was, sitting at a table with Ernesto's sicarios lined up behind him.

Ernesto shook his head. They looked more like a rag-tag bunch of men than trained sicarios. None of them were standing up straight, and height-wise, they were all over the place. Two tall men were on the far left, a shorter man was beside them, Pala (who was lanky) came next, then three shorter men followed . . . His eyes stopped going down the line when it burst into applause. The knotted rope suddenly began to feel slightly awkward, and he let it slip casually from his hand and drop to the floor.

Ramón stood up.

'Don Ernesto,' he shouted over the clapping and cheering, 'congratulations on your retirement.'

Ernesto turned a crimson face towards Ramón.

'What!'

'Your retirement! The boys and I' – he waved a hand behind him – 'have decided the time has come for you to step aside and let some young blood through.'

'Oh, "the boys" and you have decided, have you? Well, "the boys" and you can—' He was about to deliver a tongue-lashing when a hand cracked across his head. 'How dare you,' he spluttered, and before he could turn round, he was pushed into the hall. 'Do you know who I am!' he roared, giving his assailant a fierce look. It was swiftly replaced with a pained expression as he was led to the table by his ears.

'Don Ernesto,' Ramón shouted, flapping his hands to calm the men, 'please take a seat and don't go down fighting. The men would like you to join us, and I would like to see you retire gracefully. There's no need to disappoint us on either count, and I don't want Guido to have to squeeze your ears even harder.' He waved at the man to release his grip.

Ernesto spun round and glared at his assailant, who was walking back to the doorway to stand guard. Ernesto ignored Ramón and addressed the sicarios.

'Are you going to let this *Colombian*' – he said the word with embittered denigration 'with the brainpower and charm of . . .' – he paused to find the right word – ' . . . a slug, decide your future? Take what we've built through hard work, enterprise and—'

'Deceit?' Ramón completed the sentence for him.

'What!' His deep voice sounded outraged even if it wobbled slightly.

'Take a seat, *hermano*, and don't make a fool of yourself. We were all listening in on last night's conversation with Angel Man. Cut the pretence. Let's talk terms.'

Ernesto frowned. The door looked inviting, but Guido was blocking it. His ears were still sore from his strong grip, so he took a seat.

Ramón faced him.

'What the men don't know is that you've been in league with the DEA for a long time.' His voice rose and he ignored Ernesto's disparaging wave. 'You informed them of every measure I've taken to stop the assassin . . .' He paused for effect. 'Now it's only a matter of time before Popeye reaches us.' With a theatrical gesture, he called for boos for the villain that was Popeye. The hall did not disappoint, and the men stamped their feet and whistled in disapproval. After a short interval he got back to what he really wanted to share with them. 'With that in mind, I've decided to provide some entertainment in the camp as a distraction. *Señor*,' he said, staring at Ernesto, 'I challenge you to a competition. The winner gets your emeralds. If you win, then you get to keep them and retire to a quiet hacienda in Paraguay.'

Ernesto said nothing. Ramón had the backing of the compound's muscle. He could not reach his radio without passing his assailant, and even if he did, he would find little support as an informant. He was left with no choice.

'And if I lose?' he asked.

'So long as I have your emeralds, you'll be free to leave. You can forget about the hacienda.' Ernesto had the advantage of being fitter and stronger than the Colombian, and he readily accepted.

'Good, I'm pleased,' Ramón continued. 'You had no choice, although as you are fitter and stronger than me, you'll have a slight handicap.' He paused, and it was obvious that he had read Ernesto's mind. '*But* there is no way you can lose against someone with a "sandbag physique", is there, *cabrón*?' The last word was said with menace. Ernesto's mind raced back to the radio communication, and he tried to remember how many times he had used the codename Fat Toad, not to mention all the other insults. He had a sneaking suspicion that the handicap would extract revenge for his indiscretion.

Ramón picked up *The Player*. With one hand on its spine and the other cupped underneath, he presented it to the room like a sacred text, and the men once more broke into applause. Ernesto's bookmark was removed and he began to read:

Sleve McDichael shook his chains. He was a killing machine so ruthless that even his signature melted the very paper it was written on. But not today! Today Sleve wasn't signing paper, he was defending freedom! Outside, his arch nemesis Todd Smorin waited, pumped to the max for the deadly challenge set by Commandant Nogilny. Sleve knew that only one of them would survive and it wasn't going to be Todd. His chains rattled. He was tempted to rip them off yet Todd would need all the help he could get in the arena of Camp Gride with the blazing sun beating down on them like a bass drum – hard, percussive and shorn of all mercy.

Ramón put down *The Player* and looked at Ernesto.

'*Hermano*, today you are Todd and I am Sleve. You'll have to imagine we are in Camp Gride . . . and we all know you have a vivid imagination, *hijo de puta*.'

The reference to Freddie was clear, and Ernesto regretted sharing his plan over the radio. Before he could dismiss it as bragging to the DEA, Ramón continued, 'I've decided to allow some crowd participation, and parts of your handicap will be provided by the men. But enough of that, you must be curious to hear more about what we've got planned, so I'll hand you over to Commandant Nogilny.'

Pala stepped forward to a standing ovation and took a small bow.

'Today's challenge is a triathlon,' he announced. 'The first leg is a swim in the Rio Beni. The second is a ten-lap bike race followed by two or three laps running around the compound. I haven't decided on the number yet, it'll depend on how Sleve's doing.'

If the handicap suggested the competition was rigged, Pala's throwaway comment confirmed it could be deadly. The emeralds were Ernesto's only leverage and he needed to use them to his advantage, but Guido seized his arm and marched him out of the hall before he could come up with a plan.

Guido paused at the railing and Ernesto looked down. His Massey Ferguson tractor was parked in the clearing and a selection of hoes, rakes, forks and shovels were arranged around it in a neat semicircle. A large gardening implement took pride of place in the very centre of them, and Ernesto's heart nearly missed a beat. It was his STIHL FS 86, recently serviced and in full working order. Guido pushed him towards the steps.

'Get me out of here and the emeralds are yours,' Ernesto whispered as they went down. Guido showed not the least sign of being interested. 'The emeralds, *güevón*, the emeralds,' Ernesto repeated, slightly louder. 'That's three million dollars,' he insisted as they were halfway down. Still there was no reply, and he almost shouted, 'You know what I'm offering you, *güevón* – a new life. Seize it, *cabrón!*'

Ramón was standing on the veranda, and he had heard Ernesto's offer.

'Guido is deaf and mute, *hermano*,' he called down, 'although he understands hand directions.'

As Ernesto turned round he missed Guido's backhander, and it sent him crashing into the handrail and down the remaining steps. A few seconds later he was being taken, slightly dazed, across to the riverbank. Once there, Guido fastened a thick belt around his waist and another man threw a pair of board shorts at him.

Pala was there with the other sicarios.

'This is the swimming leg,' he announced. 'Both competitors must reach a large red-and-white buoy downriver. Todd,' he said, addressing Ernesto, 'you'll have a rope attached to you in case you get ideas of swimming off, and should you choose not to swim at all, then we have three caimans waiting for you.' He pointed at a line of cages on the riverbank, and Ernesto noticed a large green canoe next to them. 'The canoe is for your opponent, Todd,' Pala added. 'Think of it as your handicap.'

Ernesto gave a wry smile and Guido attached a rope to his belt. His head was still spinning from the earlier backhander when his feet left the ground and his body flew into the river. Coming to the surface, a sharp tug brought him back onto the bank.

'There will be no cheating or advantage taken,' Pala shouted. 'If you think you can dive in and get a head start, Todd, you're sorely mistaken,' and he nodded in approval at Guido. 'The race will only start once I've blown my whistle . . . not before then.'

Ramón appeared in a broad-brimmed hat and enormous shorts.

The riverbank was slippery, and it needed three men to get him down and another to carry his canoe. Ramón squeezed inside it, the men braced themselves for a launch and the canoe promptly sank into a thick, gloopy mud; a fifth man came to help and made no difference whatsoever. It was only when Guido arrived in a small boat that Ramón's canoe could be dragged into the river and the race could finally begin. As Ernesto slipped into the water, he noticed that there was a huge engine on the back of Guido's boat. It was oversized and far too powerful for simply keeping him in check . . . Then the sound of a whistle and the roar of an engine left him no time to think.

Ernesto was pulled underwater, and when he came to the surface, he realised he had been dragged sideways and Ramón had set off. He was now paddling furiously towards a broad bend where the riverbank was covered in myrtle and laurel trees. His canoe soon disappeared past them and Ernesto followed at a gentle pace. When he reached the spot, a steady current gripped his legs and took him slowly around the bend and towards the finish line. He emerged in a long stretch of river and saw a red-and-white buoy tied to an overhanging branch, bobbing gently in the water. The finish was probably no more than two hundred metres away, and Ramón should have been waiting there . . . except he was nowhere to be seen.

Ernesto twisted round too late and the sharp end of a canoe caught the side of his head. He was rammed underwater, and when he spluttered to the surface, a paddle crashed on his shoulder and sent him under again. This time he was held there until the paddle gradually fell away as water filled his lungs and his body started to sink. Then a sharp tug on the rope wrenched him up, and he emerged gasping and splashing in panic. Guido held out a pole and Ernesto clung to it.

The minutes ticked by and Ernesto slowly started to recover. Ramón was waiting patiently at the buoy and Guido was making no attempt to help him out of the water. Ernesto had no idea what was coming next, but he knew he could not swim to the finish line. When Pala's boat appeared, he prayed the caiman had not been released.

'Todd, you're running out of time,' Pala shouted officiously. 'The rules dictate that a competitor must finish each stage, otherwise they are disqualified. I can see you need assistance. I will check with Don Ramón . . . er, Sleve . . . whether or not the rules can be waived and help given on this occasion.'

Ramón gave a nod, Guido feathered the throttle and Ernesto was towed slowly up to the buoy. The race was finally over, and Ernesto stretched out a shaking hand and asked for help. What he got in reply was a curt wave from Ramón, not a helping hand from Guido, and his body spun to the roar of an engine as he lurched off in the direction of the compound.

Guido opened the throttle and the river swallowed Ernesto whole; things became a blur and all he could think of was holding his breath for as long as possible. He was coursing through the water like a human torpedo, aquaplaning some sections and bouncing through others, snatching the odd breath when he was spun onto his back and digging deep when he was carving underwater. By the time it was over, he was half drowned and too exhausted to swear at the men dragging him onto the riverbank.

Lying there, he was ashamed of the sicarios. He had given them a life with purpose and helped them grow from young saplings into powerful men. Discipline was strict, but fair. None of them had received a punishment that exceeded the extent of their misdemeanours and all of them had reaped a rich harvest. Yet they had destroyed his trust and trampled on his begonias. Now they stood over him like Roman soldiers preparing his Calvary, a pack of hyenas no better than pimps in a whorehouse. He began to recover and was about to share his views when a hand seized his belt.

'*Puta*,' he whimpered. His bones shook and his teeth chattered as Guido flapped him up and down on the ground as though wringing water from a sponge. Then he was on his feet and being led to a strange contraption that was tied to his Massey Ferguson tractor. Pala was standing next to it.

'Todd,' he called out, 'come and inspect your bike.'

It was one of the rusty deckchairs from the women's huts. Psychedelic patterned and vinyl covered, an immobile piece of furniture designed for relaxation, not travelling at speed. But travel at speed it was going to, for a set of wheels had been attached to the legs and the front axle was fixed to the tractor with a tow-rope. The wheels had clearly been ripped off his wheelbarrow, and he was about to tell Pala to fuck off when he was pushed into the deckchair. Then his body was tied to it with a ratchet strap and a bright yellow colander was balanced on his head. On it, the words 'THEY CALL ME MELLOW YELLOW' were written in large purple letters, and it was clipped around his chin with a flowery strap. By the time they finished, Ernesto had found some hidden reserves, and it allowed him to express his disapproval:

'Motherfuckers. Sons of whores . . .'

Ramón was sitting a safe distance from Ernesto's invective.

'Don Ernesto,' he yelled, '*tranquilo*, calm yourself. Today you're racing as Mr Mellow Yellow, not Conan the Destroyer.' Ramón slowly drummed his fingers on an armrest as he stared into space. 'My begonias. Yes, yes . . . I must finish deadheading them tomorrow, otherwise they'll be disappointing this year. What!' He leant forward. 'Someone has thrown them over the railing . . .' He cupped his ear as though listening carefully. '*Puta!* Someone trampled on them.'

'If you think you're going to destroy my begonias and walk away with my emeralds,' Ernesto shouted, 'you're sorely mistaken.'

Ramón stopped him dead.

'Don't interrupt me, *hijo de puta*. I haven't finished.' He picked up a baseball cap. 'I was saying, today *you* are racing as Mr Mellow Yellow and *I* am racing as Conan the Destroyer.' He pointed at the initials 'DEA' on the cap and put it on.

'I thought you were Sleve McDichael?' Ernesto replied sarcastically.

Ramón dismissed his comment with a wave and Pala took it as the signal to set off. The Massey Ferguson lurched forward, and along with it, the peculiar rig and its colander-wearing passenger. The first few laps were taken gently, then Pala sped up as the course became more familiar; by the time the fifth lap arrived, his foot hit the floor.

Ernesto shot back as the front wheels of his deckchair lifted up and the contraption hurtled down a straight section. It was all he could do to grip the armrests as Pala gave it one last burst of acceleration before slamming on the brakes and swerving to the side. Ernesto stared in horror at the reason for the sudden manoeuvre. A long ramp of earth and rough-cut planks was fast approaching. He hit it at speed and his deckchair was launched into the air as he clung on to a round of applause. However, the landing was a disappointment when compared to the flight and he crashed to the ground in a blur of psychedelic fabric and spinning aluminium poles. Ernesto's wheels disappeared into the river and a loud groan of disappointment rose from the compound.

Pala got down and tied the tow-rope to Ernesto's straps, then turned the tractor round. Waving from his Massey Ferguson, he watched Ernesto's resistance fade with each new lap of the compound he was dragged around. By the time they had finished, the colander had been ripped off and his torso was covered in blood. Whether by accident or intention, Pala stopped the tractor in front of Freddie's cage, and it was not long before the primate was shaking his bars at the man who had imprisoned him.

Pala's instinct was right. Ernesto was broken. Three men carried him over to Ramón.

'Congratulations, *hermano*, you won the leg,' he said from a comfy chair that had remained immobile throughout the event. 'That's one each. The last leg will be the decider.' He turned and pointed at a line of men holding gardening tools. 'They've been waiting to deliver your handicap for the run and there was stiff competition to use the strimmer' – a man stepped forward and raised his STIHL FS 86 – 'but first you must recover from your ride.'

The men put down their tools and gave a round of applause for his efforts, and Freddie gripped the bars of his cage and bared his teeth. It made no difference. Ernesto was finished. He had nothing left to offer. With a groan, he pushed himself up on an arm and implored Ramón to stop.

'You win. Take my emeralds. Let me recover and I'll bring them to you.'

'Pala will bring them. Tell me where they are, *cabrón*.'

There was no reply. Ernesto had fallen unconscious. The men fidgeted with their tools and Freddie wrenched the bars of his cage. Still Ernesto did not move. Ramón angrily waved for some smelling salts and Ernesto soon came round.

'Where are they?' Ramón demanded.

'What? What's "they"?' Ernesto was confused.

'Don't "what" me, *cabrón*. The emeralds.'

'Ah, those . . . They're on the *altiplano, hermano* . . .' His voice drifted off.

Ramón turned to Pala and threw his hands up in frustration. Ten laps were too much, but Pala had convinced him otherwise. Ernesto sounded like he was hallucinating, and Ramón shoved the smelling salts under his nose again. His head shot back and Ramón shook him.

'Where are the emeralds?' he repeated.

This time Ernesto looked him in the eye and half smiled.

'They're hidden on the *altiplano*. You'll need me alive to get to them, *cabrón*.'

Ramón cursed and turned to Pala, who shrugged. It was credible. Ernesto made frequent business trips to the *altiplano*.

'Okay. Let's say you've hidden them on the *altiplano*. If we take you there and don't find any emeralds . . . what you've experienced here will seem like a walk in the park.'

'They're there,' Ernesto replied. 'Somewhere over the rainbow there's an island with no water and a fish that never swims. You'll find them buried there, beneath the shadow of a man with prickly skin . . .' His voice drifted off before he could finish.

'What!' Ramón shouted.

'Run!' shouted the sicarios.

Freddie had finally torn open the bars of his cage and was careering towards the injured man. The sicarios scattered and Ramón scurried after them.

The gorilla seized Ernesto, brandished him over his head for a moment then flipped him around and locked his neck in a tight grip. Slowly at first, then gradually faster and faster, Freddie rotated on his heels and spun round like a hammer thrower at the Olympics. It was not long before Ernesto's legs had lifted from the ground and his arms were flailing as his body swung in a broad arc. The gorilla's eyes were now fixed firmly on the sparkling tin roof of the hall, and it was about to receive a direct hit when out of nowhere there was a sharp crack followed by the sound of ripping sinews . . . and Ernesto's torso flew off in the opposite direction. It shot across the camp in a curved trajectory, smashed through the railings of his hacienda and destroyed what remained of his potted plants.

Freddie was left with a severed head in his hands, and for a few seconds he looked stunned, almost puzzled . . . then he let out a huge roar and took off with Ernesto's head tucked under one arm and his ganglions dragging behind like the tentacles of an octopus.

CHAPTER TWENTY-FOUR

*S*omewhere over the rainbow there's an island with no water and a fish that never swims. You'll find them buried there, beneath the shadow of a man with prickly skin.

Ramón wondered if Ernesto had been hallucinating, although he had been lucid and there had even been a sparkle in his eyes when he had said it. He also knew that Ernesto was broken and looking for a way out. If Ramón had been in that situation, he would have done exactly the same – stalled for time by making himself indispensable. Yet something told him that Ernesto was telling the truth, and he set about solving the puzzle of the emeralds.

Taking a sip of coffee, his thoughts focussed on the DEA. Over the radio they had been insistent that Popeye reach the compound. Ernesto was right to question them. It *was* suspicious. Why go to the trouble? Ernesto was confident of killing him and he might have succeeded had the men not turned against him. After that, the DEA would have had plenty of time to assassinate their informant.

Ramón chuckled.

The hijo de puta *thought they would forget he killed one agent and tortured another!* The DEA were after both of them and there was no way a new Californian apartment was waiting for Ernesto. What bothered him, though, was that Popeye had orders to recover the emeralds. *Maybe that's the real reason to get Popeye into the compound?* If so, it meant Angel Man knew about the emeralds, and the information could only have come from someone high up in Medellín.

Piña immediately came to mind. He was in for a cut when Ramón recovered them. Maybe he was hedging his bets and also had a deal with the DEA if they got them first? Ramón knew he had to find out either way and tried to check his growing suspicion of Piña.

It was a clear night with a full moon. Ramón was on the veranda, his back arched and arms wide open. His wail rose into the night, louder and louder until his throat was raw and the moon had been challenged to do its worst, then he retreated to the bedroom.

His finger ran down Ernesto's bookmark and stopped at '1208 – 91.5 – 2245'.

The clock reached 22:45 and a gravelly voice broke the silence.

'Delta Echo Alpha, pick up,' said Ramón in his best Ernesto impression.

'Delta Echo Alpha, receiving.'

'Good evening, *hermano*. How are you?'

'Roger that, Ernesto. Fine. How's Fat Toad?'

'Exuberant,' he snapped. 'Working out and getting into shape.'

'Roger. What for?'

'The ladies. He's a handsome beast – it's his figure that lets him down.'

There was a short pause.

'Roger. What news on Popeye?'

'Still lying low in Cochabamba and making contacts,' Ramón said, then added, 'Has he been enquiring about my emeralds?'

This time there was a long silence.

'Emeralds, Ernesto?'

'My contact says Popeye thinks I've hidden some on the *altiplano*?'

Another silence.

'Who is your contact, Deep Tongue?' There was the hint of suspicion, and the use of his codename demanded a similar response.

'I can't reveal my contacts, Angel Man,' Ramón replied.

'Well, *are* they hidden on the *altiplano*, Deep Tongue?' the man asked.

'So you *have* heard about them,' Ramón answered, leaving the accusation hanging. 'Is Popeye coming to assassinate me once he's found them, or do I get killed first?'

This time there was no pause.

'Operation Spank the Hand has neither a contingency for the recovery of emeralds *nor* plans to assassinate you.'

It was a deliberate mistake that Ramón needed to correct, but the actual name of the operation escaped him. He took a few seconds to try and remember it . . . *Operation Thunder Box . . . Operation Thunder Gun . . . maybe Operation Thunder Man?*

'There's more to Operation Thunder Man than you're telling me,' he eventually said.

'Hello, Fat Toad,' came the reply.

Ramón knew he had blown it.

'It's Señor Ramón Emilio Escobar Sanchez to you, *hijo de puta*.'

'No. It's Fat Toad. And we've plans to deflate you, motherfucker.'

'Will that be when you track me down in Paraguay, *cabrón*?'

'Paraguay, or the ends of the earth.'

'Come find me. I'll be wearing a sparkling emerald crown – you won't be able to miss me. In fact, I'm leaving with Ernesto's emeralds tomorrow. Why not pop down before then and we can share an *aguardiente* together?'

The radio went dead and Ramón sat back.

The DEA knew about the emeralds. He was not sure if Popeye's orders had been shared with them, yet his suspicion of Piña grew. However, he was still determined to go to the *altiplano* and find them. Piña did not need to know. What's more, if he *was* an informant then his cut had been forfeited.

Although he doubted the DEA would believe he was going to Paraguay, they had no reason to think he was about to leave the Beni. As for Piña, well, the longer he was kept in the dark the better. Also, he could no longer trust any of the sicarios – at least one of them had released Pasquale – and all communication from the camp needed to be shut down.

He pulled out the valves from his radio and would get Pala to remove the others in the morning. That way, even though he knew the riddle would eventually get out, at least he would have a head start solving it. The fact that Ernesto had shared it so publicly was unfortunate, and he would have liked Pala to assassinate each and every one of the men who had heard it. The problem was, Pala's skill in the multiple-kill arena was unproven and his ability to survive the challenge uncertain. He quickly dismissed the idea.

The next morning Ramón rose early. He had not slept well. The idea that Piña might be in league with the DEA had given him a restless night. They had a cast-iron agreement – at least he had thought so – with him trading from Bolivia and Piña taking over Medellín. There would have been a steady supply of coca paste to Medellín, each of them would have had separate trading regions in the States, and the money would have poured in. The call with the DEA had changed everything. Instinct told him that Angel Man was after the emeralds, and that incriminated Piña.

'*Puta!*'

He went to find Pala.

An hour later Ramón was eating and talking in the dining room and Pala was standing by the table listening. '*Hermano*, arrange a flight to Guanay this afternoon,' Ramón said. 'I've some business to organise before we go to the *altiplano*.'

Pala had the good sense not to enquire about his timings and simply nodded. The radio valves had already been removed and he had packed for a trip; all that remained was to choose a sicario to run the compound. The operation would continue as normal, although none of the other sicarios would be allowed to leave and all communication would be through the man in temporary charge.

'We'll need to crack the riddle,' Ramón continued. 'Find out where Ernesto went on his business trips. We'll go there first.'

'He's got a large collection of photos in an album,' Pala replied. 'We should check it for clues.'

Ramón's suspicions were confirmed. Pala's 'thorough' search *had* been derailed by photographs. It no longer mattered. He did not suppose for one moment that Ernesto would be so stupid as to have a photograph of the secret location. However, he humoured Pala.

'Fine. Bring it. Did anything catch your eye?' he asked, without much interest.

'There's a photo of him standing under a large rainbow outside an amusement park. I don't think there was a sign, but there was a huge pot of gold at the end of the rainbow, you know, with coins spilling out and—'

'Yes, yes. I get it,' Ramón replied. 'Bring the album. Find out where the park is. We're going there.'

CHAPTER TWENTY-FIVE

Popeye was sitting at Colina de San Sebastián, a popular spot overlooking Cochabamba.

For the time being there was a hum of vendors selling cheap souvenirs and families posing for photographs. Soon all that would change. The small hill and its saintly statue were about to be eclipsed by a bigger statue on a higher hill. Not only would it dominate the city from its superior vantage point, but the newcomer also had a distinct advantage. Jesus, who in terms of spiritual kudos was in a different league to the saint pierced by arrows, would gaze down from its plinth. The new statue was modelled on Christ the Redeemer in Rio de Janeiro, except its outstretched arms would face a landscape of dusty concrete and car parks, not the golden beaches of Copacabana and Ipanema.

It made no difference to Popeye; he did not care about the changing dynamics and he was not there for the view. He had come to contemplate his next move away from the noise of the city, somewhere without distraction or interruption, for the message he had received that morning needed proper consideration.

'Beware Andrea – Chicharrón Alabaron.'

It was written on a playing card with an angel rising from hell, identical to the one delivered on the bus, although this one came in an envelope, not attached to the end of a mousetrap. Piña had told him to lie low and he had done just that. This new threat to his life changed everything. Things needed to move more quickly. He had already made contact with the *cocalero* community; now he needed to work them harder to find a way into the Beni cartel. In the meantime, the question of the mysterious 'Andrea' remained unanswered.

Yet another attempt on his life by a female assassin! He cursed Dolores and he cursed the man who preyed on his weakness for women. He did not know Andrea, although he knew Chicharrón Alabaron. Everyone did. The 'praised *chicharrón*' they served was indeed a pork dish worthy of praise, and he had eaten there several times. Somehow, taking advantage of his love of *chicharrones* was a different matter to ensnaring him with a woman, and he frowned when thinking about the distasteful combination. He traced a finger around the angel and flipped the card over. The message had not changed. It was simple and to the point. He was searching for details that did not exist and tucked it away in his wallet.

On the way down, his eyes wandered up to the other hill and the huge scaffolding that hid its emerging champion. The thought did not escape him that like Jesus, he also had a certain kudos that came from dealing with small fry like Andrea, and she would be getting a bullet in the chest when the time came. It would have to wait. First he needed to pay a visit to the clumsily named Six Federations of Coca Growers of the Tropic of Cochabamba, or 'the union' for short. He was travelling as Juan Arroyo, an independent journalist writing an article about the narco trade in Bolivia. It had allowed him to ask questions without raising suspicion, and the union was keen for him to highlight their struggle.

When Law 1008 was passed a few years earlier, coca leaf cultivation became illegal and the farmers in the Chapare valley below Cochabamba lost their livelihood. Since then, the union had organised roadblocks and demonstrations against what they saw as an imperialist attack on their indigenous culture. 'Juan' was keen for the Colombian public to learn of their plight, and insisted on an interview with the cartel, otherwise his article would only be half the story. Eventually his tenacity was rewarded. That very afternoon he was meeting a local union representative who could arrange an interview. Popeye knew he had to push hard as the warning meant he had been discovered, and the sooner he left Cochabamba the better.

He was convinced that Ramón was behind the attempt on his life and the question of how he continued to receive information weighed heavily. His thoughts turned to Medellín, yet the idea of Don Pablo helping a double-crosser was ridiculous, and Piña was ambitious but not stupid. It pointed to someone he must have met in the union, and it was odd that his meeting also coincided with the warning he had just received. He touched his Beretta. Whoever it was would regret their actions.

On his way down Calle Junin, he set about finding a way to expose them; by the time Calle Calama was reached, he had changed his mind. His priority was reaching his targets in the Beni, not exposing an accuser. With that in mind, he continued down Avenida Ayacucho and concentrated on the matter in hand. There was a small branch of Banco de Bogotá close to the junction with Calle Santivañez and he was going there for cash. A thousand dollars would do it. It would be a large bribe, but he needed to move fast. He did not have time to cultivate a relationship with the man, and money would speed up the process.

Around him, four lanes of traffic streamed down the avenue and zoomed past bland offices and small shops, all of which came from an era when concrete was popular. Popeye waited at a busy junction and crossed at the first opportunity. Looking around, he realised he had grown to like the small city despite its ugly buildings. He would be sad to leave. It was cooler than Medellín and more relaxed; things would be different when he arrived in the Beni.

The money was counted out. Four thousand bolivianos, the equivalent of just over a thousand dollars. Popeye stuffed the large envelope into his jacket pocket and left the bank. The counters had been busy and he had been forced to wait in a long queue with other customers. The withdrawal of such a large sum then needed the approval of the bank manager, and he had to wait at the counter whilst the man was found. Eventually the money was handed over and he could get on his way. It meant there was no time to check out Chicharrón Alabaron, and he decided to hang around Avenida Ayacucho instead. The union offices were only a short walk away and he had twenty minutes to spare, so he went into the church of Santo Domingo on the opposite side of the road.

Popeye dipped his finger into the holy water, made a quick sign of the cross and slid across a pew. It had not escaped him that his last visit to a church had ended badly, although there were no confessions today and he was determined to remain seated. Looking up, he realised the figure of Christ hanging over its altar was even bloodier than the one in Itagüí, and he knew there was a link between the amount of blood applied to a crucifix and the amount of suffering inflicted by the conquistadors – the greater the brutality, the more blood was added – otherwise it would have had little impact on a community accustomed to random violence. *They must have suffered badly in Cochabamba*, he thought, as the figure was drenched in blood.

He was just about to pull out his black book when something sharp pressed into his back.

'Hand over the cash, *cabrón.*'

Popeye knew it was the tip of a blade, and he raised his right arm.

'*Tranquilo, hermano,*' he said.

'Hand over the cash,' the man repeated, and pushed the knife harder.

'Of course. Let me get it. It's in my jacket pocket.'

Popeye lowered his arm slowly and reached into his jacket. In a swift movement, he swung round, jammed his Beretta against the man's forehead and cocked the gun.

'Hand over your knife, *malparido,*' he said calmly, 'and kneel down and pray. Yes, that's right, with your arms on the railing and hands together.'

The man did as he was told and knelt down, shaking slightly.

'Arms on the railing, *hijo de puta.*' He pushed the man's hands down to reveal his forearms.

'Do you have a confession, my son?'

The man looked at him blankly.

'Do you have a confession, my son?' Popeye repeated, with menace.

'Er . . . um . . .'

' "Er" and "um" have no place in the confessional. I'm going to ask one more time. If you don't answer, I'll pin your arm to the pew with this knife and you'll have plenty of time to think about it. Do you have a confession, my son?' he shouted.

This time the man mumbled quickly.

'I am a thief and a liar. I hurt people and I cheat on—'

'That's good enough. You've made a full and frank confession. Your penance is two hundred Hail Marys and two hundred . . . no, four hundred Our Fathers.'

The man looked stunned at the severity of the penance.

'Yes. That's right, *cabrón*. Shut your eyes, raise them to heaven and start praying – out loud. I'll be watching and listening. If you so much as open your eyes or stop before the end . . .' He paused to let the man take it in. 'I'll pin you to the pew with this knife and you'll finish your penance in pain.'

The man did as he was told, and Popeye left him to it. On the way out he dropped the knife into a bin and thanked God he had his Beretta with him. Although it had felt awkward having a gun in church, it had allowed him to carry out a good deed and chalk up some credit with His Almighty. Confident that the location of his charitable action would improve its profile and convinced that the amount of prayers would boost its impact, he walked off in the direction of the *cocalero* union offices with a slight swagger and the hint of a grin.

CHAPTER TWENTY-SIX

Martín was sitting outside a sunlit café and his eyes were on a man striding towards the union office. Since escaping to Cochabamba he had learnt to be careful around strangers as he knew the cartel were looking for him. The union had told him there was a reporter who needed access to the cartel, and who better to facilitate it than Martín? What they did not know was that the cartel would be delighted to see him, although he was less keen to renew the acquaintance. He first wanted to observe the man before he introduced himself.

He was quite short and powerfully built, walking confidently (almost with a swagger) and aware of everything around him. *Or is that because he's looking for me?* Cropped hair. A thick beard that made him look older than his years. *Maybe in his late twenties?* He was alone and nobody was following him. Martín had reluctantly agreed to the meeting, although he had no intention of going into the union offices. A public place was far safer.

Martín got up, dropped a five-boliviano note on the table and made his way over to the reporter.

'Hello, I'm Martín. You must be . . .' He stumbled over his words. 'Er . . . Juan? Juan Arroyo?' Up close, the man looked familiar. If it wasn't for the beard and close-cropped hair . . .

'Pleased to meet you. Shall we go inside?'

'No. There's a café nearby. The coffee's better,' Martín replied.

The man nodded, and Martín took him to a place around the corner, all the while trying to remember where exactly he had seen him.

'So, you work for the union, Martín? And before that you worked for the Beni cartel?' the reporter asked, gesturing at the waitress.

'That's right. I came up to Cochabamba for my health. Too much disease in the lowlands and the climate here is more temperate. It suits me better. You're Colombian, right? Whereabouts?'

'Bogotá. Big city in the south. Like Cochabamba, but prettier.'

The banal conversation went on for a bit, each of them gathering information and sizing the other up. When Martín made a flippant comment about Colombians and their love of *chicharrones*, the man gave a broad grin, and Martín nearly choked on his coffee. It was none other than the guy he had seen in Rurrenabaque! He knew it now. He was the one in the photograph with Pablo Escobar, beaming down on the men playing pool. That same charismatic smile . . .

The shock of recognising the man opposite him soon turned to horror. He was facing the Medellín cartel's top hit-man and his life was in danger. The sicario was there to avenge Horqueta's death . . . and he had been so careful up until now.

'You okay, *hermano*? You've gone a little pale.'

Martín pretended to finish his coffee then leapt up. Popeye grabbed his arm.

'*Tranquilo*, take a seat. I don't mind you joking about *chicharrones*. Everyone jokes about them!' He dragged Martín down. 'Listen, you look pressed for time, and I have a proposition to make.'

Sicarios did not make propositions, they made demands, usually with a threat of violence. Martín relaxed a little and realised it was unlikely that he would be killed there and then. He decided to take the initiative.

'*Señor*, I know I've offended Don Ernesto and that means I've offended Don Escobar. Before you do anything hasty, please consider my wife and family.'

'What?' Popeye looked puzzled.

'I admit my role in Horqueta's death, but he was a psychopath.'

'Okay,' Popeye replied.

'I know you're Jhon Velásquez, not Juan Arroyo. Let me explain what happened, there's no need to kill me, it's all been a big mistake.'

Popeye sat back and roared with laughter.

'So *you're* the guy who killed Horqueta? I heard all about it. That *hijo de puta* had it coming. He was boasting about replacing me and you probably saved me a job. No, the way you did it was impressive . . .' He paused to catch his breath. 'Congratulations, *güevón*.' And he held out a hand.

Martín shook it and tried to recover his composure.

'So you haven't been sent to kill me, *señor*?'

'The name's Popeye . . . just Popeye . . . as in Popeye the Sailor Man.' His stock phrase produced a weak smile, and Popeye waved for the waitress. 'Of course not. I need your help. We're on the same side, *cabrón*.' Another wave and the waitress arrived.

'*Aguardiente*. One glass,' he ordered. 'You need a drink, *hermano*!' He patted Martín's cheeks to bring the blood back to them.

CHAPTER TWENTY-SEVEN

It was early evening and Popeye and Martín were in a small hall awaiting the president's annual address that marked the anniversary of the Villa Turani massacre. Martín had recovered from his earlier shock and they had spent the afternoon in a nearby bar. It had not been long before the union rep had been calling the sicario Popeye and the latter telling *chicharrón* jokes (all of which seemed to involve disguised pork rinds and Venezuelan vegetarians), and it was one of those rare occasions when something clicked in an instant. Sometimes it's a common interest or a similar set of beliefs, other times a passion for music or films; this time it was a shared sense of dark humour.

Martín must have mimicked Horqueta struggling with his carabiner and smashing flames from his head a dozen times, but every time it brought Popeye to his knees. ' . . . And then the *hijo de puta* disappeared round the corner with his arm up. I didn't know if he was waving or giving me the finger . . .' Popeye had told him about the man in Santo Domingo and wondered if *he* was still on his knees, then Popeye was on his knees and Martín was timing him praying. Eight seconds for a Hail Mary and twelve seconds for an Our Father – it meant the man's penance would have lasted around two hours. With much laughter they raised their glasses to the mugger and declared him winner of the regional stage of Mr Penitent 1992. After that the sicario even went on to describe his ordeal in the confession box, which said a lot – he didn't normally share those sorts of details.

Around them, rows of wooden chairs were filled with farmers and the hall buzzed with chatter. Bottles of homemade alcohol were everywhere and most of the men were already drunk. Hanging from the ceiling, a mirror ball sent shafts of light across a stage where a large banner marked the occasion with the words 'Cocaleros Unite Against the Imperialists' in bold red letters. The date of the massacre was commemorated underneath in a small black font: 27th June 1988.

It was a new experience for Popeye, and whilst he did not understand a word of the Quechuan being spoken, at least Martín had explained the banner to him. Back in June 1988 a protest had been organised by the *cocaleros* in Villa Turani that had turned into a confrontation with the police. Eleven farmers had been shot and their bodies later thrown into the Chapare river. It brought about the consolidation of the Chapare coca grower unions into the Six Federations of Coca Growers of the Tropic of Cochabamba, and it hardened attitudes to the government and its collusion with the United States. This evening was a rallying call to its members. It had been rescheduled several times after the authorities had cancelled their bookings, and it was only at the very last minute that the event could go ahead when a venue became available unexpectedly. Normally the hall was only used for low-key weddings, and its disco ball was ill suited to political meetings, but the intimacy of the venue heightened the sense of anticipation and charged the atmosphere.

Evo Morales strode onto the stage.

'Don't be a thief . . . Don't be lazy . . . Don't be a liar.'

His speeches always started with the three rules he learnt as a child.

'Long live coca! Death to the Yankees! *Hermanos*, we produce our coca. We bring it to market. We sell it. That's where our responsibility ends.'

The room erupted with whistling and stamping feet.

'So, gringos, if we give up our coca in El Chapare, do you think the market in the United States will collapse? No! The problem will move to Los Yungas, where Law 1008 doesn't apply. Meanwhile we all starve. No, *hermanos*. We take the fight to the Imperialists.'

Even Popeye was on his feet now, swept along by the fervour of the passionate, undernourished men around him. The money received from their crop was a fraction of the money made by the Medellín cartel, and the difference in their circumstances was hard to ignore.

Evo's speech continued, sometimes rousing the men, at other times plunging them into despair, yet always lifting them up towards the end. It was a long path, and they would face it together. The DEA would eventually be removed from the Chapare, and once he was elected president of the republic, they would be banished from Bolivia altogether. Coca farming would flourish and the profits generated would help fund free education and healthcare.

It produced another raucous applause. A bottle of homebrew swung towards Popeye and he politely refused it. As he looked around, his admiration grew for the man who inspired others and had a vision for his community. Later, when he was leaving the hall, he knew he had not heard the last of Evo Morales and that one day the accomplished speaker might well become president of his poor country.

Popeye left Martín and wandered down Calle Lanza, across the Plaza Central and up Calle Colombia. In front of him, the rustic, pink-painted walls and clay-tiled roof of Chicharrón Alabaron dominated the street and a small queue was lined up outside waiting for tables. Popeye walked straight past and turned up a small alley that led to its kitchen. The sound of crashing pots and sizzling frying pans could be heard and there was a delicious smell that was hard to resist, but resist it he did. Knocking on the door, he pushed it open and got the chef's attention.

'*Hermano.* Go and get Andrea for me,' he said with a wink, as though he were her boyfriend. 'And take this for your trouble,' he added, offering a fifty-boliviano note.

The man looked surprised. Popeye tapped his finger and pretended to put on a ring, then the penny dropped and the man grinned. It was clear that Popeye intended to propose, and he kept up the pretence by going down on one knee. The fifty bolivianos were taken with a laugh, and the chef raised a finger to his lips and promised to keep the man's romantic secret.

Popeye backed away from the door, slipped into the shadows and pulled out his Beretta. He was curious to see what his imaginary and soon-to-be-dead girlfriend looked like. Most of the Andreas he knew were plain, and there were plenty of them. A couple of them had pretty smiles, although in the main they were not his type. He did not have to wait for long. As the chef reappeared in the doorway, Popeye retreated further into the shadows and cocked his gun, but Andrea must have been shy, and he could hear the chef trying to convince her to come out. Eventually he lost patience and she was shoved out of the door. Another Andrea followed in quick succession, then another. Finally, three Andreas stood there, and the chef joined them.

'*Hermano*, come out,' he shouted. 'We've got several Andreas. Which one's your girlfriend?'

Popeye had forgotten the reason why he knew so many of them. It was a popular name, not just in Medellín but throughout Latin America. He put away his gun and emerged from the shadows.

'*Señoritas*, I'm sorry for the subterfuge. Please excuse me.' He began to laugh at the bizarre circumstances. *Please step forward, Andrea number two, for execution!* Looking at the girls lined up, he hesitated for a moment, then realised it was another opportunity to demonstrate his merciful streak. He seized the moment and reached into his jacket. Pulling out the envelope, he started counting out notes, and when he looked up, the girls were fidgeting awkwardly, not knowing what to do. One of them must have worked on the front desk as she was wearing a sparkling red dress; the others were all in black with long white aprons.

'*Señoritas*, I am a member of a charitable organisation that distributes cash to worthy people,' Popeye announced. 'Last week we were rewarding ladies named Zita. This week we have returned to the letter "A", and this is your lucky day.'

The chef looked confused and the girls were bewildered. Then one of them quickly grasped what was going on. Her red dress darted towards him, and Andrea explained how she was far more deserving than the others as she did not get any tips on the front desk, and greeting customers was hard work. It was met with a howl of protest from the other Andreas, and they rushed over to present their case. Popeye was not interested. They were all getting the same amount and it quietened them down. Handing over a wad of notes in turn, he looked carefully for any sign that would give away the assassin. They were all perfectly composed, and Popeye had no idea which of them was his would-be killer. He took a step back to let her know that he was not fooled.

'*Señoritas*, not only is this a lucky day for all of you, it is also a very special day for one very lucky woman,' he said. It was directed to the assassin, and he knew she would understand. 'The next time we meet she won't be quite as lucky. If I were her, I would take the money and get a better job.' Then he turned on his heel as though he had delivered some profound advice.

And that was as close as his behaviour got to the crazy old woman's performance back in Medellín; whereas she had ended her tirade and disappeared with a sketchpad and paintbrushes, Popeye simply vanished empty-handed into the night.

CHAPTER TWENTY-EIGHT

The next day Popeye was waiting for Martín. He had been in the café for over an hour and was growing impatient. He was also irritated that he had not asked Martín for his address. There was every chance that he was having second thoughts, and it would be hard to track him down.

Maybe he's just hungover? Popeye was glad he did not drink, although it would have to be one hell of a hangover to keep him waiting that long. *Maybe it was the* aguardiente *talking last night and he had no real intention to help?* He doubted it. He was a good judge of character and was confident that Martín could be trusted.

A moment later, Martín walked in, pale and flustered.

'*Hermano*, you're an hour late,' Popeye said, pointing at his watch. 'I was about to come and find you.'

'Sorry, I got some bad news.'

'Not a sore head then?' Martín didn't answer. 'What bad news?'

The waitress came over and Martín ordered an espresso.

'Something's happened. The compound's been locked down.'

'What compound?' asked Popeye, leaning forward.

'Don Ernesto's compound.'

Popeye sat back and took a sip of his coffee. For a moment he thought he was being duped, that it was a crude attempt to delay him. Looking at Martín's trembling hand, he suspected he was telling the truth; even the most accomplished actor would have struggled to deliver that performance, and his pallor would have challenged the best makeup artist.

'Drink your espresso, *hermano*. Start at the beginning, slowly, and take your time,' Popeye said, as though he were back in Itagüí, debriefing a prospective sicario.

Martín nodded.

Popeye listened to his story. If what he was being told was true, he had missed his chance. He was surprised that Ramón had managed to kill Ernesto. It was his compound and he had plenty of sicarios for protection. It seemed strange. Once more he wondered if he was being played, and pushed for more information.

'And your brother-in-law. What's his connection? How does he know all this?'

Martín shrugged. 'Santiago's lab ran out of coca paste. When they couldn't reach the compound, another lab in Santa Ana confirmed it.'

'So it's a rumour?'

'No,' Martín said, shaking his head. 'Shortly after the compound was locked down, Don Ramón and Pala visited Guanay. They banned all flights to and from the compound and caught a plane up to La Paz. It's not a rumour, I know it's locked down. My brother-in-law heard it directly from the airport director. I don't know what they're up to, but Pala's bound to come after me once he's finished whatever it is they're doing.'

It was strange that Ramón had broken cover, unless there had been a major change in his plans. It backed up Martín's story, to a point.

'Why kill Ernesto? And what about his sicarios?'

Here Martín's information became hazy. It appeared the compound had turned against Ernesto, although he did not know the reason. However, by incredible good fortune, his cousin Luis was in temporary charge and Martín's brother-in-law was speaking to him later. He would have more answers that evening.

'You've got some useful family connections,' Popeye said, suspicious that he was being fed false information. It sounded too convenient to have a cousin running the compound and a brother-in-law who knew Ramón's movements.

'We're all tied into the cartel. There's no other way to make a decent living in the Beni.'

There was some truth to that. A lot of men in the business were related.

'And Luis is the one with the flamethrower?'

Martín nodded.

It was Luis who had alerted Martín to the threat he had faced. Whilst the form of Horqueta's punishment had been unclear, both men knew it would be severe. There was every chance Martín might not survive the ordeal and it had left them no choice. It was a brave decision by any measure, although if what Popeye had heard was true, then it was entirely justified.

Popeye shook his head. Apparently that *hijo de puta* had taken to increasingly theatrical displays of brutality once he let it be known he would be replacing the Medellín sicario. *As though disembowelling victims isn't dramatic enough.* According to Martín, on one occasion Horqueta had arrived in Ronaldo's – or Ramudo's, he could not remember the name – for a game of pool with a scrotum sack dangling from his belt. Martín said he had carried on as though it was perfectly normal and nobody had dared say anything, even when he placed it on the side of the table to take a shot. On his way out he popped its shrivelled contents into the produce section of Ronaldo's, and they only came to light a few days later when a woman mistook them for baby onions. What she had confused for a flavour-enhancing vegetable were totally unsuitable for her soup recipe; they were also totally unsuitable for the use to which the previous owner had put them, although he would not be missing them. He had lost his life when Horqueta's punishment for his misdemeanour 'got a little out of control', and the memory had stuck with Martín ever since.

Popeye understood why he had chosen the path he was on. The threat of a deadly punishment would have convinced him to do the same. Yet after that, things seemed to completely unravel. If Martín were to be believed, Ramón had killed Ernesto. However, tracking him on the vast *altiplano* was going to be a challenge, and the question remained about Ernesto's emeralds. Ramón would not have ignored them. It meant he either had them with him or he would be returning to the compound for them. Popeye needed to know either way, and he decided to join the call that evening.

It was just after seven o'clock and pitch black. Martín was renting a room in Temporal Pampa, a poor neighbourhood on the edge of the city. Most of the houses had small yards that were protected by tall iron gates and high walls topped with broken glass. None of them had numbers and there were few distinguishing features. Martín's place had a large water tank alongside a spiral staircase that made it stand out. The staircase was bolted to the outside of the building and led to four small rooms across a flat roof. His room was at the far end, with a red door.

Popeye was glad his watch had luminescent dials, as there were no streetlights. He checked the time. The call was in twenty minutes. Martín had told him there was a payphone in the hallway. It would not be as private as Popeye would have liked, and he would have preferred to dial out, but the owner was old and deaf and Martín's brother-in-law had insisted *he* phone them. He spotted the water tank, rang a bell and set a dog barking. A moment later the owner appeared and shone a flashlight in his face.

'Open the gate, *hermano*,' Popeye bellowed, surprised by his nimbleness. 'I'm a friend of Martín.'

'*Tranquilo*, I'm not deaf,' the man replied. The gate opened and Popeye saw he was probably in his late thirties. He pointed at the water tank, and Popeye climbed the stairs.

On his way up his eyes wandered across to Serrania de San Pedro and its emerging statue. Christ was rising over the city with his back to the impoverished district of Temporal Pampa. *Not unlike the church in Cochabamba*, he reflected. He knew the cartel did more good for the poor than the church ever did and the statue would have no real impact on their lives. Popeye was glad to be part of something that made a difference. He knocked on the red door.

'Open it!' Martín shouted, and Popeye stepped inside.

Martín was sitting at a small table, and he raised a glass.

'*Hermano*, come and join me,' he slurred.

Popeye spotted a half-empty bottle of *aguardiente*.

'No. I don't drink, remember?' Seeing Martín was drunk, Popeye was glad to be on the call. 'Finish up,' he added. 'We'll wait in the hallway in case your brother-in-law calls early.'

'No need,' Martín replied. 'I just spoke to him.'

'What?'

'I just spoke to him,' he repeated. 'He wanted me to get the good news as soon as he found out.'

'Found out what?' Popeye asked, his temper growing. Then he remembered the man did not work for him, and he checked himself.

'I can return home,' Martín answered with a wide grin. 'It's true. Don Ernesto's dead and Pala isn't looking for me. It was Pala who killed him. He was a DEA informant. Pala's not coming after me and I'm safe to return. Luis is going to find me some work when I get back.'

For a moment Popeye was stunned into silence. Whilst he could follow Martín back to the Beni, it was pointless if his target had flown. He needed information, quickly, and Martín was the only one who could provide it. If there was no longer the threat of a severe punishment, it would have to be money that convinced him to stay. He liked Martín. He really hoped that the promise of money would work. If not, then there was always force. He decided to humour Martín's good luck before getting every last detail of the call.

'That's good news, *hermano*. I'm pleased for you.' It was irritating that he had missed the call even though he had arrived early. 'When are you leaving?'

Popeye spent the next ten minutes politely asking about Martín's travel plans and hearing all about his young daughters. Then he extracted the information he needed about the incident at the compound, and if his recent experiences had seemed bizarre, they were nothing compared to what he was told.

The account of the deadly triathlon was sort of believable, and Ernesto hiding his emeralds on the *altiplano* was credible. They were his retirement fund and personal insurance. He would want them as far from prying eyes and a bank deposit as possible. Yet the monkey attack and the silverback gorilla episode sounded like a rumour that had got out of hand. *Swinging Ernesto around the compound, then ripping off his head . . . Don't expect me to believe that.*

At least he knew why Ramón had left the compound. Popeye believed that, along with the mysterious riddle. Ernesto was a lawyer. Crafting words into a string of important-sounding and confusing sentences was what they did best.

Somewhere over the rainbow there's an island with no water and a fish that never swims. You'll find them buried there, beneath the shadow of a man with prickly skin.

Luis had heard the riddle. All the sicarios had heard it, yet none of them had the faintest idea what it meant. Neither had Martín's brother-in-law. Popeye got back to it once Martín had finished describing the presents he was going to buy for his wife.

'What do you make of the riddle? You knew Ernesto. Would he make it up for the fun of it?'

Martín laughed.

'You never met Don Ernesto, did you? Other than tending his plants, he only had fun when there was a purpose to it.' His voice lowered. 'His punishments were certainly fun . . . for him at least. No, he was a serious man. The riddle would have meant something – it's not just a rhyme.'

'So, what does it mean?'

'The first bit's obvious. It's the Wiphala.'

Popeye shrugged.

'The flag of the *campesinos*. You know, the square rainbow-coloured flag they carry on marches?'

Popeye was none the wiser.

'It must be a reference to the *altiplano*. The rest makes no sense.'

As Popeye already knew the emeralds were hidden on the *altiplano*, it did not help. He decided to press Martín about Ramón's travel plans.

'All I know is they flew to La Paz.'

'What for?'

'I'm not sure.'

'Can you find out?'

'I can ask.'

Popeye decided to convince Martín to help.

'*Hermano*, you know I said we're on the same side?' Martín was topping up his glass and only half listening. Popeye could tell that he was growing tired of the conversation. 'Well, that's still true, even though Ernesto's been dealt with. How would you like to get rich?' he asked.

Martín smiled.

'I'm already rich.'

Popeye knew he was referring to the family about which he had heard so much.

'No, I mean *really* rich. So wealthy that you and your family never have to worry about money again.' This got Martín's attention. 'You want to provide for your family and I want to reach the man who can make that possible'. Popeye decided to come clean. 'I've been sent here with two objectives: kill Ramón, then recover the emeralds. I can only do it with your help. Without it, Ramón will find them and disappear for good, probably to another country. Stay here and help me and you'll get enough emeralds to start a new life. That is, unless you prefer driving boats up and down the Rio Beni . . .'

He could see that Martín was interested. He was offering a rare opportunity that would set him up for life. Martín did not need much convincing, and he agreed to use Luis and his brother-in-law to get the information. It came with the strict condition that he was the only one who made contact with them, and Popeye guessed he was worried about being cut out. He was determined to get the information first-hand before much longer, and he got up and left Martín to finish his *aguardiente*.

Standing at the door, he made a flippant comment about the health of the Bolivians in general and the amazing sprightliness of the old men in Cochabamba in particular. Martín just smiled and said nothing.

CHAPTER TWENTY-NINE

Three days later they were on the *altiplano*. Popeye was drinking coffee and Martín had a beer. In front of them, Lake Uru Uru lay oasis-like beneath Cerro Quinchata. Snowy peaks surrounded the shallow lake and hundreds of Andean flamingos gave the water a pinkish hue that turned blue again whenever they flew off. For now, it was full of gabbling birds strutting around with their heads held high. They were making a show of finding a mate, performing a ritual that stretched back thousands of years. Their ancestors had been doing the same long before coca was cultivated and mining discovered, millennia before the arrival of the Spanish and the colonisation of Bolivia.

It was a quiet spot and they had time to reflect. Ramón and Pala were on their way to Luna Land, an amusement park on the outskirts of Oruro, and Popeye planned on being there when they arrived. For now, though, he was lying low in a cabin on the far side of the lake, far from prying eyes and careless chatter. The cabin also came with a cook, and for the past two evenings she had made them dinner as they huddled around a wood stove. The warmer days were spent on the veranda.

He knew Ramón and Pala had already visited four amusement parks looking for the emeralds. The first had a rainbow over its entrance, the next two offered prizes for plucking plastic fish from a glass box, and the last one had a ten-foot Desperate Dan welcoming visitors as he stroked his prickly chin. Popeye knew they were clutching at straws. Luna Land had several rides, one of which was named Treasure Island, and they probably thought it was the 'island without water' in the riddle. Popeye doubted it.

Whilst Ramón and Pala were no closer to solving the riddle, neither were Popeye and Martín. They had sat on the veranda for two days looking for inspiration. Yet despite the lake being a revelation and the flamingos a spectacle, nothing had arrived. Eventually the conversation turned to Popeye's profession.

'I've got to ask,' said Martín, breaking the silence after another long contemplation, 'how can you live with killing so many people?' It was obvious that he had been mulling over that puzzle rather than Ernesto's riddle.

Popeye was used to the question.

Normally he did not bother justifying his life. Instead, he would trot out concepts of excitement, loyalty and comradeship that people might not agree with but would understand. On a day like today, with the glorious scenery around him and the tranquillity that came from long periods of reflection, he decided to present his case properly and in sufficient detail so that Martín would be under no illusion. Not only was his lifestyle fully justified, his actions were morally correct.

'I do it in the name of liberty, *hermano*.'

'Liberty?'

'We're all blessed with the freedom to make decisions. It's a gift and I've seized it, unlike most people. Their lives are run according to the rules laid down for them. And those rules aren't even decided by a broad consensus. They're the will of the most active part of society, not the majority. Anyone taking a different path to what the elite have chosen is oppressed by violence and social exclusion.'

'So you're a freedom fighter?'

'No. I'm not fighting for society. I just refuse to be crushed by the pressure of prevailing opinion. I'm free to decide the life I lead. I won't have a narrow bunch of people impose their ideas and practices on me. They're not going to crush my individuality or restrict my actions to what *they* deem acceptable.'

'Which means that you have no rules of conduct other than your own?' Martín asked, laughing. 'And what if those rules are completely wrong?'

Popeye smiled. He was confident in his moral judgement.

'Other than God, who can decide what's right and what's wrong? What suits one age is abhorrent in another. You think the Spanish condemned the conquistadores? Of course not. And slavery was accepted for centuries. It's custom that decides whether something is acceptable or not. And the guiding principle behind that is what feels right to the active minority. So, in practice, whether something is right or wrong depends on the ideas and prejudices of a small group. Society is judged according to their customs and forced to act as it suits them, not the individual.'

'Religion isn't the custom of an elite group. The church is God's representative on earth, so are you saying we shouldn't listen to their teachings?' Martín knew Popeye was a believer and decided to press home the point. 'Does the church approve of your lifestyle?'

Popeye paused. He had wrestled with its condemnation and come to his own conclusion.

'The church has its own ideas and prejudices. Its teachings are as much the prejudices of a small group as the society that it attempts to influence. Its ideas of morality have changed over time, and that makes them customs, not God's word. His teaching is universal and doesn't blow in the wind. The church blessed crusades and approved the Holy Inquisition. Are you saying they were right and we should accept their judgement without question?'

Martín shrugged and Popeye continued.

'I'll go further. As a small group of people, they've imposed their will over individuals more than the elite have done over society. Theirs has been a rod of excommunication for dissenters and execution for heretics. And even those who broke with the church were as unwilling to allow a difference of opinion as the very church they had left for the same reasons. No, *hermano*, we can't look to priests and religious teachers for guidance on what is right and what is wrong.'

'So what do you suggest?'

Popeye turned to the scales of judgement that were his moral compass.

'None of us live perfect lives. Everyone does good and bad. What's important is that the good outweighs the bad. It's not an isolated error or a moment of charity that's the judge, it's the sum total of our lives. The difference we've made to other people. The improvement we've made to their well-being. Even the church and their cabal of holy men acknowledge that a man's life is measured at the end.'

'What, like a sack of potatoes?' Martín tried to inject some humour into a conversation that had turned serious.

Popeye wasn't deterred. He was determined to finish. It felt good to be challenged and defend his decisions. After all, he would have to do it properly one day.

'No, not like potatoes, *cabrón*. You know the church appoints a devil's advocate to challenge their decision to make someone a saint?' Martín looked blank. 'Come on, *hermano*. Don't tell me you didn't learn about it at school?' The shrug confirmed his religious education had been less extensive than Popeye's. 'Not even the holiest of men can avoid their lives being measured. A devil's advocate lays out his faults, and the Pope and his cardinals weigh them against his good works. Only then can they be granted sainthood. It just reflects what happens on Judgement Day.'

They were interrupted by the sound of the cook approaching on the back of a motorbike. She was gripping a bowler hat and clutching a large bag. As the motorbike grew louder and louder, the flamingos flew off in a mass of pink wings and spindly legs. It broke the conversation, and Martín took the opportunity to return to more mundane matters.

'I'll look for the scales so Cusi can weigh her ingredients and get to work with the sacred frying pan.'

'Get me a coffee whilst you're at it,' Popeye said, before going to help the woman with the food.

Two hours later Cusi had served up a meal of cheese, sweet potato, broad beans and fried meat. Yesterday it had been llama, tonight it was mutton; both times the men had been left with an indifferent feeling about the food, though no longer hungry.

They were now sitting around the fire as she washed up. Martín was enjoying a glass of *chicha*, a homemade maize alcohol she had brought with her. It played havoc with his stomach, but the *aguardiente* was finished and he had saved the beer for the daytime. The screech of the flamingos returning to the lake reminded Popeye that he had something to say about them, and he turned to Martín.

'Those flamingos are like the Colombians, *hermano*. Slaves to custom. Doing what their ancestors have done down the ages and never once thinking about it.'

'Birds return to water for safety. It's not just a custom—' Martín tried to explain.

Popeye cut him off.

'No, *cabrón*. Not returning to the lake. Prancing around it in a mating ritual. Thousands of years ago there would have been a dominant male that the whole flock followed. Now they all do it without a thought to its meaning or utility. Maybe he was a genius and the flamingos have benefited? If he was a lunatic, then they're blind fools. Any flamingo that doesn't join in won't get a mate. They'll be outcast. If they were in Colombia they'd be hunted down and killed for the decision.'

The *chicha* had warmed Martín more than the fire. He decided to rise to the challenge and continue their earlier discussion.

'I understand liberty and choosing your own path. That's fine so long as the consequences affect you alone and nobody else is harmed. The government's hunting you for your assassinations and bombings, *hermano*, not your ideas,' he replied.

'Assassinations, yes, bombings, no,' Popeye answered, shaking his head. 'That's El Gordo. I work with a sharp focus. I don't kill women and children indiscriminately.'

'All the same, your freedom needs to be restrained if it harms society.'

'I don't harm society.'

'You kill people.'

Popeye paused like he had at the earlier mention of the church. It was the same criticism he had received from his family, and it had driven a wedge between him and his father. Cocaine trafficking was tolerated; killing was not. It was a mortal sin. He was going to hell and no amount of justification was going to change that. Popeye knew his father was wrong.

157

'I believe an individual has the same right to kill as the state. The state shouldn't have a monopoly on sanctioned violence. What I do is in defence of our organisation or to remove a threat to our existence. That's no different to an army defending a country or removing a neighbouring despot. Take Luis Galán, for example.' Martín looked blank. 'He was one of our presidential candidates. When he started attacking us, running on a ticket of "extradition for the narcos", I assassinated him.'

'*Hermano*, that's democracy!'

'No, *cabrón*, that's no argument,' Popeye replied, growing irritated. 'Look at history; it'll show you democracy isn't always right. Democracy put Adolf Hitler in power.' And he went further. 'If an individual had killed the *hijo de puta* when he was still an unknown artist, that bullet would have saved millions of lives, *cabrón*. Yet at the time, society would have condemned his actions and executed him.'

'So Luis Galán was Colombia's Adolf Hitler?' Martín asked, laughing, surprised at Popeye's leap from an unknown politician to the century's most notorious dictator.

'I doubt it. But I know he would have destroyed our cartel and thousands would have suffered as a result. I killed an individual to protect the universal good. What's more, when it's put on the scales of judgement, the benefit of a thousand people will far outweigh the loss of an individual.'

'Not if Luis Galán has anything to do with the scales,' Martín said.

'Listen, *hermano*, he was just an ordinary man who deserved to die,' Popeye said, exasperated. 'Society lost nothing. He offered nothing new. He was the same machine from the same mould that's been used to forge our leaders for the past century. Bland individuals promoted by an active minority. They've stifled Colombia. Our people have lost the desire to progress and improve. The customs forced on them have killed the strong impulses we need to make geniuses, and society has no idea how to create the geniuses it needs. Pablo Escobar is a rare talent. He needs to be defended for his creativity, not attacked for his vision.'

At the sound of the fugitive Colombian's name, Cusi's washing-up came to an abrupt end. Popeye immediately regretted mentioning him. They needed to remain undiscovered if he were to catch Ramón off guard. Now he may have unwittingly given himself away. He decided to see what Cusi knew before worrying about what to do with her.

'*Señora*, leave the dishes. Your meal was delicious. You deserve a rest. Come and join us at the fire,' he said.

She dried her hands and joined them.

'Do you know what we're doing here, *señora*?' She shook her head. 'I have a business in La Paz and my friend is a keen birdwatcher. I needed a break and he likes watching flamingos.' Popeye winked at Martín. 'The cabin was a perfect find, and your cooking has made it even more memorable, thank you.'

The compliment brought a wide smile, and she relaxed a bit.

'Would you like some *chicha*, *señora*?' Popeye asked, and waved at Martín to pour her a glass. 'We were talking about the flamingos and then all of a sudden the conversation was about killing and politicians!' He laughed. 'I don't know where that came from. *Chicha*'s too strong, it always brings out the worst in me . . . Of course I haven't killed anyone.'

The woman looked blank. The penny dropped, and Martín realised why Popeye had invited her over. 'My friend's a complete softie, *señora*,' said Martín, chipping in. 'He runs away at the first sign of trouble.' Popeye nodded reluctantly. 'He's such a coward that we call him Captain Custard. Yellow skin and mushy insides.' Popeye attempted a smile and ended up scowling. 'Ask to see his underpants, *señora*. Double reinforced and specially lined for those awkward moments when Captain Custard is in hasty retreat.' Popeye was no longer making any attempt to hide his irritation. It was only the woman's burst of laughter that broke the tension.

'No, thank you! I've got a husband and don't want to see his underpants. He doesn't look like a killer to me either,' she said, grabbing Popeye's hand and running a finger across his palm. 'Look how soft his hands are!'

Popeye knew that she had not been listening. It was only the mention of Pablo Escobar that had got her attention. The woman turned to Martín.

'Are you a bird expert, *señor*?' she asked. He was slightly startled by the question and began mumbling about being an amateur, just someone who enjoys the outdoor life, when Popeye jumped in.

'Oh yes, he's an expert. He's just being modest. Birds are his passion and flamingos are an obsession. He's even got a flamingo suit at home. When we're out looking for *señoritas* in a bar, he's strutting around the street trying to attract the attention of any woman passing. You know, head up, twisting it from side to side. He'd wear the suit if it didn't get him arrested.'

The woman gave Martín a strange look, and he was about to deny it when she asked:

'Do you know why the males behave like that?'

'The males?'

'The flamingos.'

For a moment Martín was thrown. Popeye's earlier rant about customs came to mind and he fell back on it.

'It's an ancient ritual handed down through the generations, something that binds the flock together. A custom that lets the females know they have proud and virile males from which to choose a mate . . .'

He said it without conviction, as though he were speculating more than answering the question. She shook her head.

'No. You've read that from a book. You don't know the real reason. Anyway, it's not written down. We know. It's one of the stories we sing to our babies.' Martín rolled his eyes as she poured herself another glass of *chicha*. 'A long time ago the world was only inhabited by birds. The most majestic of them was the flamingo, and the flamingos on the *altiplano* lived in paradise.' Clearly the local explanation of the ritual was going to be provided whether they liked it or not. 'At that time they lived on a vast lake in a wilder part of the *altiplano* and were ruled by a wise king and his beloved queen. Their home was a large island in the middle of the lake.' She turned to the men. 'And it's still there. We call it the Island of the

Fish.' By now Popeye's eyes had glazed over from a lack of interest, and Martín was struggling to focus, having consumed almost an entire bottle of *chicha*. The woman carried on regardless. 'One year, after a violent storm, the birds noticed the lake had turned salty and was starting to lose water. None of the flamingos could understand where the water was going, until one day an eagle arrived from the East and explained it to them.'

Popeye could contain himself no longer.

'*Señora*, I'll finish the washing-up. Carry on explaining it to my friend.' He got up and patted Martín on the back.

'The reason for the water turning salty and then disappearing,' she continued, 'was because fish had been created. They needed an ocean for a home and the lake was stolen. It broke the queen's heart and she died shortly afterwards. The king buried her on the island and gave it the name that we use today, the Island of the Fish, after the creature that drained their lake. Once the water was all gone, the flamingos left to find a new home.' She stopped and stared hard at Martín. 'The flamingos on Lake Uru Uru are descended from the ones that fled the lake. Each mating season they used to parade up and down in front of the king and turn their heads back to the resting place of his queen. It's the same now, except there is no longer a king.'

Popeye rushed back to the wood stove.

'*Señora*, that story – song, or whatever it is – does it have the line "there's an island with no water and a fish that never swims"?'

She mouthed some words to herself . . . then nodded.

'What's the name of the lake?'

'The Salar de Uyuni.'

Martín jumped like he'd been stung. It had been staring him in the face all along. Although his religious education was poor, his knowledge of geography was second to none. The Salar de Uyuni was the largest salt lake in the world, about the same size as Jamaica. In its very centre was the aptly named Island of the Fish, and it was only a hundred and fifty miles away.

CHAPTER THIRTY

The next day a motorbike disturbed the flamingos once more, although this time Popeye was riding and Martín was sitting behind him. They were on their way to Luna Land, where Pala would be arriving later that evening. Martín's information was that Pala was going to check out Treasure Island and then report back to Ramón. Popeye would be following him on his bike.

Martín had insisted he come along, and Popeye had pushed back. He did not like working in a team and he hated depending on other people. However, on this occasion it made sense to bring him. Martín would recognise the sicario whilst Popeye only had a description to go on. The thought of spending the evening following the wrong man around the park sealed the decision.

Luna Land was on the outskirts of Oruro, and Popeye and Martín had stopped there on their way to Lake Uru Uru; now they were returning to a small bar and restaurant called Button's Bar at the amusement park's entrance. It was the perfect place to look out for Pala, and an ideal choice for Martín, who was running low on alcohol. Not only that, but from Martín's perspective, at least, it got better. Popeye had insisted Martín should remain in the bar all evening. It would avoid him being spotted, and he had agreed without much argument.

The two of them were bouncing towards a cluster of adobe houses, throwing up a cloud of dust in the process. As they approached, a lady in a pink apron sprang from her seat and pointed at a metal tray on the ground. It was full of bright red strips of llama flesh, salted and drying in the baking sun. Popeye stopped to give the woman ten bolivianos and waved away the crusty offering she tried to force on him. A few minutes later they arrived at the highway and took a ring road around the drab city of Oruro.

Although it had once been the powerhouse of Bolivia, Oruro was now in decline. The mountains and its rich minerals had not changed; it was the price of tin that had collapsed. New mines in Brazil and Malaysia had flooded the market and they operated at a fraction of the cost of those surrounding the city. Luckily, the amusement park had been built at the start of the 1980s; any later and it would have gone under.

The name given to the park was a misnomer. The only experience Luna Land offered anywhere close to the adventure of space travel was a rollercoaster with cars shaped like rockets. The whole place had been shipped across from the States and was a vision stuck firmly in the late 1950s, well before the age of moon landings and UFO sightings. It had served the population of Higginsville, Missouri, perfectly well until Button Bros. of Missouri went bust in the 1970s. A local entrepreneur from Oruro had bought the park lock, stock and barrel, and its Big Dipper rollercoaster now boasted a ride climbing nearly four thousand metres higher than the original. It also came with Treasure Island, which was the real attraction for Ramón and Pala.

Pala was a tall man with black hair. Whilst his height was a distinguishing feature, his hair colour was not. All Bolivians had black hair, or at least that was how it seemed to Popeye. He also had a long stride and a slightly pinched face. The additional details made no difference. Popeye had pointed out five prospective targets, and each of them had been wrong. Now that it was almost dark, it would be even harder to identify him. Popeye wanted to be out there mingling with the crowd and stalking his target, but he knew he had to be patient. He remained inside and pushed Martín's glass away.

'*Hermano*, I need you to focus on Pala, not Pilsner.'

Martín reached for the glass.

'*Tranquilo*, it's not *chicha*, I can drink these all night,' he said, raising it. 'Besides, we need to blend in. You're not drinking. Two men in a bar and neither of them drinking? That's suspicious, *hermano*.'

To emphasise the point, Martín glugged down half of his beer, then quickly lowered the glass.

'There he is,' he said, nodding casually at the entrance.

Popeye looked out. There were at least three men who matched Pala's description.

'Which one?'

'In the red jacket.'

Popeye dropped fifty bolivianos on the table and reached for his coat. 'Don't move. I'll be back for you.'

The man in the red jacket was strolling into the park. He was alone, and nobody appeared to be following him. Popeye almost wished Ramón had joined him. It would have saved him the trouble of tracking down the *hijo de puta*, and even though the park was too public for an assassination, he was certain he would have found a quiet spot for it. He shook his head. Pala was an amateur. None of his sicarios would have worn a red jacket for a job that needed a low profile.

Popeye stepped outside and joined a steady flow of people. They were being drawn to a large Ferris wheel like moths to a flame, and he could see Pala was amongst them.

Popeye shadowed him. As the attraction got closer he realised it actually had two wheels. The smaller one was barely above the ground and the larger one towered over the park. They were separated in the middle by a rotating globe that was dominated by the stars and stripes of the United States; the rest of the world was left a neutral grey. As the larger wheel rotated, orange and green strip lights flashed in sequence and a string of red bulbs lit up its passenger cars. Pala queued for a ticket and Popeye waited a short distance away. He approved of Pala's choice. It was a good decision. He would have done exactly the same: survey the park from a vantage point then head over to Treasure Island.

'Aren't you going for a ride?'

Popeye turned round. A group of girls were trying to squeeze through, and he was blocking the way. He stepped aside.

'No, I don't like heights,' he said, and they laughed on their way past.

'There's always the smaller one,' one of them shouted over her shoulder. 'My nephew loves it,' she added, and turned round with a sweet smile. It did not escape him that she was the most confident of the group and by far the prettiest. He watched them disappear up the stairs to the big wheel, then shuffled back, further out of the way.

Once the Ferris wheel had completed two full, slow rotations, Pala finally stepped off, and Popeye followed him as he meandered past prize stalls and minor rides (though in the opposite direction to Treasure Island). The Cyclone Waltzer was ignored, along with Button's Melter Skelter, and he had no time for the amusement arcade or the vibrating conveyors of Button's Fun House. Finally Pala arrived at Windmill Corral and joined a group of prospective sharpshooters, each of whom had twelve attempts to hit six targets on a rotating windmill. The prize was a goldfish in a bag. Pala came away empty-handed and lined up for a ticket on the Super Sensational Ghost Train instead.

This time Popeye avoided the paying customers and watched from a distance. It just so happened that the same group of girls appeared out of nowhere and joined the queue, and it was not long before they spotted him. '*Señor*,' the pretty one shouted, 'we know you're scared of heights – are you also scared of ghosts?' Before Popeye could answer, she had turned back to her friends and whispered something that made them laugh.

Popeye took a step back and hoped Pala had not noticed. He gave her a dismissive wave, pretended to be searching for a different ride and walked off in the opposite direction. When he reached a prize stall he turned round. The girls were now at the front of the queue and Pala had gone inside, so he returned to the ride and waited for him to reappear. Every fifteen seconds or so a recorded scream reached fever pitch, the ghost doors banged open and a car covered in alien stickers burst through. One car contained a laughing couple, another a cool teenager, another a mother with a crying child. Yet there was no sign of the Bolivian sicario. Then

Popeye heard some muffled shrieks growing louder and louder, almost drowning out the scream. Three cars exploded through the doors in quick succession, full of screeching girls.

'*Puta!*' Popeye swore. It was the same girls from the queue. Pala had given him the slip, either intentionally or by accident. If it had been intentional then he must have spotted Popeye, or it could have been that Pala changed his mind at the last minute? His eyes darted around the park and he breathed a sigh of relief. Pala was bent over a prize stall. It made his mind up – he was going to join Pala on each and every ride he took from now on. If the girls were nearby then he would join them and blend in with the crowd. He just hoped that the next attraction would be Treasure Island; it was odd that Pala had avoided it so far.

In the event, there was no need to look for the girls. They found him.

'Señor Scaredy Cat!'

He looked round and they were walking towards him. This time there was no running away.

'Scaredy Cat? You were terrified on the ghost train,' he said. 'I could hear you miles away. You were screaming like the kids on the merry-go-round.' He nodded towards the hurdy-gurdy sound of its spinning horses and unicorns.

'Oh yeah. Take me on it and we'll see who screams the loudest,' the pretty girl replied, and linked her arm through his. 'What's your name, *señor*? I can't call you Señor Scaredy Cat for the rest of the evening.'

Popeye kept his eye on Pala, who was engrossed in hooking a plastic fish. She tugged his arm and asked if he was looking for his girlfriend.

'No, it's not that,' he said, laughing. 'I'm just trying to decide whether to visit Treasure Island or The Big Dipper. My name's Juan.'

'Maya. The Big Dipper's fun.'

Pala was on the move. Popeye placed his hand on the woman's arm.

'The Big Dipper it is then.'

She left her friends behind with a wave, and they followed Pala. He seemed to be making his way over to the rollercoaster, then veered off towards Treasure Island.

'Actually, let's go to Treasure Island,' Popeye said, leading Maya away from The Big Dipper. Pala must have had a change of heart, for he stopped abruptly and swung round. He was now striding straight towards them, and Popeye crouched down to tie his shoelace.

'Are you okay?' Maya asked. 'We don't have to go on a ride if you're scared.'

Popeye fiddled with his lace for a bit and watched Pala out of the corner of his eye. There was no queue at the booth for The Big Dipper and he was soon inside the ride.

'Sorry, big dippers faze me a bit. No, let's try it out,' he said, linking arms once more.

The Big Dipper was a classic rollercoaster with three large waves and a sweeping lower section. The whole thing was constructed with crisscrossed girders and thick beams like a nineteenth-century railway bridge crossing a deep gorge, except this one had a solar system bolted to its side and spacemen floating between its planets. The rails were hidden from prospective punters by long planks painted the same colour as The Big Dipper's rocket cars. The intention was to create the illusion of a space flight, although its rickety tracks put paid to any sense of an interstellar journey. Each peak was approached with a good deal of shaking and some brutal shuddering, then a whiplash launched the car over the crest: nothing like the smooth acceleration of sleek spacecraft in the movies.

Pala was two peaks in front. Maya clung to Popeye's arm, screaming on the way down and laughing on the way up. He played the perfect gentleman: consoling, encouraging and cajoling, all the while watching his target blast through space ahead. It was a mystery why Pala had chosen to ride the rollercoaster. There were no clues to be found on The Big Dipper. Maybe he was just having a good time and not bothering with the job? *Puta* amateur. It did not matter just so long as Pala took him to Ramón. He knew the only secret on Treasure Island was a skeleton pointing towards a fake treasure chest, and his bony finger was not guiding Pala anywhere close to the Island of the Fish. The ride ended, and *finally* Pala made his way across to Treasure Island.

It was an extensive attraction with a huge Spanish galleon painted on its hoarding. In front of it, a wooden booth with a glass box sold tickets for 'Long John Silver's Adventure'. A plastic parrot sat on its sign and a dummy pirate was standing behind a man selling tickets, peering over his shoulder as though checking his work. Popeye bought two tickets from the odd couple and followed Pala at a distance.

A small doorway was carved in the bottom of the galleon, and it led to a world of exotic island paraphernalia. Large plastic palms formed a path up to a long quay that was decorated in coiled ropes and lit with a row of spotlights. A line of ships with pirate flags and miniature crow's nests awaited their passengers, and none of them resembled Spanish galleons; they were more like toy speedboats on a boating lake. A shadowy light came from a line of small bulbs strung between the palm trees which allowed Popeye keep close to Pala yet remain hidden. When Pala stopped at a barrel of 'Long John Silver Rum', Popeye slowed down.

'Don't tell me you're having second thoughts about this ride as well?' Maya asked as he stopped to admire the plastic trees. She encouraged him with a pull on his arm, then gave up and carried on, shaking her head. Popeye watched the sicario leave the barrel and step onto the quay. By now Maya was nearby, and he could have sworn that Pala acknowledged her with a slight glance before he got into a boat. Popeye put it down to her being attractive and waited for Pala to leave.

The ride attendant insisted that every boat had a full complement of passengers and a further three were needed before the boat could 'set sail'. Popeye stepped to the side and waved through some people behind. He noticed a man and woman deliberately hang back, pretending to admire the trees, and he knew there was nothing remotely interesting about them. He took a closer. They were local *campesinos*. The man was short and the woman was carrying a large material bag . . . Then Maya was calling him and he turned back to see Pala drifting away from the quay.

Popeye and Maya sat on a narrow bench at the front of the boat. The *campesinos* were directly behind them and another couple were ushered onto the last bench. Maya grasped Popeye's hand, and they set sail past a collection of rubber monkeys and through a screen of jungle creepers. The sound of a sea shanty rang out as they entered the land of treasure and their boat floated alongside a fibreglass beach. It was covered in starfish and sparkling shells, and two palm trees were in its centre. A spotlight burst into life and picked out a large map stretched between two trees. A few seconds later the sea shanty cut out, there was a loud wail and a skeleton wobbled out on a hidden rail. Sure enough, when it reached the map, it raised a bony finger and pointed at a red cross in one corner. Maya snuggled up to Popeye. Her hand ran across his chest and his arm was around her shoulder, then a bolt of electricity shot down Popeye's neck.

Maya lunged for his Beretta. Popeye fell forward and crashed into the front of the boat. His arms wouldn't move. They were paralysed by the shock. Maya was tugging at his jacket. The stun gun bore down again. He twisted to avoid it and a blast hit Maya. She screamed. His arms were hanging aimlessly, but he managed to twist round and headbutt the *campesino*. Maya came for him. He struggled to raise an elbow in defence and kicked out instead. Then a garrotte was slung around his throat. Popeye was dragged back. Maya was once more pulling at his jacket. The rope tightened and he gasped. Her hand pulled out his Beretta. His throat felt like it was being sliced in two. He turned his body towards her and tried to clamp her arm. The garrotte yanked him back. Now she was fumbling with his gun, trying to flip off its safety. Popeye's shoulder arced and his elbow managed to catch her chin. This time it was more powerful, and she dropped the gun. His hands instinctively tore at the garrotte and seized the arms twisting it. Maya scrambled for the gun, and he stamped on her hand. Then he lunged forward and rolled his shoulder. The smaller man flew into the water. The garrotte was released. Another elbow strike dropped Maya.

Now the *campesino* was clambering onto the fibreglass shore and the Beretta was in Popeye's hand. His first shot missed as he dodged behind a tree. The next one caught the skeleton and took its arm off. Maya was groaning, and he put a bullet in her chest. Then the man scurried off into the next scene. With perfect timing, the boat moved slowly towards the treasure map. Popeye was furious. He had been ambushed and was in no mood to lose the man. He jumped onto the foreshore and went after him.

Popeye's arms were still heavy and his neck was burning. Pala's boat was just ahead, and he had been alerted by the gunfire. A shot flew past Popeye's shoulder. He couldn't hold the Beretta well enough to return fire accurately, and he took cover. His boat caught up. The *campesino* woman was cowering in her seat and the other passengers were on the floor. He knew they weren't a threat. Turning back to Pala, he watched him disappear around the corner, then a one-legged pirate dropped out of the ceiling and Popeye shot it.

Pala was gone and he needed to get ahead of him. He felt along the wall for an exit and eventually found a loose section of timber. It did not take much to kick through it, and he found himself behind the scenes of the ride, surrounded by huge timber boxes, each one twice the size of a shipping container with large numbers on their side – he had just emerged from box two. He ran up to the box labelled six. The one-legged pirate that had dropped into the previous scene had given him an idea. Climbing a ladder attached to the box, he found a trapdoor in the roof. Scene six did not come with a plummeting pirate, yet it had an opening should the need ever arise. Popeye lifted its cover and waited patiently for Pala. This time he could support his arm, and he knew his aim would be accurate enough for a hit.

There would be another way to reach Ramón. Right now, he was determined to kill the sicario trapped in Treasure Island.

In the event, when Pala's boat appeared he was nowhere to be seen. Popeye jumped up, swearing, and caught a glimpse of Pala running back into the park. His chance to take revenge had gone. His temper boiled over, and he vowed Pala would regret the subterfuge. It was personal now. Then the sound of sirens reminded him that he too needed to disappear, and he clambered down.

Back at Button's Bar, Martín was a little worse for wear and looked startled when he saw Popeye.

'*Hermano* . . . what's happening out there?'

People were panicking and streaming out of the park. Flashing blue lights were blocking the entrance and a police cordon was being set up.

'We need to leave.'

Martín went to get up, but his hand slipped on the chair and he fell heavily to the floor. Popeye left him there and stormed into the kitchen, making a beeline for a large bin. Popeye returned to the bar and duly emptied its contents over Martín. An old cabbage leaf was rubbed around his head and Popeye shoved his Beretta inside Martín's jacket.

'*Puta!*' Martín mumbled as he was propped up and led outside.

The crowd parted at the stench of rubbish and the sight of a staggering man, and they were soon at the checkpoint. A senior officer was there in a heavily braided hat, striding up and down as he gave instructions to three officers. Popeye approached the one that looked the most junior.

'Step back!' the man shouted, then cast his eyes over them. 'What's going on, *señor*? Who's your friend?'

'It's my brother. He's drunk and he's been in a fight. I've come to bring him home,' Popeye replied, pulling his jacket collar close to his neck to hide the ligature marks that were still burning.

'With a bin?'

'The other guy fought dirty.'

'You're Colombian? Papers, please.'

'Felipe!' a voice boomed across the checkpoint. 'Is there a problem?'

The young officer looked slightly flustered by the attention. He quickly shook his head at his boss and focussed on Martín.

'Step forward so I can search you.'

Popeye made sure Martín bumped into the man's uniform. Sure enough, a cabbage leaf dropped on his shoe and some fish skin rubbed on his jacket.

'*Hijo de puta!*' the officer swore, and swiped it off, leaving a grey smear down his tunic and a couple of fish scales on his buttons.

'Felipe! We need to get these people searched. What's the problem?'

The officer was about to search Martín but thought better of it. In the end, he patted down his legs and arms and missed the Beretta in his jacket. Once Popeye was searched, they were waved through.

CHAPTER THIRTY-ONE

The following day Popeye was still fuming. His neck was red-raw from the garrotte and ached from the stun gun. A trap had been set and he had walked straight into it. When the time came to face Pala, he told himself there would be no mercy. A bullet in each kneecap, then one to the chest. Ramón would come later. There was no ointment in the cabin, so he had rubbed a little butter on the wound, which was rancid and smelt slightly. Whilst it eased the soreness, it stung where the skin was broken. He planned to get some antiseptic cream in Oruro, then phone Martín's brother-in-law. After that he would put a call in to Piña and update him on his progress.

He was convinced that Martín's relations were working for Ramón. The question remained whether Martín was innocent or not. A loud snore from the bedroom reminded him that Martín had been too drunk to be questioned last night – it had been enough to get him home in one piece. He had seemed shocked when Popeye had returned to the bar, almost as though he had seen a ghost. Then he chuckled. Martín had woken from his drunken stupor into a scene straight from a horror movie: panicked people running out of an amusement park. No wonder he was shocked! *Puta* Treasure Island. Popeye felt stupid falling for it. He had underestimated Ramón and taken him for a fat buffoon. He would not make the same mistake twice, though first he wanted to see what Martín had to say for himself.

'*Hermano*, wake up,' Popeye said, shaking his shoulder. 'We need to talk. What do you recall about last night?'

Martín rolled out of bed and looked for his clothes.

'*Puta!* Where are my clothes?'

'Outside. They stink. You fell in a bin.'

'Fell in a bin? How could I fall in a bin?'

'I've no idea. You were covered in garbage, so you must have. Last night – what do you remember?'

'Not much. Some flashing lights. Falling off a bike . . .' Martín touched his forearm gingerly. 'What happened to your neck?' he asked, looking puzzled. 'And did you find Ramón?' Wrapping a blanket around his shoulders, he went to make coffee. 'When are we going to the Salar de Uyuni?' he added casually.

Popeye took a long look as Martín walked over to the sink. He did not seem surprised that Popeye was still alive, and he had made no mention of Pala. He was just a harmless drunk, a family man trying to make his way through life, not a double-crosser who cheated people. It was his relations that were scheming. Two could play that game. He decided he could trust Martín, yet he needed to hide his suspicions.

'I got ambushed in the park.'

'What?'

'I took my eye off the ball. Let's just say it was distracted by an attractive girl . . .'

'*Hermano!* Not again.'

Popeye had already told Martín about the pilot Dolores, and 'taking his eye off the ball' needed no further explanation. Popeye shrugged.

'I was distracted and Pala sneaked up on me. Luckily I only ended up with a sore neck. He managed to get away, and we're no further forwards. It means I'll have to speak to your brother-in-law, or cousin, or whoever it is that knows their movements.' Martín raised no objection, and it removed any lingering suspicion that he might be working with them.

'Are we safe here or will Pala come looking?' Martín asked.

'I chose this cabin for a reason. Anyone approaching sets off the flamingos,' Popeye replied. 'He knows he's missed his chance. Ramón and him will have moved on, and your contacts will know where they're going.'

'Why not just get the emeralds, *hermano*? We know they're on the Island of the Fish – you can deal with Ramón afterwards.'

Popeye stared at him. Was he trying to divert him away from Ramón? Then he remembered Martín was only really interested in the emeralds.

'You've never met El Patrón,' he said. 'He likes instructions to be followed. Kill Ramón, *then* get Ernesto's emeralds. If I returned with the emeralds and Ramón was still alive . . .' His voice trailed off; there was no need to explain the consequences.

Martín brought over the coffee and they sat down.

'Who's best to speak to? Your brother-in-law or your cousin?' Popeye asked.

'Santiago gets his information from my cousin. It's too risky for Luis to communicate openly in the compound. He liaises with my brother-in-law. We'll speak to him.'

'And they still want some emeralds for helping out?'

Martín nodded, and Popeye held back his anger.

It was the weekend and Martín was confident he would be able to contact his brother-in-law that afternoon. Santiago would be watching the Boca Juniors match in Raul's Bar.

This time they travelled into the city in a pickup rather than the motorbike as it was out of commission with a long scrape down its side. Popeye had assured Martín that he would be paying for the damage; if he had not fallen off the back, Popeye would not have lost control.

On their way out, Popeye stopped again at the adobe houses. The poverty in Medellín was nothing compared to what he had seen on the *altiplano*. No running water or electricity and a poor diet. At least in the barrios there was the chance to break out; after the closure of Oruro's tin mines, the only escape for the *campesinos* was to relocate to Potosí and work in their deadly silver mines, or leave the *altiplano* for good and find work in the coca business. Several of the houses had already been abandoned.

'Señora Llama!' he shouted.

She appeared at a door, and he waved her over.

'Don't bother with the llama,' he said as she turned back.

She came over with a beaming smile and a listless child in her arms.

'I found this hidden away in the cabin,' he said, and pulled out a wad of cash. It was the last of the money taken out in Cochabamba, three hundred and fifty dollars or so. 'It's not mine and it's certainly not the owner's. Will you look after it?' He winked. 'In fact, I think you should keep it.'

The woman looked astonished at her good fortune. She accepted the money with a shake of her head and a broad smile and turned back to the house. Popeye knew what she had in mind, and he shouted after her.

'No, *señora*. No llama . . . *please*, no llama!'

She went inside anyway and emerged holding a bottle of cloudy liquid. It was *chicha*, the one thing that helped pass the dark, cold nights. Popeye could not refuse it, nor could Martín, and they carried on their way.

Their first stop was a pharmacy where Popeye cleaned his wound. The antiseptic cream stung slightly and the white dressing made him look like a priest in a dog collar, and it gave Martín the opportunity to request blessings and forgiveness for his sins as they drove round looking for a bar. For Popeye, not only was it a painful reminder of how close he had come to death, it was also a wakeup call that there had been no warning from the fake priest this time. Maybe the rules of the game were changing?

Their next stop was a quiet bar on the edge of the city, where Martín was soon ordering drinks. Popeye watched him chatting amiably with the bartender and realised he was in his element – drinking beer, sharing a casual conversation and cracking jokes.

When he returned, he had a soft drink for Popeye.

'We can use the bartender's phone and pay him instead. It'll be more private than using the payphone,' he said, nodding towards a door behind the bar. 'I'm going to call my wife first.'

Popeye got up to join him.

'*Hermano!*' he said, laughing. 'What a man says to his wife is private. Give me five minutes and I'll be back for you.'

Popeye sat down and raised his glass of lemonade.

'Don't be long. We want your brother-in-law to concentrate on us, not the game,' he said, pointing at a large television set on the wall. 'It'll start in fifteen minutes.'

Martín disappeared through the door and returned after a couple of minutes.

'I've got Santiago on the phone.'

Popeye got up.

'I thought you were phoning your wife?'

'I did. Then I called Raul's to make sure he was there.'

'How is she?'

'Who?'

'Your wife, *cabrón*.'

'Oh. Yeah, good thanks.'

The room behind the bar stank of alcohol. A mess of amber-coloured plastic pipes connected a row of barrels to the bar and most of their seals were leaking. Martín and Popeye avoided the pipes spread out on the floor and went across to a small table where a phone receiver lay on its side.

'*Hermano!*' Martín shouted into it. 'I've got Popeye with me.' He handed over the phone.

A thin, reedy voice crackled through the receiver.

'It's an honour to talk to you, Popeye. How's your neck?'

Popeye stayed calm; Santiago would pay for that remark.

'Martín told me you were attacked with a stun gun. And in the back of your head! That must have hurt?'

Popeye vowed Santiago would experience extreme pain when he caught up with him.

Santiago was exactly as he expected: confident, even cocky on the end of the phone, and Popeye was now convinced that he was working for Ramón, safely hidden away in Guanay and about to lead him into another trap. It was often like that with inexperienced men: they gave themselves away with careless chatter. Popeye had been careful not to mention the stun gun to Martín, and only Ramón or Pala could have told him. Santiago was closer to their plans than he had let on.

'Not as painful as the bullet Pala is going to get,' Popeye replied, ignoring the comment. 'I need to know where they are going. Have you spoken to them?'

'Not personally. Luis has a call every morning.'

'And?'

'They're going to Potosí. It's a mining town about five hours away by car.'

'I've heard of it.'

Potosí was where the Spanish found their pot of gold in the Americas. Well, more truckloads than a pot, and not gold but silver – enough to build a solid bridge across the Atlantic if the history books were to be believed. Popeye did not believe them, although childhood memories of schoolbooks showing conquistadores riding horses across the ocean had stuck with him.

'Why Potosí?'

'They found a photo of Don Ernesto down one of the mines and it caught their attention.'

'Why?'

Popeye knew he was being drawn in.

'He was standing next to Huari with a large lamp.'

'Who?'

'Huari, the god of the underworld that protects the miners. There's a large shrine down there with an effigy of him on its altar.'

'Okay.'

'He's got a sharp, pointy beard, and they're convinced he's "the man with the prickly skin" from the riddle.'

'And they think being down a mine is the same as being buried?'

'Exactly!'

Popeye could tell Santiago thought he was hooked.

'So where are the emeralds buried?' he asked.

'Don Ernesto was holding up a new lamp in the photo which was much larger than the others on the altar. They think it has a false compartment and the emeralds are hidden inside it. The lamp is chained to the altar, and only the high priest and his acolytes have access to the shrine.'

'How does Ramón know that?'

'What?'

'How does he know the lamp is chained to the altar?' Santiago went silent, and Popeye offered up an explanation. 'Maybe there's another photo of the lamp chained to the altar.'

Santiago seized Popeye's suggestion.

'Yes, that's it.'

'So what are they doing about it?'

Popeye heard a slight chuckle on the end of the phone.

'Pala's going to organise an out-of-hours visit to the shrine with the acolytes. You would like them – apparently they're stunning beauties. There's three of them . . . Sabrina, Eva . . . and I think the other one is called Leyna.'

'Why involve all three acolytes, *hermano*?'

'There's no choice. There are three locks on the door to the shrine and each of them holds a key. It can only be opened by all of the acolytes at the same time. Listen, if you get ahead of Pala, you could trap him down there in the mine.'

'And how would I do that exactly?'

'The acolytes work in the Temple of Huari. A hundred dollars would do it. Get the girls to unlock the shrine for you and beat him to it.'

'What about Ramón?'

'Oh, you won't catch him there. The ladders down into the mine are too weak and steep for Don Ramón. He'll be waiting in the temple for Pala to bring the emeralds to him.'

'Where's the temple?'

'It's directly opposite the road that goes up to the pithead.'

'And when will Pala get there?'

'Three days from now. Don Ramón has some charitable work to perform, and they're making a slight detour to fit it in.'

Popeye asked if Santiago knew what time Pala was visiting the mine. Of course he did. It was planned for six in the morning. Popeye also suspected the acolytes would be in on the plan to trap him, and he decided to be careful around them.

He put the phone down and joined Martín in the bar.

Sergio Martínez, Boca Juniors' star striker, had just scored and was running to a corner flag. As he gyrated his hips against the pole, the commentator was roaring 'GOAL!' and Martín was cheering, but Popeye was grinding his teeth. No wonder Santiago had chuckled when mentioning the acolytes. It was their in-joke. Taking the first letter of each of their names and adding them to those of Dolores, Andrea and Maya spelt 'DAMSEL'. It was an obvious reference to his weakness for women. He was going to enjoy planting his Beretta on Santiago's forehead and asking him to tell another joke before he died.

CHAPTER THIRTY-TWO

If Oruro had seemed drab to Popeye, Potosí took it to a new level and added another four hundred metres of altitude. Perched on a cold, barren plateau dominated by Cerro Rico, the city spread out from the mountain and filled every valley and hilltop with window-less blocks of concrete and bare brick. It was the mother of all mining towns. The ghosts of eight million perished souls were said to haunt the mines of Cerro Rico, drifting through the maze of tunnels and shafts that radiated out from its conical peak. The city came with a pedigree of death. It was the perfect place for Pala to die.

Popeye and Martín headed straight for the Temple of Huari. All around were signs of a place where people passed through and spent as little time as was necessary. For the unfortunate people who ended up staying permanently, an extensive municipal cemetery neatly tucked away their remains, one on top of the other in concrete alcoves layered eight stories high. For those still living, they woke each morning to the sight of the mountain of death and a view across buildings that would never be completed: corroded rebars poking from their tops like stubble after the harvest and water ponding on concrete slabs that were never designed to be a roof. Even the rubbish seemed to follow a course out of the city, and piles of it grew ever more frequent as Popeye and Martín drove to the foot of the mountain – yellow and green plastic bags that gave the dry banks a splash of colour.

The Temple of Huari was opposite a slag heap that had grown monumental from centuries of mining. Above it, sifting plants and dusty conveyors spilled out unwanted material and a narrow railway carted away the valuable rocks to a large processing pond. The temple had a prime position, reminding the miners of the grinding destruction into which they were heading and the offerings that were needed to survive the ordeal. Their car pulled up alongside a smart-looking Mercedes jeep and Popeye got out.

Inside, the temple was like any shop peddling cheap knick-knacks at a religious shrine, except this one offered cigarettes, bags of coca leaves and bottles of *chicha*, rather than crucifixes, icons and bottles of holy water. Behind its counter, a girl sat reading a paper. As Popeye had been told, she was certainly pretty, although she was not wearing any vestments. In fact, when she stood up, Popeye saw she was wearing a low-cut blouse. He could not fail to notice it as she gathered up her long jet-black hair.

'Hello,' she said, tying it up.

'Sabrina?' Popeye asked.

'No, Leyna,' she replied, brushing a strand from her forehead. 'What can I get you?'

Popeye glanced around the place. It was a shop, not a temple, stocked with everyday items: booze and basic foodstuffs next to the altar essentials.

'I'll take two of the Huari figures,' he replied, pointing to a shelf on the wall.

Leyna leant on the counter and gave a glimpse of her cleavage.

'If you make it three, I'll give you a discount. This afternoon it's ten per cent.'

'And if I return tomorrow?'

'Oh, tomorrow you'll get fifteen. Julia—' She quickly corrected herself. 'No, Sabrina will be working, and she's a softie.'

'You're sure it's Sabrina, not Julia?'

She raised a hand and flicked away another strand of hair.

'No. Definitely Sabrina. Julia works on Wednesdays and Thursdays.'

Popeye knew she was lying, and it confirmed his suspicion that the acolytes were working for Ramón. She disappeared behind a curtain and returned with a small stepladder. 'Hold this for me, *señor*, and I'll get them down. If I fall, at least it'll be into your arms!' she said, laughing.

'The name's Pop—er, Juan, Juan Arroyo,' Popeye replied weakly. 'It's a long story,' he added automatically as his willpower was tested and he fell back on his stock introduction.

She was wearing tight jeans that emphasised the curve of her hips, and climbing up to reach the Huari models, she made no attempt to hide the shapeliness of her body. Popeye gripped the stepladder and tried to remain disinterested. It was difficult, though a shake of the ladder seemed to do it. She screamed and grabbed it, and the spell was broken.

'That's not funny, *señor*,' she shouted, clutching two Huaris. 'The offer's over,' she said on her way down. 'You can take two at the normal price.'

Popeye laughed. 'I'm sorry, Eva, I couldn't resist.'

'It's Leyna, not Eva!'

She was obviously irritated. There was no swing of her hips on the way to the counter. 'How do you know her?' she asked snappily.

'Well, seeing as you ask. A friend of mine recommended the shop – er, temple – to me and said there were three acolytes who worked here.' With his fingers he counted them out. 'Sabrina – or is it Julia? – Eva . . . and you.' He emphasised the pronoun with a flourish and pulled out his wallet. 'Could you arrange an out-of-hours visit to the shrine?' He put two fifty-dollar bills on the counter. Leyna fingered the notes with a long fingernail as she considered them.

'Another fifty would do it,' she answered, looking directly into his eyes. 'A hundred and fifty split three ways is better than a hundred.'

'Does the extra fifty come with a stick of dynamite?' Popeye asked, pointing towards the locked cage he had seen when holding the stepladder.

'No. That comes with a licence to buy explosives,' she replied tersely, then checked herself. 'But I'll throw in the Huari models – after all, you'll want to leave them at the shrine.'

OR REDEMPTION

Popeye guessed that she resold them after visitors left as a way of making some extra money. Rather than pick her up on it, he decided to charm her and leave on good terms. How long had she worked in the temple? His sister could do with some of her shampoo, it made her hair shimmer. No! She was twenty-eight? He had thought she was ten years younger . . .

Eventually a miner came in and the conversation petered out, but not before arrangements had been made and Leyna had started to come round. She would meet him with the other acolytes the day after tomorrow. Five fifteen in the morning in the temple car park. They could use her Mercedes and she would provide a jacket, helmet and lamp for him. Did he need to bring anything? No, just a small offering for Huari: some coca leaves, a packet of cigarettes or a shot of *chicha* would do it. When he mentioned the bottle in his car, her face lit up. She clearly preferred drinking alcohol to chewing coca leaves. They parted, if not exactly friends, then certainly not enemies. At least that was how it felt to Popeye. He had been treated to another flash of her cleavage on the way out and guessed it was not offered to any old Tom, Dick or Harry.

As darkness fell, Potosí descended into its own underworld. Young girls, shivering in short skirts, hung around its corners as men got blind drunk and dogs barked alongside the thudding that echoed around Cerro Rico. Popeye would soon discover the pounding continued all night, sifting rocks into those that were valuable and those destined for the slag heap. The whole city was a slag heap. Anything of value was quickly spirited away. What remained was a collection of dysfunctional individuals seeking riches and an assortment of substandard buildings more than happy to house them.

The following day Popeye went for a walk and Martín found a bar. The only evidence of the immense wealth that had sprung out of Cerro Rico was the cathedral and an old colonial mint on the plaza. They were similar to hundreds of other monuments in Latin America, built when missionaries were converting souls and slavery flourished. Many of the dead souls of Cerro Rico were indentured labour from the neighbouring Portuguese empire, and it reminded Popeye of a sign he had seen outside a school in Oruro.

'A town of the educated is a town of the free. Education is the only way to escape slavery.'

It was meant for the pupils arriving at school – strolling around Potosí, the message seemed profound. The men still pouring into the city were simply exchanging one form of bondage for another. It was a town of willing slaves who had swapped the grinding poverty of the *altiplano* with the physical struggle and danger of the mines. The only way to break the cycle was to educate their families and raise their standard of living; he was proud to be doing so in Medellín. Cocaine produced an unending supply of dollars that went on improving their lives; the vast quantities of silver produced by Cerro Rico had been squandered on monuments and expensive jewellery.

Later that evening, Popeye and Martín sat down to a tasteless meal in a tatty restaurant. The food was atrocious, although Martín was too drunk to notice. Popeye pushed his plate away and turned in early. He was keen to deal with Pala before dawn and leave the city for good. This time he did not need Martín to identify the sicario, and he was going alone.

It would not be long now, only a few more hours and the hunter would be caught in his own trap.

Popeye's headlights picked out three figures lined up in front of a Mercedes jeep. They were wearing cream-coloured robes that stretched down to their feet and their hair was arranged with garlands of flowers. Each of them slowly raised an arm as Popeye pulled up, and the mock theatricals were taken even further when he got out. This time they raised both arms and greeted him as though he had stumbled upon a pagan ritual. He struggled to keep a straight face and turned to the first one.

'Leyna, nice vestments—'

She cut him off. 'I'm Sabrina.'

They looked identical in the gloom of the car park. Same height, flowing hair and slim frames. When they climbed into the jeep, he saw they were similar, but not identical. Each of their robes had an image of a leering face on the front (which he recognised as Huari) and they wore a thick set of beads: alternate red and black stones that matched the red face and black beard of their god. The garlands were quickly removed.

They set off into the night with Eva driving. It was pitch black and the only light came from the luminous glow of the dashboard. Leyna sat behind the driver and Popeye was next to her. Sabrina was in the passenger seat, and she started the conversation.

'I love your accent, *señor*. Are you from Colombia?' she asked. 'Colombian men are the most attractive in Latin America and your accents are so sexy,' she said, twisting round. 'I guess all the girls say the same?' she added, with an inviting smile.

'I don't know. I prefer the company of men to women, *señora*,' Popeye replied, with difficulty. 'Most of my boyfriends comment on my broad shoulders, not my accent.' Ignoring the brush-off, she turned to Leyna.

'Leyna tells me you've brought some *chicha* for Huari?'

Leyna nodded, and four shot glasses suddenly appeared out of nowhere. He knew what was coming next: a toast before they descended into Huari's kingdom, and his glass would be laced with something to slow his reactions.

'No, *señorita*. Your devil's going to drink every last drop of my *chicha*,' he said, and gripped the bottle firmly in his hand. 'You ladies crack open a hip flask if you want, don't mind me.'

Once more, Sabrina was thrown. She turned back without a word and Leyna stepped in to fill the awkward silence. How was Popeye coping with the altitude? Did he find it colder than Colombia? He didn't answer and instead turned the conversation around.

'Ladies, I have a question for you. Which one of you has met a Colombian the size of your slag heap?'

Silence.

'Okay, maybe I'm being unfair. Let's just say he's probably the largest man you've ever seen.'

Silence.

'Okay. How about a tall man with a pinched face who goes by the name of Pala? He's Bolivian, not a sexy beast from Colombia.'

Popeye waited several seconds, in fact almost half a minute, before sighing loudly and pulling out his Beretta. He placed its grip on his leg, then leant forward and pushed the barrel into the upholstery of the passenger seat. The *crack* of a bullet ricocheted around the confines of the vehicle and the women screamed.

Popeye had been determined that Pala should suffer from his indiscretion in Luna Land and his Beretta was loaded with dumdums that exploded on impact. It had an unintended effect in the narrow confines of the car. The woman's stomach burst out of her gown and covered the luminous dials of the dashboard. Blood was all over the Mercedes and Popeye had to wipe some gunge from his face before continuing.

'I'm glad the small talk's out of the way. I didn't feel I had your attention, ladies . . . Do I have your full attention now?' he asked, turning to Leyna for reassurance. She was splattered all over and mumbling to herself, something about the car being a rented vehicle and there being penalty charges for any damage. Eva had taken her foot off the accelerator and her hands were locked on the steering wheel. The car rolled to a stop and stalled with a violent jerk when she forgot to release the clutch. She was in shock and staring straight ahead.

Popeye leant forward and pressed his gun to her temple.

'Eva, or *puta* Julia. Whatever your name is. Can I trust you to drive?' he asked, and eventually she nodded.

'If you make any sudden moves, that's going to make me jumpy. And if I'm jumpy your friend back here is going to end up like Sabrina. Neither of us want that, so start the engine again and drive slowly in a straight line, and let's see if we can work this out.'

The woman nodded again and did what she was told.

'Good. Here's what we're going to do. First, you're going to explain what's planned for me. After that you're going to have to try and convince me not to kill you. Let's start with the plan and see how we get on.'

The Mercedes crept up the road and Popeye listened.

Three sharp corners and a long straight later, it came to an abrupt stop. Popeye got out, and Eva handed him the keys and climbed in the back. Then the dead woman was pulled out. Popeye flung her carcass over a flimsy barrier and climbed in the front. Tearing up the road, he passed a small cross by a sharp drop around the same time that Sabrina was careering down the slag heap. The entrance to the complex was reached as she disappeared into a small dip and came out spinning like a bouncing bomb. She was sprawled in a pile of rubbish by the time Popeye pulled over, and her friends died in the backseat not long after the scavenging dogs reached her body.

CHAPTER THIRTY-THREE

It was still night. There was a cluster of lights coming from an isolated building that looked like it was an amenity block; other than that, the mine was plunged in darkness and would not come alive until the dayshift arrived. Only a skeleton workforce was manning machinery that hammered and bashed rocks all night and sent the pulverised material rattling down a long chute and onto a conveyor.

Popeye swung the jeep past a large warning sign – 'Restricted Area, No Unauthorised Personnel' – and parked behind a huge dumper truck. He needed to hide the jeep from prying eyes as it looked like a prop from a gangster movie; its windows were plastered with blood and a long smear across the driver's windscreen gave a glimpse of what lay inside: an interior covered in gore and two headless corpses slumped in the back seat. When Leyna's and Eva's heads had exploded, Popeye vowed never again to use dumdum bullets in a confined space.

He got out and threw his coat into the boot and put on a miner's jacket. It was an inspired choice, as were the sticks of dynamite alongside it. Tucking three of them into a bag, he went to put the last one in his jacket pocket and noticed a small zip running down the inside of its arm. Ideal for a stick of dynamite! In it went, and he slung the bag over his shoulder and slammed the boot. Just before their demise, the women had told him that Pala planned to lock him behind a blast-proof door and blow him up with dynamite. He did not even have the balls to face his target, never mind look him in the eye. '*Hijo de puta*,' he mumbled, and picked up his bottle of *chicha* from the back seat and stuck it in the bag.

Pala was waiting for him in a nightwatchman's cabin close to the pithead. Once he had gone inside with the women, Pala was planning to follow at a safe distance. The plan had been for the girls to show Popeye the shrine, then leave with the promise they would return 'wearing something more comfortable'. He would be waiting there expecting a vision of beauty to appear; instead, a stick of fizzing dynamite would roll across the floor and the door would be slammed shut.

Popeye had a better idea.

He sneaked up to Pala's cabin. It was a flimsy structure built with expediency in mind, just like the city below. The ground in front of it had been scraped level and the earth was piled up behind it. Popeye crept onto the mound and put his shoulder against the panels of the hut. With a sharp push, it toppled forward and smashed into the ground, shattering its window. Popeye rushed round and tore open the door. The hut was empty other than a stool on its side and some broken crockery. When he turned round, he was staring down the barrel of Pala's gun.

'Raise your hands, *cabrón*, nice and slow. You were stupid to stop the car. I knew something was up.' He noticed that Popeye was drenched in blood. '*Malparido!*' he swore. 'What did you do to those girls?'

Popeye said nothing and cursed. The long straight was too exposed; he should have stopped on a corner that hugged the mountainside.

Pala rammed his gun into Popeye's side and told him to walk up to the pithead.

'I could shoot you right now. And that's exactly what I would have done a few months ago, except Don Ramón has taught me to savour the finer moments of a kill, and who better to kill than a cheap stalker with a Beretta?'

'You should kill me now, *hijo de puta*. You won't get another chance,' Popeye replied calmly. It was not the first time he'd had a gun pressed up against him, and he knew the suggestion would make the sicario do the exact opposite. 'If you take me down the mine you'll regret it. Do it like a man, here and now. Blowing up someone behind a locked door is for cowards and little girls.'

It was obvious that Popeye had no respect for the sicario, and Pala repaid the insult with the butt of his gun. It cracked on the back of Popeye's head and his knees buckled. Pala shoved him forward and they approached the pithead.

Its entrance was supported by heavy timbers and a small lantern was hanging from one of them. Popeye was pushed forward, the bag ripped off his back and the dynamite removed. Then Pala seized Popeye's Beretta and tied a rope across his chest and shoulder. Popeye was told to fasten the other end to his waist. With a sharp tug, Pala checked the rope was tight and waved at the passageway inside.

'Down we go, *hermano*. Into the depths of Cerro Rico,' he said with a chuckle, and pushed him towards a shaft at one end.

Santiago was right. The ladder had wooden rungs that looked as ancient as the mine, and it plunged into a void so deep that the light from Pala's head torch barely touched its edges. As Popeye climbed down, he knew Ramón would not have been able to follow, yet he was surprised he was not there for at least the start of the performance.

Pala followed with one hand on a rung and the other holding his gun. His head torch swung up and down as he checked on Popeye before changing grip; Popeye soon realised it was a rhythm, and the upswing was his best chance of catching Pala at a disadvantage.

The shaft dropped precipitously and they passed fresh tunnels lit by small bulbs every four or five metres. They ran perpendicular to the main shaft and each of them had a small platform for the miners to reach the ladder and haul their tools back up. Two lines of a winch ran down the side of the shaft and several platforms still had some tools laid out. The winch must have been broken, otherwise the tools would have been locked away safely. The lower they got, the more frequent the tools became, and Popeye guessed it was because the miners wished to avoid an arduous climb with them swinging on their backs.

Eventually the bottom of the mine shaft was picked out in the flickering light of Pala's head torch. Popeye knew this was his chance. He waited for an upswing in the torch and leapt off. Pala was torn from the ladder and they fell heavily onto a platform, rolled off its timber planks and plunged headlong into the void. The platform broke their fall only slightly and they hit the floor hard, followed by tools clattering around them. They were stunned, but lucky; the mining authority had recently laid out matting as a basic, last-ditch safety measure.

It was a race to recover. Popeye came round first and tugged at the rope. It was broken, and he groped around for a tool to batter Pala. His hand gripped something firm and he smashed it over Pala's head. It was a kneeling pad that made his head torch shake, then cut out, and they were left in total darkness. Popeye rolled away. He expected a shot, though it would be risky in the small area as its ricochet could come back to bite if the target was missed. The sound of shuffling feet told him Pala thought the same. He was on the move.

Popeye levered himself up and checked nothing was broken. His eyes were growing accustomed to the dark and he spotted the tunnel down which Pala had escaped. His shuffling had turned into echoing steps and Popeye knew he had no time to lose. He grabbed the first tool that came to hand. It was a long pitching chisel – cold, heavy steel – and he took off down the tunnel.

There were no proper lights. It was either a service tunnel or part of the ventilation system. Popeye hoped it was the latter, otherwise Pala would disappear down one of the tunnels that it passed. He was lucky again. It led to a ventilation shaft, and a metal ladder was bolted to the bare rock. It was designed to ventilate the mines, not access them, and he could hear the ring of Pala's shoes on its metal rungs. He was climbing to the surface. Popeye needed to reach him . . . and fast. With a renewed vigour he gripped the ladder and pulled himself up. Higher and higher he climbed. His shoulder was in agony and his knee gave way on more than one occasion, yet he needed to reach the man if he were to avoid a bullet. If Pala arrived at the exit, he would have no chance – it would be a turkey shoot once his gun was pointing down on him.

Finally he felt he was closing in on his target. Popeye was growing tired, but Pala was slowing down fast and his outline appeared just ahead, caught in the ambient light at the top of the shaft. He was almost there, and it spurred on Popeye. Pala's foot was only three rungs above him, and with an effort he sprang up and grabbed it. The boot that landed on his head made him lose his grip and he lashed out with his chisel. It clanged on the ladder and Pala moved on to the next rung. Pala was now scrambling for the finish and Popeye lunged again. This time he seized a leg. A shot was fired. Popeye swung his chisel and it connected. The gun tumbled down the shaft and the chisel followed it. The narrow chamber reverberated with ringing metal and splintering rock, and Pala was almost at the top. A large steel cage protected the shaft. It looked like he was trapped. Then it suddenly opened, and a face appeared.

The man quickly pulled away when Pala emerged. Popeye tried to pull him back and got a boot in the face. Pala limped off through the open cage and Popeye crawled out of the shaft, wiping blood from his nose, and lay on the ground for a moment to recover his strength. There was a light wind, and he saw a lantern swinging slightly through the mesh of the cage and realised the pithead was nearby. He jumped up to see if Pala was heading there, but there was no sign of him. Then, turning round, he caught sight of a shadow limping off in the opposite direction.

Popeye ran across to the pithead and retrieved his bag. Around him, the tin buildings were ringing from a heavy rain and potholes were filling with water, yet he barely noticed them. His focus was on catching Pala.

CHAPTER THIRTY-FOUR

Popeye had a sense that something was running beside him, and whatever it was filled him with a powerful adrenaline that made him feel invincible and almost superhuman. His heart was pounding with energy. It was like the angel of death had joined him. It was no longer enough to kill Pala; now he had to destroy him. He launched himself after the sicario in a fury.

Pala was hugging the shadow of a long building, trying to avoid the light that was coming from the amenity block, but Popeye had him in his sights and there was no escape. Pala reached the end of the building and swung round the corner, and Popeye was hot on his heels. The ground was wet, and as he turned the corner, Popeye lost his footing. A loud *clang* rang out and a bullet tore through the corrugated tin above his head. It was the slip that had saved him. Pala had Popeye's Beretta, and he was making off towards the sifting plant. Popeye got up and ran straight after him, interrupted only by another shot, another miss.

Popeye crashed into Pala's back and sent him tumbling into a puddle. His arm pinned Pala's hand to the ground and the Beretta fell to one side. Pala's face was buried in the puddle, and he thrashed wildly, bubbles breaking the surface. Popeye held him down for almost a minute before dragging him behind a shed.

A funnel appeared from Popeye's bag and the bottle of *chicha* was opened. The funnel was forced into Pala's mouth. Alcohol flew down his gullet. Half a bottle to start with. A short pause to allow him to breathe. Coughing and retching, then the rest of the bottle followed.

'Keep it down, *hermano*,' Popeye shouted as some of it shot across the ground. 'Think of it as pain relief.'

He cocked his Beretta, pressed it against Pala's kneecap, and its recoil echoed around the buildings.

'That's one for dragging me around that *puta* funfair.'

Pala rolled around, wailing in agony.

'Here's another for getting me on a rollercoaster. I fucking hate rollercoasters.'

The other kneecap exploded and Pala almost passed out.

'Chop, chop. Don't fall asleep on me,' Popeye said, and lifted Pala with almost superhuman strength. He slung his limp body over his shoulder and marched off towards the sound of hammering.

The workers scattered as he appeared in the sifting plant. Popeye was like a vision from hell, covered in blood and carrying a man whose legs were half hanging off. One hand held Pala tight against his shoulder, the other gripped his silver Beretta. He cast his eyes around the machinery before striding with purpose towards a line of small carts. They were moving slowly along a narrow track, dragged along by a ratchet chain. When they reached a conveyor belt, their contents were tipped out and they swung back for more material.

Popeye slung Pala into one of the carts and watched it shudder down the track and tip him onto the conveyor. His hands clawed at the handrails slipping past and his body twisted and arced. It made no difference; despite his frantic struggle, there was nothing he could do to stop the inevitable.

Pala went into the pneumatic hammer.

Two smashes of its iron ram and it was all over. An automatic arm scooped his pulverised mess off its base and shovelled it down a long chute. His mangled remains slipped slowly down onto another conveyor and were fast-tracked to the slag heap.

Popeye turned round and walked away.

The rattling and smashing of the sifting plant gradually faded into the distance. The rain was starting to clear, and as he made his way towards the jeep, the red mist also began to lift; it was as though he had uncorked an evil genie and it was now back in the bottle. It was the first time he had gone from assassinating a target to destroying someone. He had a deep sense of something evil having taken control of him, and he felt empty. Pala was victim number two hundred; killing him should have been a cause for celebration. Instead, he felt despondent.

The last thing he remembered was the windscreen of the jeep splattered in blood before something slammed into his head. He fell to the ground and another blow left him senseless.

CHAPTER THIRTY-FIVE

When Popeye came round, it was dark and cold with a faint smell of incense in the air and a damp chill in the building. He blinked and tried to make out where he was. Moonlight was streaming through a row of rectangular windows, and he could just make out the hard angles of some furniture. It looked like a line of benches that were regularly spaced down a long corridor, and it was impossible to see anything beyond them. Other than the sound of rain outside, everything was deadly silent.

Then he started to move.

He was strapped to a chair that was gliding just above the ground, taking him slowly down the corridor and towards a dim light that had appeared at its end. Then he realised he was not in a corridor at all but in the nave of a church, and its bells were beginning to chime. Thirteen strikes in all, and he was in front of the altar, except there was no altar and he was facing a monstrous pair of old-fashioned scales with a dish attached either side of a large fulcrum. Something clanged, like a metal handle locking into place, and the building burst into light.

Popeye was not in a church . . . he was in the Cathedral of Potosí.

He shrank in his chair. A large eye was floating where he expected to see a crucifix, and it was like no eye he had ever seen – it had a deep blue pupil and an iris of concentric turquoise and white rings that were shimmering slightly. The eye blinked and he turned away. The cathedral reeked of symbolism – a Scales of Judgement presided over by an All Seeing Eye – and it looked like a ceremony was about to begin with Popeye in its very centre. He struggled with his bindings and shouted at the *hijo de puta* organising the performance to show himself, but his words echoed around the cathedral and the lights grew dim, then a dense incense swirled around the scales and a dark silhouette appeared.

It had sharp, pointed ears that rose above the incense, and Popeye relaxed.

The fake priest had clearly been busy. Whoever was in the Batman suit would regret it once he was freed, at which point he would deal with the fake priest. The All Seeing Eye was the very same one that appeared on dollar bills, and he was sure the Scales of Judgement were somewhere on the larger notes. The lights came on again and the rest of the incense lifted.

Popeye froze.

Standing before him, a two-metre-high figure towered down. It was half man and half beast. The sharp, pointed ears were those of a jackal, not Batman, and there were two striped ribbons on its shoulders, not a bat cape. Its snout was jet black and its nostrils were flared. Brilliant yellow eyes glared at him and a long iron staff was gripped in its right hand. It was no cartoon superhero. It was Anubis, the ancient Egyptian god of death.

Popeye knew he was in danger.

Suddenly the chair shot up and he was taken to the cathedral pulpit, although the pulpit had been removed and all that remained was a large platform. When the seat came to rest, Anubis had disappeared, and the symbolism slowly began to make more sense. Anubis was the mythical figure who guided individuals across the threshold of the living and into the world of the dead. Before that, a man's heart was placed on the Scales of Judgement and the All Seeing Eye ensured it was properly weighted against 'the feather of truth'. If the scales tipped the wrong way, Anubis was there to drive the man's soul straight into hell with his iron rod.

Popeye knew he was about to be judged.

Footsteps echoed loudly on the cathedral's stone flags and Popeye turned towards the sound. A new figure appeared. This one had the head of a stag and the body of a man. He was wearing a dark red robe with flames rising from its hem, and his antlers were gnarled and twisted with sharp white points. He passed underneath Popeye and strode up to the scales. Two identical chairs were now either side of them, carved out of teak with ornate arms and long backrests, more like thrones than ordinary seats. The figure walked to the left of the scales and Popeye breathed a sigh of relief. Unlike Anubis, its head was a prop, and the man was now removing it. Once it was placed on the chair, he swung round and glared at Popeye.

Popeye almost jumped out of his skin. The bushy hair and thick moustache were unmistakable . . . It was none other than Luis Galán!

He was still trying to make sense of it when there was a sharp blast of a trumpet from the far end of the cathedral. Another figure was standing there – it was a magnificent angel with a dazzling breastplate over his chest and silver greaves on his shins. As he strode up to the scales, the cathedral was filled with a sweet perfume that rose high above the nave, and a slight glow followed him. He stood to the right of the scales and declared in a clear voice:

'I am the Lord's Herald. Summoned to bear witness to the good deeds performed by Jhon Velásquez. I call forth an angel for each and every one of the poor and needy saved by his actions.'

Two heavy doors swung open from where he had come, and a wave of shimmering light poured down the nave and spilled over the pews opposite him. And the angels kept coming and coming, hovering over those seated below them in a brilliant, swirling light.

'I place four thousand two hundred good deeds on the scales,' the Lord's Herald finally announced, and sat down. The scales lurched to the right, and Popeye felt sure his soul was saved.

He looked down at Luis Galán with contempt. He was sitting with the ridiculous stag head in his lap. The man had been a corrupt politician, not a symbol of noble purity, and he was sorely mistaken if he thought turning up with a stag's head would magically give him those qualities. Luis stood up and put the prop to one side.

'I am the Devil's Advocate,' he announced, and Popeye felt like giving him the finger, 'summoned to bear witness to the evil performed by Jhon Velásquez. I call forth a downcast soul for each and every one of his dead victims.'

Good luck, cabrón, Popeye thought. *You're four thousand short.*

There was a clap of thunder and a small section of stone flagstones burst open. A bony hand appeared, then a skeleton emerged from the crypt, followed by a stream of others. The pews opposite Luis Galán filled with bleached bones, and femurs scraped across their hard benches: two hundred in total . . . and Popeye was counting. The scales barely moved. Popeye knew he was home and dry. He waited for his chair to be lifted to paradise, but Luis Galán was far from finished.

'I call forth a downcast soul for each and every one of Jhon Velásquez's victims who are still alive.'

Popeye leant forward.

'Fuck off, Galán. You've had your chance, now piss off,' he shouted.

Luis turned to him.

'I'm not finished. You miscalculated badly, *cabrón*. The living dead need to be added to the scales. The people you destroyed, yet remain alive: mothers, fathers, wives, husbands, sisters, brothers . . . the loved ones of your targets.'

Popeye watched in horror. More and more skeletons rose from the crypt and filled the pews, then jostled the others standing by the door and pushed them into the plaza. His sense of assurance was shattered. He had never given any thought to the indirect consequences of his work. He had no idea there were so many other victims, and the sheer numbers overwhelmed him. When he looked at the scales, they were dropping slowly to the left as his sins were added.

'I place four thousand two hundred evil acts on the scales,' Luis Galán announced, and sat down.

The scales were now level, and Popeye wondered what it signified – perhaps a stint in purgatory? Then a foul smell of rotten cabbages and old rags swept through the cathedral. A sinister figure with a fishtail and an up-pointed bird's head was struggling down the nave. She was gripping a belly that was swollen and was walking with difficulty. When she passed underneath the pulpit, Popeye could see that she was pregnant. She stopped in front of the scales and turned to address the bizarre congregation.

'There is one more victim to add. The unborn child of Sabrina, torn from her stomach by ravenous dogs. I carry her child as evidence of this crime and demand it be added to the scales.'

She said the words with confidence and they filled Popeye with dread. There was the slightest tilt in the scales, and it was enough to bring down judgement on him and for Anubis to reappear. This time he had a dark shadow billowing behind him like an approaching storm and the iron staff in his hand was glowing red hot. Popeye's chair spiralled down from the pulpit, and the Lord's Herald and his shimmering souls vanished.

A primeval fear gripped him. He was damned. A gloom descended over the cathedral and a deep pit opened up in the middle of the nave. Popeye didn't notice; he was focussed on his rib cage, which had started to swell violently as though it was about to burst. The pain became intense, and Popeye gripped his sides as the sweat poured down his face, then there was an almighty *crack*, his sternum fractured and his heart burst out and flew across the cathedral, spraying blood over a line of skeletons as it was sucked down the fiery pit. The skeletons jumped to their feet, the cathedral rattled to the sound of their raucous applause and Popeye struggled to escape from his chair. It was no use. Anubis' hand was now on his throat and Popeye was in the air. Luis Galán was cheering. The fiery pit loomed. Anubis' burning staff seared his neck and Popeye was rammed down the pit . . . straight into hell.

CHAPTER THIRTY-SIX

'NO, NO, NO, NO!'

Popeye woke in a cold sweat. He was in a dark room and the bars on the window told him it was a police cell. He was lying on the floor. In horror, he realised his leg was manacled to a chain, and the chain was fixed to a thick ring on the wall. He tried to get up and fell back down.

The next thing he did was to feel inside his jacket. His Beretta was missing. Worse than that, he was absolutely shaken to the core. His confidence was completely shattered; the nightmare was no dream, it was reality.

He had destroyed countless lives. The bony skeletons had been real people, broken by the loss of loved ones. They were innocent victims, paying the price for something that did not concern them.

He was immobile, staring into space, destroyed physically and emotionally. His neck was in agony and his soul had plunged into a place so dark that it could only be the edge of hell, teetering there, waiting for Luis Galán's last push. His whole life had been flipped over and made pointless. He had dragged himself from poverty and helped others do the same. Now he bore the fruits of his labour and his soul was damned.

His head was pounding and he lay down and placed it on his arms. The floor was covered in smooth, damp cobbles and he was glad of the miner's jacket. He started to fall asleep again and jumped with a start. He was determined to stay awake and avoid the world of Anubis and Luis Galán.

Sitting up, he pulled the chain. It was long, with stubby links that clanged on the cobbles. The ring to which it was attached lay directly beneath the window. Other than that, there was nothing of note in the bare cell apart from a small alcove in a corner. Popeye decided to see what was behind it, and when he tried to stand up, his legs gave way. He knew he needed to rest, but it seemed the chain would reach the alcove, and he was relieved to at least be able to move around his cell once he recovered.

He tried to stay warm by sitting on the back of his jacket. He felt more than just sorry for himself; he felt cheated. It was the accident of birth that had placed him on this path. He had been born in Colombia, where opportunities were in cocaine, not the tech sector, and he had been raised by loving and supportive parents, but poor ones. Had he been wealthy and educated then he could have campaigned for the Senate and used his power legally and comprehensively. Instead, his options were limited to organising marches and designing banners or embracing the narco culture that was illegal but pervasive. He chose the world of cocaine, and he now realised that it had destroyed his soul. His head was pounding and he struggled to stay awake.

Daybreak eventually arrived, and with it a sliver of light came through the small window and its iron bars. It was open to the elements and its cool breeze reminded Popeye of being in the cellar with Pablo Escobar. It felt like an age ago, and sadness washed over him. His gravesite should be in the lush mountains of Colombia, not the barren *altiplano* of Bolivia, and he knew he had to do whatever he could to return home. His body was exhausted and his soul had grown tired of death. He wanted to die. He needed to lie down in a narrow box under six feet of soil. And it had to be in Medellín.

A guard came in with a paraffin lamp and a bowl of thin soup. No words were spoken. A spoon was handed over, a lump of bread was fished out of the guard's pocket, and he threw it on the floor. The lamp was left behind so Popeye had some light, and the door was slammed shut.

Popeye was still struggling with the nightmare and finding it difficult to focus. The image of the fish woman and her swollen belly kept coming back to him. If he were also liable for unborn children, his victims would stretch into thousands, if not hundreds of thousands! *The children that would have been born had I not killed their parent.* If it were really that bad then the mountain he faced would be impossible to climb. Once more a dark depression tore at his soul.

Popeye played with the soup. It was lukewarm and watery, yet it tasted better than the food being served on Potosí's streets. With the bread broken into it, it started to revive him. The next moment he heard a voice through the window.

'*Hermano.* Are you in there?'

There was no mistaking it.

Never had he been so pleased to hear Martín's voice. Popeye pushed himself up gingerly and called back; two hands went to grip the bars but failed.

'What are you doing in jail, *hermano*?' Martín shouted. 'The police came for your things. When you didn't return I thought you'd gone after Ramón?'

Once more his fingers grasped, and once again he failed to get a hold.

'I can't reach the window. They won't let me see you. Tell me what you need, *hermano*,' Martín said.

Popeye thanked his blessings that he had a friend to rely on. His brain was whirring. He knew he needed to find a way out and it needed to be quick. He guessed he was in a police cell whilst charges were being drawn up. After that he would be moved to a prison to await trial, probably later that morning. Any chance of escape would disappear once he was locked in a high-security cell behind a perimeter fence. If he were to escape, it had to be that morning.

'Bring the car round and park nearby. I'm leaving this morning. Throw me a cigarette in case I need a smoke.'

'What? You don't smoke. Nor do I.'

'Just get one and toss it in,' Popeye replied, and he eyed the lantern that he knew would soon disappear. 'And give three sharp blasts on the horn once you've arrived. Be quick, I haven't got long.'

A few minutes later a cigarette landed on the floor, and the guard returned for the bowl and the lantern. Once he had left, Popeye turned to the chain and its narrow ring. A large padlock was fastened at one end, and it jammed in the ring as he reached the alcove. A foul odour confirmed his suspicion. It was a small latrine, and a bucket of water was next to a stinking hole. It suited his plan perfectly. All he had to do was bide his time until Martín arrived: after that, he wasn't sure how it would play out.

There was a blast of a horn and he sprang into action. Four sharp thumps on the door. Ten seconds later it swung open. The guard appeared and pointed a gun at Popeye.

'Do that again, *cabrón*, and I'll shoot you in the leg.'

'Okay. Give me a light first,' Popeye replied, the cigarette in his mouth.

The guard shook his head.

'No. Hold on, you *hijo de*—' Popeye's foot went to stop the door, but it slammed in his face and the chain did its job – it stopped his foot in mid-air, and his other one slipped on the damp cobbles. He fell to the floor and the cigarette broke in two. He was left with a crushed filter and some tobacco strands in his mouth.

'Motherfucker!' he shouted.

The cigarette was useless. He got up and banged on the door. This time it burst open almost immediately and two guards appeared, not one. They rushed at him and seized his arms. A large club swung at his head, and he only just managed to duck and avoid it. The men pushed him against the wall and the club was rammed into his stomach.

'No, no, *hermanos* . . . I just want a smoke,' Popeye gasped. 'I'll make it worth your while.'

That did the trick, and the men held back momentarily. Popeye seized the moment.

'I have a valuable watch. It's yours if you give me a cigarette,' he said, and nodded at his left wrist. The man released his grip and Popeye pulled up his sleeve. Its luminescent dials stood out in the gloomy cell and both arms were freed. A cigarette was handed over in exchange for the watch, and the men stood admiring their timepiece.

'And a light?' he reminded them.

Popeye took a drag on the cigarette and blew the smoke across the cell, trying not to cough. Its end glowed with a sharp point as the men turned and left. Popeye went across to the window and gave a short whistle. Then he whispered Martín's name as loudly as he dared. There was no answer.

Popeye reached for the zip running down the inside of his arm and pulled out the dynamite. He'd known it was an inspired choice, he just hadn't known when it would come in handy. Far better for the moment to present itself rather than rush it, and way better to harness its power rather than make an explosion for the sake of a spectacle. Popeye was confident the very moment had arrived, and what's more, it would also provide a breathtaking spectacle. He took another drag of the foul smoke and touched the cigarette's burning end to the fuse.

It fizzed for a moment before he placed it under the window then shuffled over to the latrine, where he crouched with his arms wrapped around his head. He estimated it would take around thirty seconds to burn through, although explosives were not his thing and he had no idea what was about to happen. Maybe it would blast through the wall or the whole place would collapse on top of him? All he could do was shut his eyes tight and hope for the best.

An almighty blast yanked him into the alcove wall and a block of stone flew across the street. It smashed through a shop window opposite like a cannon ball from six hundred years earlier and decimated an extensive display of ethnic doll souvenirs. The ring was still attached to the block, and Popeye was lucky the blast had broken a link in the chain, otherwise part of him would have been lying in the street alongside the debris.

Light was now streaming through the gaping hole in the wall. Popeye lost no time and scrambled to his feet. As he reached the opening, something made him pause there for a moment – it was an overwhelming urge to roar and beat his chest in defiance, a rush that came from blasting out of captivity. He felt invincible, like a superhero, except he was clad in a ripped miner's jacket and his ears were ringing.

Martín appeared and Popeye jumped down. A car door slammed, tyres screeched, and the car raced through the streets of Potosí and out onto the barren *altiplano*, pursued by the city's finest.

CHAPTER THIRTY-SEVEN

Popeye had shoved Martín out of the driver's seat at the first opportunity and it had been like being back home: tearing away from the police, taking corners late, locking out the back end with the handbrake, weaving through oncoming traffic . . . The road behind Cerro Rico had soon narrowed into a series of dips and bends, past processing plants and heavy lorries coming and going. One of them had nearly smashed into them on a tight bend and the police cars following had not been so lucky. Popeye had sped off to the sound of screeching tyres and crunching metal.

Now they were off the road, parked down a quiet side street, Popeye turned to Martín and stretched out a hand.

'You saved me, *hermano*.'

Martín shook it.

'And you'll get a proper reward when we get the emeralds,' Popeye added. 'Do you know where we are?'

Martín ignored the question and stared at him.

'What happened in Potosí, *hermano*? Did you get Pala and Ramón? And what were you doing in a police cell?'

'Don't worry about it. Another time. Too much to explain.' Popeye brushed the questions aside and rubbed his neck. The adrenaline was wearing off and it was starting to throb. 'We need to swap the car. Any idea where we can find a garage?'

Martín shook his head. A road atlas was on the back seat and he grabbed it.

'If we follow this road, it comes out on the highway. There's bound to be one on it,' he said, tracing out a route with his finger.

'The police are going to set up roadblocks to trap you, *hermano*. It could be risky.'

Popeye swung back onto the road in a cloud of dust.

'We'd better be quick then.'

Thirty minutes later they were in a 1972 Volkswagen Beetle. The mechanic in the garage had bought it in Peru and driven it back over the border. It still had Peruvian plates, which was not ideal, though less conspicuous than the other car they had been offered: a 1964 Ford, in bright pink. Basic paperwork was swapped with a handshake and the mechanic waved them off with a smile. No money changed hands and he ended up with a four-wheel drive that was far more valuable.

Popeye needed to lie low, somewhere to hide in plain sight where the police would not think to look. Maybe a small mining community with no need to provide ID and fill out forms, not a small town with an inquisitive receptionist at a hotel desk? Besides, he had no money and Martín would have to pay. A couple of cheap rooms would be ideal.

There was a place on the map called Agua de Castilla that he was going to check out. It looked like it was no more than ten kilometres away, and the police would never think to search there for him. They would assume he was fleeing the country, not staying as a guest in a miner's house under their very noses.

It would also give him time to decide what to do next. Not only was his ID gone but his Beretta had been taken. For the first time since leaving Colombia, he felt exposed. What's more, he also knew that his life as a sicario was over. He could no longer kill for a living. He had to find redemption, and it was not waiting for him down the barrel of a gun. He was not going to assassinate Ramón, even though the *hijo de puta* had it coming. Besides, right now he had no idea where to find him. He could still be in Potosí for all he knew; he would have fled if he had seen the evidence of his jailbreak.

Popeye knew he had rare talents and he needed to use them. He had to find redemption, to save his soul from eternal damnation and avoid that *puta* iron staff that had rammed it into hell. He subconsciously rubbed his neck, and it felt like a painful reminder of Anubis, not the *malparido* who had sneaked up behind him with a cosh.

The sign for Agua de Castilla appeared and he pulled off the highway. It looked like the perfect spot. An unmade road led to a ramshackle collection of houses that ended in what appeared to be a dumping ground for old cars. There was only one prominent building, a community centre, the kind that offered rudimentary healthcare during the day and alcohol and football coverage at night. They parked the Beetle and went inside.

A large group of poorly dressed women sat huddled in a corner and ragged children were running everywhere; there was no sign of a clinic. He was right about the evening entertainment; a large television had been bolted to the wall, and below it, a long, box-like structure was fixed to the floor. It looked like it came from an old cafeteria. It had a long wooden counter for serving drinks and a metal shutter was rolled down and locked with a heavy chain. There was no sign of a door, and it seemed likely that alcohol was stored inside.

'*Señoras*,' Popeye said, walking up to the women, 'do you have any accommodation here?'

One of them looked up and said nothing. Martín stepped in.

'We're looking for a room for the night. Does the community take in guests?'

She stared at him before answering.

'Which mine have you come from?' she asked.

Now the whole group turned round. Twenty pairs of eyes glared at Popeye, and he felt the entire weight of Agua de Castilla's female curiosity boring into him. For a moment he wondered if there had been a news alert about his escape and they had recognised his face. Then he remembered he was wearing a miner's jacket that was covered in blood and dust, and he probably looked like he had been in an accident.

'No, ladies, we're not miners! We're tourists on our way down to Chile,' he said, and dusted down the arms of his jacket. 'I told my friend here I could climb the slag heap in Potosí. Of course, I was drunk at the time,' he said, laughing, 'and it became a challenge I was stupid enough to try.'

He did not need to say anything more. A glass of water was brought for each of them, some children hung on to their legs, and after some conferring, two rooms were made available. A meal was included in the price, which was a relief as they had not seen any shops or restaurants on their way in. Popeye knew he had to change his appearance as soon as possible and decided to try his luck.

'Señora,' he said, turning to a middle-aged woman who seemed to be one of the community leaders. 'My clothes are ripped and covered in dirt. Is there anywhere I can buy new clothes?' He knew the answer. There was nowhere, and he hoped it might persuade her to dig out some old garments from her husband's drawer; instead she led him to a small room. Boxes were piled up inside and each one was branded with a large Red Cross stamp and the words 'Donated by the USA' underneath. She sized him up and down and pulled out a box marked 'Medium'.

'Here, take what you need. If they're too small, try those other boxes in the corner.'

The scissors he had been given were blunt and Martín's razor was old. It took Popeye most of that afternoon to shave off his hair and beard. His head was sore and revealed old wounds. His face was itchy and spotted with dried blood. The ligature marks were more noticeable, and a pasty shadow outlined the area where his beard had once been.

Walking into the community centre later that evening, he was no beauty and his clothes were winning no contests: a beige Bart Simpson sweatshirt, a pair of teal-green tracksuit bottoms and a duffle coat. He'd had to delve into the 'Large' box to find anything that fitted. Luckily he had also found a pair of leggings that were now underneath the Nike shell suit bottoms, otherwise he would have frozen. There was also a selection of beanies, one of which would keep his shaven head warm. None of the men at the tables seemed to notice him, and the women were gone. He found a table in the corner and Martín went to the bar.

He returned with two beers and Popeye raised his eyebrows.

'I know, *hermano* . . . you don't drink beer,' said Martín, putting them down. 'The "drunkard from Potosí" who doesn't drink alcohol . . .' He left the words hanging, and Popeye knew it might look suspicious if he was not drinking.

He raised his beer and took a sip. It tasted foul, and he decided to swap it with Martín's empty as soon as he could. It did not take long before the opportunity arose. Martín went up for another beer and Popeye clasped Martín's glass as evidence of his drinking prowess. All the men were drinking beer and the only soft drink available was pineapple juice, kept aside for the children on the rare occasion that they were allowed into the hall of an evening. The women were at home cooking.

Martín was chatting at the bar, the men around him were playing cards and smoke filled the room. *Pantanal* was on the television, and this week's episode of the Brazilian soap opera was coming to a climax. A woman was lying sobbing on the street, and a man was driving off at speed as she screamed after him, then the scene suddenly switched to a rotating logo of the national news channel and a camera zoomed in on a sharply dressed presenter. He waited until the logo had disappeared before putting down the sheet of paper he was pretending to study.

'—ing news . . .' The bartender was too slow with the volume control. 'This morning Potosí woke to a daring escape from its police station and a massive manhunt is now under way. Gustavo Guzmán is live for us in Potosí with the latest. Gustavo, what can you tell us?'

A young man with a large microphone beamed down from the television set.

'Thank you, Jorge. Yes, that's right. Pandemonium this morning as a dangerous criminal blew his way out of captivity.'

Popeye looked around. The card games had stopped and the men were glued to the screen. Gustavo carried on:

'It appears an explosive device supplied by an accomplice was used to blast a hole in the wall. It's still unclear exactly how the prisoner managed to survive the explosion. He's believed to be an expert in bombs and munitions and the charge was clearly carefully prepared.'

The camera turned to a scene of destruction behind the news reporter. A half-collapsed shop was cordoned off with police tape and a row of cars with smashed windows stretched down the street. The camera returned to Gustavo, and he pointed to some timber supports that were holding up the police station.

The men at the table in front of Popeye burst into applause.

'Jorge, the authorities believe the police station may need to be demolished.' Gustavo continued.

The applause grew louder as other men joined in.

'It's still to be confirmed, but from where I'm standing, it looks like Potosí is about to lose another historic building.'

Then back to the studio.

'Gustavo, what do we know about the man who escaped? Is he a danger to the public? And what's known about his accomplice?'

Gustavo picked up his cue after a short pause and raised his microphone.

'Thank you, Jorge. Yes, the public are being told not to approach either man, each of whom are considered extremely dangerous. The escaped prisoner is believed to be none other than Pablo Escobar's top sicario, Jhon Velásquez, who goes by the nickname Popeye.' A grainy black-and-white photograph appeared on the screen, and Popeye hurriedly shielded his face with a glass. 'I understand Jhon Velásquez's true identity was only discovered when he was taken into custody. At this stage it remains unclear why he was arrested, although there are reports of multiple bodies being found at Cerro Rico.'

The photograph slipped into the corner of the screen and Gustavo's microphone reappeared.

'His accomplice is thought to be a notorious drug dealer, possibly Bolivian.'

Martín returned, looking shocked.

'*Hermano*, they're making out I'm a notorious drug dealer,' he whispered, and looked to Popeye for reassurance.

'At least they haven't got your photo,' was the best Popeye could come up with.

The coverage turned to the scene of the road accident. Two police cars were being craned onto the back of a lorry and the road was ablaze with the flashing lights of rescue vehicles.

'That was the road out of Potosí earlier, Jorge. Absolute carnage. Jhon Velásquez fired at police cars and then blew up the road with sticks of dynamite.'

This was the moment the room erupted with cheers and whistles. Popeye was left in no doubt that the miners of Agua de Castilla approved of the manner in which he had made his escape, and it was clear that their allegiance lay with those fighting the authorities, not the police. He felt like standing up to the applause and was struggling with the temptation when Martín grabbed his arm and raised it above his head like a champion boxer.

'*Hermanos*, fellow Bolivians,' he announced, banging his glass on the table, 'please raise your glass to Jhon Velásquez, my indestructible friend from Colombia.'

The whole room turned and stared at the man in the red beanie, beige sweatshirt and teal-green tracksuit bottoms. He stood up as the applause grew louder, removed his beanie, gave a deep bow and revealed a bald head marked by scars.

CHAPTER THIRTY-EIGHT

Three days later a triumphant Popeye turned onto the highway. It was hard not to feel triumphant after the send-off he had received.

The whole community of Agua de Castilla had turned out. His dusty-white Volkswagen had bounced down the street to a cacophony of cheers and hands slapping its roof, and emerged through a line of school-age children vigorously waving Wiphala flags. It was the first time he had seen the seven colours of the rainbow stitched together in a patchwork of squares that fluttered and rippled like prayer flags in the wind.

He was buzzing and enthusiastic.

The same could not be said of Martín, who was quiet and withdrawn. A call with his wife the other night had not gone well; at least, that was what he had told Popeye. Now he was having second thoughts about joining him on the Salar de Uyuni. It was only the reminder of the wealth coming his way that had convinced him to stay. He was staring straight ahead and seemed troubled.

'*Hermano*, cheer up. The police aren't about to catch us,' Popeye said. He guessed Martín's wife had seen the news coverage and taken exception to her husband being a fugitive. He also knew she was far from enthusiastic about him being described as a notorious drug dealer; Martín had told him as much.

'And what about the cartel?' Martín asked. Clearly he was less concerned about the police catching them than the cartel. He had asked the very same question back in Agua de Castilla and had gone on to remind Popeye that the emeralds were only supposed to be recovered once Ramón was dead, not before. Alongside the disapproval of his wife, it was another excuse to avoid the lake and return home. 'I don't want anything to do with disobeying orders, *hermano*. I've spent long enough away from my family going down that route . . .'

Popeye had laughed off Martín's whingeing and told him Piña had fully approved his new plan. Anyway, it was pointless trying to pursue Ramón. He had probably returned to the Beni now that he had no protection. There was also a nationwide hunt for Popeye, and he had no weapon. The only option was to recover the emeralds and return to Colombia. It was common sense.

Popeye's explanation had failed to reassure Martín the first time. Now that Martín was raising it again, he became irritated.

'I told you. Piña has authorised it. Stop worrying,' he snapped. 'You'll soon be heading home with a handful of emeralds, and you can start a new life in Paraguay if you want. Anyway, the police aren't going to identify you, and there's no reason for Ramón to suspect you. And even if he does, then your cousin Luis will have your back like last time. Just sit back, *cabrón*, and enjoy the ride.' Then, as if to emphasise the point, he swung the car off the highway and onto the gravel of the hard shoulder. The Beetle raced down its loose surface with narrow tyres that barely gripped, and as the car twisted and shook, Popeye spun the steering wheel sharply one way, then another, to try and keep it on a straight course. By the time he realised it was no rally car, it was too late.

Martín clung to his door as the swerving became more desperate, and as they lurched from side to side, his head crashed against the window. It was only a matter of time before the car flipped over and disappeared down a ditch that was growing steadily wider and deeper as they flew alongside it. Suddenly the road veered to one side. A deep ravine was directly ahead and the car was careering straight for it. Martín slammed his hands on the dashboard and Popeye locked his arms on the steering wheel. The car raced towards the abyss, its axle shuddered and its wheels spun wildly . . . then at the very last moment, it dropped into a small dip in the hard shoulder, whipped across a sharp camber and flew back onto the road like a missile from a slingshot, tyres screeching and rubber burning.

Popeye roared with laughter and Martín remained sullen, but with the hint of a smile. It was enough for Popeye to know he was coming round. Twenty minutes later they passed a sign for the town of Uyuni, and he knew it would not be long before Martín had forgotten all about his worries.

Martín was on his fourth beer. All that remained on his plate was a purple-coloured thighbone from half a roast chicken, and he looked content. Popeye glanced at the man who had not only become a friend but was also responsible for his rescue in Potosí. He felt he should warn him about his relations, or at least one of them, and he decided to come clean.

'You know I killed Pala on Cerro Rico . . .' he said. Martín nodded. 'What I didn't tell you was that I was lured into a trap. Pala was expecting me and I was lucky to survive.' Popeye looked straight at Martín. 'It was your brother-in-law, Santiago, who set me up. Cerro Rico was to be my grave, not Pala's.' Martín looked shocked.

Popeye continued.

'After Luna Land, I knew he was working for Ramón. I only went along with the ridiculous plan at Potosí to catch him out.'

'And you said nothing?' Martín asked.

Popeye ignored the accusation that he had not been forthcoming.

'Don't trust your brother-in-law, *hermano*. Tread carefully. If he has any suspicion you were involved in what happened to Pala, you'll be in danger. That's why I didn't tell you. Best you had no idea what was going to happen. Never let on that we worked together. Tell them I had a gun to your head the whole time and you were forced into helping me track Ramón and find the emeralds. Just be careful when you return home.'

'And why would Santiago help Ramón?' Martín asked, a little defensively.

Popeye sighed. 'Money, *cabrón*, and normally Santiago would be getting a bullet in the head. I can't explain this to you easily, and it's going to sound odd . . .' He paused. 'But I know your brother-in-law did me a favour in the long run.' Popeye wasn't about to bare his soul to Martín, yet he still wanted to share his minor epiphany. 'I've come to realise, *hermano*, you can't micromanage the scales of judgement.' He laughed, and warmed to his explanation. 'You never know quite how bad your bad is going to be, and you can't depend on the good being quite as good as you expect. No, I've done enough killing for one man. Time to build up some reserves of merit. Time to leave the life of a sicario behind.'

Martín was too drunk to engage in a proper discussion. He had paced himself in the cabin by the lake; since arriving in Uyuni he had taken full advantage of the more extensive facilities on offer. It meant he did not have the faculties to delve into Popeye's metaphysical ideas, and it also meant he did not think to ask how his retirement would go down in Medellín; instead, he peered over his glass, shrugged and accepted Popeye's explanation.

'*Salud, hermano*,' he replied, and took a long drink. 'Merit it is then. Join me in a toast before I finish this one off.'

Popeye shook his head, but Martín waved for a shot of *aguardiente*. Once it arrived, he nodded at the glass, and Popeye decided to humour him.

'Here's to your future merit, and here's to my future wealth.' The toast was made and Popeye took a sip of the fiery liquid.

Five beers later, the evening drew to a close. Popeye wanted to be up early and get as much information as he could about the Island of the Fish; Martín was ready to stagger up the stairs and collapse in a drunken stupor. Fortunately, there were rooms above the bar, and the landlord showed them upstairs with a promise of breakfast and a strong coffee in the morning.

The following morning Popeye bought a shovel and a hunting knife from a shop next door and found somewhere selling a local map and a compass. Martín was fast asleep when he took the money from his wallet, and he did not bother to wake him. Whilst he would have preferred a gun to a knife, the blade would have to do, and the shovel could always double as a secondary weapon if necessary.

When he returned, Martín was drinking coffee.

'Sore head?'

'No, sore wallet,' Martín replied, shaking it at Popeye.

Popeye shrugged and held up the shovel, map and compass. 'I could have woken you . . .?'

He sat down and poured himself a cup. The red beanie stayed on. It was now an essential item of clothing, and without it his head froze. In fact, it only warmed up when the midday sun appeared, and he was beginning to regret scalping it quite so severely. He was unfolding the map when some toast and scrambled eggs arrived.

The map caught the attention of the old man serving them, and he asked if they were tourists. Popeye knew he would have to engage in conversation.

'Yes, on our way to Calama and Chilean beaches.'

'You got a permit?'

'What for?'

'Crossing the border,' the man replied. 'ID and vehicle documents need to be certified in a police station. You won't get through without it. There's a national search for a dangerous criminal, and each person and every vehicle needs a permit number.' The man turned to Martín in an attempt to bring him into the conversation, but Martín was stirring a small whirlpool of powdered milk around his coffee and was not in the least bit interested. 'It's pointless,' he added, returning to Popeye. 'If he's got any sense he'll have disappeared into the lowlands and is on his way to Paraguay.'

Popeye pulled down his beanie and lowered his head as though studying the map.

'Well, if we need to sort out a permit, we'll be staying a bit longer. What's worth seeing around here?' he asked, avoiding eye contact.

'There's the cemetery.'

'The cemetery?'

'The train cemetery. Most people wander around it then visit the *salar*. It's a graveyard of rusting steam trains—' Popeye cut him off.

'No. I hate trains. What about the *salar*?'

The man leant over and waved his finger over the large white blob that covered the map.

'Take your choice, there's enough of it. Nothing for miles other than Colchani on its very edge. Most people visit Colchani to see the salt being mined.'

Popeye decided to end the conversation before the man grew more inquisitive. Thanking him for his help, he picked up a fork and was about to tuck into the scrambled eggs when the man shouted over from the bar:

'You can get a permit from the local police station.'

Popeye looked up.

'What! To visit the lake?'

'No, to cross the border. Oh, I forgot . . .' Popeye sighed; the man was now on his way back. 'There's a weird hippy camped out on the Island of the Fish,' he said, and pointed to a small dot on the map. 'It's a long way out, but you might think about visiting him.'

Popeye's ears pricked up.

'Why?'

'He's like John the Baptist, preaching in the wilderness. I haven't met him myself, but he likes visitors and relies on handouts. And don't bother bringing any dried llama if you visit, he's a vegetable man.'

'A what?'

'A vegetable man. Doesn't eat meat. Dangerous. Means he's got bad eyesight and wears dark glasses. Also, his skin burns easily.'

Martín stopped stirring his coffee.

'Don't tell me he's an American. Goes by the name Sol?'

The man paused for a moment, then nodded.

'That's him. Harmless, but letting vegetables destroy his body.'

Martín took a sip of his coffee.

'I've heard about this guy,' he said to Popeye. 'He spent some time with the *cocaleros*. He's a gringo hippy. Everyone liked him in Cochabamba and Evo Morales took him under his wing. One day he just left, saying he needed time to meditate and was heading for a desert. It must be the same guy.'

CHAPTER THIRTY-NINE

The Salar de Uyuni is neither a well-known lake nor a hospitable one. It stretches across the *altiplano* with a thick salt crust that sparkles up close and shimmers in the distance, and its pancake-flat surface spreads out in hexagonal-shaped deposits that seem to lock together and bury anything trying to break through its impenetrable surface.

Popeye and Martín drove onto it with a cheap compass and a second-hand map.

It felt like the ideal place for a person to disappear and for the sun to bleach their bones. Popeye did not intend staying there any longer than necessary, and he was gripping the wheel tightly; meanwhile, Martín was holding the compass and looking at a map that told him nothing much at all. There were no distinguishing features to guide them to the Island of the Fish, and only the slow descent of the sun indicated they were heading west, towards the rocky outcrop. The car was stocked with water, quinoa, bananas and potatoes for the gringo, and chocolate, bread, cheese and ham for them. They had not managed to find any sleeping bags and would have to make do with some thick blankets for the cold evenings. At the last minute, Martín had also decided to have another conversation with his wife, 'to bring her round'. It did not work, and Popeye wondered what it was that was pulling him home. It had to be the kids, as she did not sound like the sort of woman he would be rushing home to see.

Their destination was due west of Colchani. Anything more complex and they would never find it. Popeye had visions of driving straight past, and he kept checking that Martín had the compass needle pointing due west. He was also nervous of running out of petrol, and they had filled a jerry can in Colchani to be on the safe side even though the fuel dial was showing full. Other than a large black Land Cruiser parked on the station forecourt, there was no sign of life in the small settlement, and the possibility of someone venturing onto the *salar* and stumbling across them if they got stuck was remote.

They drove straight, unswervingly, due west. No testing of the Beetle's handling on the salt crust. No attempt to raise Martín's spirits. They were a small white dot on a huge white plain, perfectly camouflaged other than the sun reflecting off their windscreen. Popeye was timing their journey. They should cover sixty kilometres in two hours and twenty-eight minutes, and the island would be directly in front of them. He had allowed for a ten-minute contingency either side – if they travelled any longer without finding it, they had gone wrong.

Around the two-hour mark, a thin brown line appeared on the horizon and Popeye's concerns disappeared. What started as a blot on the sparkling landscape soon turned into a strip of land, and by the time they got closer, it had grown into an extensive island covered in large boulders and brightly flowering cacti. Salt plates surrounded the island and it had a rocky coastline; otherwise, there was nothing to suggest any connection with fish. It rose gently to a small peak in its very centre, and a man in a bright red coat was standing there, next to a particularly tall cactus. He stood watching them approach, then turned round and disappeared behind it.

CHAPTER FORTY

Popeye stopped at the edge of the island and they got out. The salt under his feet crunched slightly and he bent down to take a closer look. It was rock solid with a razor-sharp joint that gave the salt plain its distinctive appearance. It was hard to believe anything could survive out there, and the cacti gave the place an oasis-like quality. Up close, the island was much larger than Popeye had imagined, and he wondered where the man had gone, or if he was hiding from them. Without his Beretta, he decided to drive around the island and find *him* before he found *them*. Whilst he was not expecting any trouble, there was no harm being cautious, and he told Martín to jump back in.

They drove round the island in an anti-clockwise direction, and Martín kept a close eye out for the gringo. Eventually a large tent appeared on the opposite side, and the man in the red jacket was sitting there, watching a pot of coffee coming to the boil as the sun cast his shadow over the rocks behind him. Popeye got out and Martín followed. The man looked up and waved a mug.

'Would you like some coffee?'

Popeye walked over and introduced himself. The guy had quite a set-up. Two deckchairs were waiting for them around a small table, and a large canopy had been rigged up for shade. Another canopy was stretched over a row of boxes and some water containers were neatly stacked beside his tent.

'We've brought you some food and water,' Popeye said, wondering if there was room for more supplies.

'That's good of you. Hi, I'm Sol, welcome to my home. Grab a seat in the shade and I'll bring the coffee over.'

Martín joined him and Sol arrived with the drinks.

'So, what brings you here?' he asked, opening some powdered milk.

'The cacti,' Popeye replied.

The whole island was covered in them. At its peak stood a magnificent one with two huge arms and a crown of tall spikes. It towered over the shorter ones dotted around the island and made them appear perfectly ordinary.

'The one at the top's impressive,' he added, twisting round.

Sol reached for a spoon and did not bother looking up.

'That's Old Man Time. Apparently he's two hundred years old. I stood up there and watched you approach. Ten metres high. He's like a sundial. His shadow was just touching the *salar*, so I knew it was mid-afternoon. In the morning he reaches over there, around eleven o'clock.' He pointed to a small outcrop of rocks on the edge of the island. 'They reckon he holds two hundred gallons of water after a downpour. He's sacred, which is why no one touches him.' He turned to the men. 'I guess you're staying the night?' he asked.

'Yes, in the car,' Popeye replied.

'I can fit one of you in my tent,' Sol said, looking up with a smile. 'You choose.'

Two cups of coffee later, Popeye nodded at Martín to keep Sol occupied and returned to the car. It took him ten minutes to climb to the top of the island and another five to finish taking in the stunning view. After that he set to work with his spade. Old Man Time had to be the man with prickly skin in the riddle, and his shadow would fall anywhere on an east–west axis. The sun would reach his crown by midday and fall to the other side in the afternoon. All he had to do was dig along the axis and he would find the emeralds.

Although the compass was still in the car, the shadow of Old Man Time pointed towards their tyre tracks, and he knew they had come from the east. The shadow marked out a rough strip where his search should begin: east this afternoon and west in the morning. Half an hour later, the first section of topsoil was removed and he was ready to dig. It was tough work and he regretted buying only one spade. On his own it could take several days, not the few hours he'd imagined. Then he got lucky. He hit a patch of softer earth, his spade clanked on something, and he fell to his knees and began scooping away the soil.

His nails ran across a smooth surface, and when he brushed away the dirt, he was looking down at a thick metal plate. He grabbed his shovel, scraped away the soil and lifted one of its edges. Soon it was in his hands, and he was staring at a plastic pipe buried in the ground. He tried to control his excitement. The pipe had a groove cut across its top and a small metal bar was lodged in it with a rope attached. Something had to be on its end. Popeye prayed that he was not about to be the butt of another practical joke and slowly lifted the bar and pulled up the rope.

And there it was – a slender metal tube about the length of a man's forearm. The words 'Property of Muzo Mining Company, Boyacá' were stamped on it in bold red letters, and Popeye knew he had found the emeralds. It was no practical joke, and a rattle of the container told him he had three million dollars in his hands.

He stood up and had to stop himself from shouting with joy. He had reached the end of his journey. One door had closed and another was about to open. He did not know where it would take him, but wherever it was, it would be far away from cocaine and assassinations, and as he stared at the salt plain, he felt an overwhelming sense of relief.

He knew he needed to cover his tracks, and putting the emeralds to one side he used his shovel to break off the arm of a small cactus. It slid down the pipe with a little help from the shovel, and he replaced the metal plate. It seemed a shame for Ramón or some other *hijo de puta* to find the hiding place empty, and the cactus would provide a painful memory to add to the one of deep disappointment. The soil and rocks were soon back in place, and he was strolling down with a spade over one shoulder and the cylinder gripped in his other hand.

He stopped for a brief moment before reaching the bottom. The temptation to hold some of the emeralds was too great, and he twisted the lid of the canister. It would not budge. He tried again with it clamped between his knees. No luck. When he looked closely, he realised the lid was soldered and impossible to twist open. Breaking it apart with the shovel would only risk damaging the emeralds, so with a degree of reluctance, he accepted he would have to wait until he found a hacksaw in Uyuni.

Popeye took a slight detour and approached the car from the other side of Sol's tent. The men were still deep in conversation as he put the emeralds safely in the boot, and when he walked back towards them, it was with a smile that was difficult to hide.

CHAPTER FORTY-ONE

The sun was sinking into the salt lake to the sound of sizzling pork. The temperature was now falling quickly, and Sol had lit a small charcoal brazier. As it glowed next to the gas stove, the sky was turning dark blue and the stars were beginning to sparkle.

Martín had spotted Popeye putting something into the boot and guessed his relaxed demeanour was more than just having visited Old Man Time. He had waited until Sol had disappeared into his tent before pressing his partner. Popeye had given nothing away, other than to confirm that he had dug along the east axis and was relieved that part of the search was now over. Martín was having none of it, and he had gone over to the car to check his suspicions. Soon the emerald canister was in his hand, and he was back with Popeye and slapping him on the back. Martín then spent several minutes trying to persuade Popeye to drive them back to Uyuni before nightfall, but Popeye refused.

Sitting facing the brazier, Popeye knew it would have been madness to attempt the journey. Once the stars were out, darkness had fallen with lightning speed and an inky-black curtain had covered the lake. It would have been crazy to drive across it with only the headlights of a twenty-year-old car as a guide. The sizzling meat also reminded him that his decision to intervene with a packet of dried herbs had been a good one. Had he not stepped in, they would have been eating flavourless cubes of meat, not seasoned strips of pork, and he turned with a smile to the man who was in charge of the frying pan.

'You could have just said that you don't like llama,' he said. 'Vegetarians aren't trusted in Bolivia.'

'I know. I've tried and it hasn't worked. People keep showing up with dried llama.'

Popeye empathised, although Martín was not convinced by the excuse.

'And I know you Colombians are suckers for fried pork,' the gringo added, 'otherwise it would have been lentil and potato stew for you.'

Popeye knew he was going to get on with the gringo.

'Mind you,' Sol added, 'I also thought Colombians had a sense of style? I've got to say, dude, those teal-green bottoms and that Bart Simpson sweatshirt aren't doing it for me.'

Popeye laughed. If the gringo had any idea who he was making fun of he might have behaved differently. It was rare to be with people who behaved naturally in his company, and he was warming to him.

When they finished eating, Sol produced a bottle of *aguardiente*, and Popeye was surprised to see Martín refuse a glass. Some excuse about all the *chicha* he had been drinking and a sore stomach . . . It meant Popeye was forced to join the gringo, otherwise it would have been rude. Then Martín said he needed an early night and took himself off to Sol's tent.

Popeye was astonished.

It was the perfect time to celebrate, yet Martín had chosen to have an early night? However, the first bite of alcohol pushed the thought from his head, and by the second one he was ready to spend an evening chatting to someone who was a local attraction. He was curious to find out why people drove two and a half hours to visit him – was it because he had something to say, or was it really to admire Old Man Time?

'How long have you been out here?' he asked.

'What, on the island, or Bolivia?'

'The island.'

'Just over two months.'

'And you're on your own, apart from the people who visit?'

Sol nodded. 'Well,' he said, laughing, 'I get regular visits from the police.' Popeye raised his eyebrows. 'They drive over once a week to "check I'm okay" . . . The real reason is they're worried I'll eat Old Man Time. You know, if I run out of food! That's fine. We have a coffee and a chat. I guess it gives them something to do. They usually bring over some vegetables and water, which is cool.'

'And what *do* you do?'

'I meditate.'

'And preach?'

'What?'

'I heard you preach to visitors.'

'Listen, dude. Whoever you've been talking to is seriously confused.' Popeye was about to mention the bartender and his views on vegetables, but Sol had carried on before he had a chance to do so. 'All I do is share a coffee and sometimes an *aguardiente* with visitors. Occasionally we talk about life and the bigger picture. That's not preaching, dude, it's being sociable.' He turned to Popeye. 'And what about you?'

'What about me?'

'What do *you* do?' He repeated Popeye's question with a smile.

'I'm between jobs,' Popeye answered calmly. 'Seeing where things take me right now.'

'And where do you want them to take you?'

Popeye hesitated, and it gave Sol the opportunity to disappear for some provisions. When he returned, he was holding two small bottles and a large joint.

'Here, take this. It's apple juice. Soothes the throat.' He lit the joint and passed it to Popeye.

'I don't smoke.'

'Dude, everyone who spends the evening here smokes. It's not optional.' He pushed the joint towards him. Popeye shook his head, yet took it reluctantly. If the gringo knew the real identity of the man he was hustling, he would be far less pushy. He almost felt like telling him to see his shock – it was only the thought of a police visit and the added risk of being caught that stopped him. He took a tiny drag, reached for his apple juice and passed over the joint, trying not to cough.

'So, where are you going?' Sol asked.

'Back to Uyuni. Tomorrow morning,' Popeye replied.

'Very funny,' Sol said, laughing. 'If you find the question scary, then try this one. What's the purpose in your life? Once you know the purpose, the path you need to follow is much clearer.'

Popeye sat back and felt his arms tingle and his chest swell slightly. It was like nothing he had ever experienced. It also came with an odd sensation of being connected in some strange way with the stars glistening overhead. He took a small sip of his apple juice and waved for the joint. This time its end glowed red as he took a proper drag.

'Redemption,' he answered. 'Redemption for the harm I've done without realising it.'

Sol was silent, and Popeye felt he had bared his soul and confessed his sins, except it wasn't to a priest but to the entire universe. He took another drag and passed the joint back.

'We're all on that path, dude,' Sol eventually replied. 'It's called universal guilt. A sort of Adam and Eve thing.'

Popeye knew Sol did not know the enormity of what he had done, and how could he?

'I've tried to educate and feed the poor, though it turns out I caused more harm along the way than good,' Popeye continued. 'Now I'm trying to figure out how to make amends. So I know my purpose. It's the path that isn't clear.'

He shrugged. The gringo could no more imagine his experience than he could imagine the experience of a wild animal. The brazier was glowing red hot and the temperature was plummeting. He decided to end the conversation and sit back and enjoy the sensation of being in the middle of somewhere that was timeless. Pulling a blanket around his shoulders, he did just that, and reached out for the joint. However, Sol was busy with it. Popeye watched him inhale deeply then blow a stream of smoke across the brazier before turning to face him.

'The most violent element in society is ignorance, dude. Whatever harm you think you've done, educating people goes a long, long way to remedying it. People can't unlearn what they've been taught, and a lot of what they've been told to believe has its foundations in hatred.' The joint stayed firmly in Sol's hand and he took another drag. 'No one is born bad. They're taught to hate. It's learned behaviour. If you're teaching people to think for themselves, to question the ideals and values promoted by the active, self-interested group in society, then you're already on the path, dude.'

Then he passed the joint over to Popeye. 'You'll find redemption on that path,' he said, and took a sip of apple juice. 'Ignorance breeds hatred, education brings freedom. The freedom to think clearly, not blindly accept rhetoric. The ability to recognise that we're all different, to accept those differences and live in harmony. It's not the differences that divide us, dude, it's hatred that prevents us from accepting and celebrating those differences.'

Popeye turned to Sol and offered his hand.

'The name's Jhon Velásquez, güevón. Not "dude".'

CHAPTER FORTY-TWO

Popeye woke with a splitting headache. He had made the mistake of parking the car facing due east and it felt like the rising sun had burned a hole straight through his forehead. Then, as though the decisions taken the previous day were all coming home to roost at the same time, something deeply unpleasant started rising up his throat. He grabbed the door handle and yanked hard. Nothing happened. In a mild panic he lurched for the window handle. His hand whirled round. He started to retch as a pane of glass shuddered down. A dribble of liquid splashed down the door and a jet of semi-digested pork shot across the salt crust.

Popeye sat back and moaned. He had managed to recline the seat in order to sleep, and as he stared up at the nicotine-stained ceiling, he regretted having taken up smoking and drinking. It was too late though, as were his reactions. He did not see Martín approach, and the tip of a blade pressed into his throat before he had time to move.

'Don't say anything, *hermano*, and things will turn out fine. Both hands on the steering wheel.'

Popeye sat up and did as he was told. A length of rope with a hoop was thrown onto his lap.

'Tie it around your left wrist, slowly – no sudden movements.'

Popeye picked up the rope.

'Okay, pull the knot tight . . . now back on the wheel. Tie your hand to the bit in the middle. Okay, stretch out your other hand.'

Martín kept the knife at Popeye's throat and slung a new rope over his other wrist. This was also tied like a lasso, and he tightened it with a sharp tug.

'Okay, hand on the wheel.'

Martín passed the rope through the steering wheel and removed the knife to finish tying it. Popeye jerked forward and headbutted him, but it was not enough to stop his hand from being fastened tight. He braced himself for a blow in retaliation, but Martín had stepped back and was fiddling with something on the door handle. Popeye realised he must have run a rope underneath the car and tied the driver and passenger doors together. The driver's door opened and Popeye saw a length of mountaineering rope on the ground.

'This can go one of two ways, *hermano*. Either you can try and headbutt me again and I can beat you senseless, *or* you can chill and neither of us are in pain. Whichever one it is, you're still going to end up tied to the seat.'

Popeye nodded, his seat sprang upright and his torso was quickly strapped to it. Popeye looked across at the tent and Martín shrugged.

'I know. It would be good if our gringo friend came to the rescue. Right now he's sleeping off the chloroform and sleeping draught I gave him. I've had them ever since we left Cochabamba. That was Don Ramón's original plan for you, a bullet when you were asleep; then it switched to a more dramatic death. It changed again once you cracked the riddle, and when you lost your Beretta you became a treasure hunter, although Pala was determined to finish you off in the mine and Don Ramón let him have a go.' Popeye looked at him in bewilderment. 'I'm sorry, *hermano*. I like you. I didn't want it to come to this. Remember, I kept trying to get you to turn back? I even tried getting you off the *salar* last night . . .'

Popeye said nothing and let Martín speak. He seemed to want to unburden himself. Pulling over a deckchair, he sat down outside the car.

'You've been set up, *hermano*. Your boss is playing a double game. It was Piña who gave Don Ramón the details of your flight out of Colombia; it didn't take much to get the information from Pala, he was always slow-witted. He also said Piña and Don Ramón are going into business. I guess Piña knew the attempt on your life

THE MAN WITH THE SILVER BERETTA

would fail, but maybe he wanted to gain Don Ramón's loyalty by providing the information?'

'And what about you, *cabrón*?' Popeye asked.

'What about me?'

'Why are you doing it? You had a new future with your family. Why lose that?'

'What family?'

Popeye looked him in the eye, stunned by what he had just been told. The *hijo de puta* never had that precious family he was always talking about. It must have been clear what Popeye was thinking, for Martín quickly broke the silence.

'No, no . . . I've got a wife and children, *hermano*,' he said, shrugging again. 'The thing is, I also have a brother-in-law who betrayed them for a few hundred dollars. If I hadn't helped, there would *be* no future.' He looked down at his feet. 'They're locked up in Guanay, *hermano*,' he mumbled. 'My wife and kids. I got the call when I was in Cochabamba.' He looked straight at Popeye. 'You know the meeting when I arrived late, after the massacre in Villa Turani address . . . – well, that was when I was given the choice: either help Don Ramón or lose them.'

'So, all those calls weren't to your wife, but some *malparido* working for Ramón?'

'No. Some of them were, but most of them ended with the phone being snatched away and a threat being made.'

'And what now?'

'We wait for another two hours.'

'What happens then?'

'Don Ramón arrives from Colchani. We leave with the emeralds. The gringo wakes up in a few hours and then you escape.'

'I won't be *escaping* anywhere, *cabrón*. I'll be coming after you.'

'No, you won't. You'll be escaping if you've got any sense. When Don Ramón reaches Colchani he'll be calling the police. The "anonymous caller with a Colombian accent" will tell them a dangerous fugitive is hiding out on the Island of the Fish, and he'll give a detailed description . . . you know, teal-green tracksuit bottoms, Bart Simpson—'

'Yes, I get it,' Popeye said. 'Using the police to cover his tracks . . .' He shook his head. 'And you trust someone who works with the police and betrays his own cousin?'

Martín shrugged.

'I don't have a choice, *hermano*, and nor do you. Don Ramón has promised he won't kill you, and I believe him. He's got no reason to. All he wants are the emeralds. If you keep heading due west, you won't be caught. There's a small crossing into Chile about a hundred kilometres away. You've got plenty of water and petrol to reach it. You can bribe your way across and be safe before nightfall. I was given some dollars as a contingency, and I'll leave them with you.'

'Why did you bother to save me back in Potosí, *cabrón*?'

'The emeralds, *hermano*. Plus, you're a friend.'

CHAPTER FORTY-THREE

A black Land Cruiser crunched over the *salar* and stopped by the tent. It was the same one that Popeye had seen in Colchani. It remained for a few minutes with its engine running and its exhaust destroying the ambience of the camp before its engine cut out, the driver's door opened and a large man eased himself onto the running board. It was unmistakably Ramón. He climbed down and turned round.

'You must be Martín,' he said, walking over. Martín went to introduce himself and Ramón brushed past the hand he was offered. 'Nice to put a face to a name,' he said over his shoulder, and carried on to the Beetle. He leant through its window, and Popeye received a warm smile and a pat on his cheek.

'*Cabrón*, how are you? It's been a while. Come on, let's see your new hairstyle,' he joked, whipping off the red beanie and throwing it in the back seat. 'Nice!' he said, laughing, and ran his finger down a long scar. 'Not your best look, *muchacho*. But no, seriously, I haven't come to admire your cunning disguise.'

Popeye stared back at the young guy, who had changed little from the annoying, overconfident *hijo de puta* who had joined the cartel three years earlier. If he had not been strapped in, he would have caught Ramón's hand and crushed his fingers before it reached the beanie. Instead, he returned the smile.

'Nice to put a face to a name,' he repeated calmly. 'I don't remember you, but you're El Patrón's cousin, right? Piña told me I couldn't miss you – the fat man with an annoying laugh who sweats like a pig.' Ramón stepped back and Popeye looked him up and down. 'Just how much *do* you weigh, *cabrón?*'

Ramón waved a finger and shook his head.

'If you think by insulting me you'll improve your situation,' he replied, laughing, 'you seriously underestimate me. No, you're staying tied up. Maybe not in the Beetle and definitely not upright, but you aren't going anywhere.' Then he roared with laughter. '*Puta*, forget that. You're going to Colchani – I'm not sure why I said that.' He waved across to Martín. '*Hermano*, fetch me a seat. Your friend and I have some catching up to do.'

Martín had the good sense not to offer one of the deckchairs. He managed to find a large cooler box, and Ramón lowered himself onto it.

'First off, I want to thank you for finding the emeralds for me. Pala was useless. All we had to go on was a photo album and some hunches he had from working with Ernesto. Without you, we'd still be scratching around this godforsaken place.'

Popeye said nothing.

'Secondly, I want you to know that you've been played. Piña is working for me. My cousin sent you to kill me and Piña made sure that wasn't going to happen. I've known your every move, and once you attached yourself to Martín – oh, and thank you for selecting him, I wasn't sure if you'd stick to your plan after Peru – it was easy to lead you around the *altiplano*. I was hedging my bets. I gave you time to solve the riddle and at the same time had a bit of fun, to see if you would survive . . . and you did! If you weren't such a *hijo de puta* I'd have you work for me.'

Ramón waited for a response, but Popeye stayed silent. He was thinking through the accusation that Piña had betrayed him. It would explain how Ramón had been tracking his movements. Yet, if Piña wanted to set up on his own and replace El Patrón, he certainly did not need Ramón to do it. He needed someone who could remove Pablo Escobar and provide protection. Ramón offered neither of these. That only came from the government and the DEA, not a fat *cabrón* with coca paste, and Popeye realised that Ramón was not in the position of strength he thought he was in.

'If you kill me you'll burn your bridges with Piña. You don't want him as an enemy. He hasn't sanctioned my death, otherwise I wouldn't have made it this far.' Popeye was guessing, and the change in Ramón's demeanour told him he had guessed correctly.

'I run Bolivia, not Piña, *hijo de puta*. I don't need anyone's approval to protect my territory,' he snapped. 'You'll be collateral damage recovering the emeralds.'

Up until now Martín had been keeping a safe distance. He had moved his deckchair away to respect Don Ramón's privacy, yet he could still hear the conversation. The mention of Popeye being killed made him jump up.

'Don Ramón, I'm sorry to interrupt. I've got what we agreed.' He walked over with the canister of emeralds. 'We should leave now, there's no reason to delay.'

'What!' Ramón shouted, snatching them from him. 'What do I have to do for respect around here?' He pointed at the Beetle's passenger door. 'Get that rope off. If you don't want to hang around, fine, let's leave.'

Martín stood staring.

'Er . . . what do we need it for?'

'*Chucha madre.* Don't "er" me – just get the rope.'

Ramón turned back to Popeye.

'*Puta*, your friend's impatient. And I thought we were having such a nice chat. We can continue it in Colchani, although you won't have any ears. In fact, there won't be much of you left.' He waved at the Land Cruiser. 'You're going to join me in the back . . . well, I'll be in the car and you'll be attached to the tow-bar. I'm interested to see how long you'll last. That salt looks as sharp as a billion razors. Two and a bit hours being dragged across it will be painful . . .'

Popeye looked at Martín and saw he was uncomfortable. Their eyes met and he knew he had an ally. They could easily overpower the *hijo de puta* if they chose their moment.

Ramón then told Martín to get Popeye out of the car, and Popeye made it easy for him. The rope that bound him to the seat was untied and fastened around his upper arms and chest, and the ropes around the steering wheel were cut. Popeye was led over to the Land Cruiser and nothing was said. The men knew this was their chance.

Martín swung round and ran at Ramón. He was still sitting on the cooler box and made no attempt to move. Then his Colt. 45 blew off Martín's face.

CHAPTER FORTY-FOUR

Popeye just stared.

'What?' Ramón asked, shrugging. 'You expected me to show up without a gun?'

He pushed himself up with an effort and waved his Colt. 45.

'Over to the car, *cabrón*,' he said, and gestured at the Land Cruiser. 'That's it, now lie down by the bumper.' Ramón untied the rope from the Beetle and followed him over. 'Hands together, like you're praying.' Popeye did as he was told. 'That's it,' he said, and tied Popeye's wrists together. 'Now, lie back. Any kicking and you'll get a bullet in the ankle.'

Ramón opened the boot and pulled out another length of rope.

Popeye lifted his head and noticed a small silver cylinder above the tow-bar. It was a winch with a large hook dangling from its end.

Ramón laughed when he caught Popeye staring. 'Did you expect me to drag you around and not enjoy the show?'

He beckoned at Popeye to lift his legs. 'I can play you out on the winch and then pull you back – that's right, feet together – and watch in the rear-view. I'm going to try out some cornering – okay, feet down – and see if I can get you to roll. We'll have to see how it goes.'

Ramón clipped the hook to the rope around Popeye's ankles.

'You know, we could have made a good team, *cabrón*. Pala was pretty useless, even though he was gradually improving, whereas you're the finished article.'

'And Martín?' Popeye asked.

'What about him?'

'You shot him in the face.'

'Oh . . . I thought you were asking if he was improving? He was stubborn and took some persuading, as it happens. Having his wife on the end of the phone helped,' he said, laughing. 'Come on, don't say "shot him in the face" like it's something you've never done! I heard what you did up at Cerro Rico – that was some weird shit.'

Popeye said nothing and closed his eyes. If his end *was* coming, then he would have to rely on noble intentions to save his soul. The opportunity to use the emeralds for a good cause was gone. The charitable foundation he was going to set up was not going to happen, and the Colombian poor would continue to lack basic education.

When he opened his eyes, it was as though his prayers had been answered all at once.

A set of black tyres was fast approaching. He could see them underneath the Land Cruiser, although the rest of the vehicle remained hidden. It swung to the side and Popeye saw another set following. Both vehicles disappeared, and his eye caught something sparkling. It came from the small rocky outcrop on the edge of the island, the very same one that Sol had mentioned. It must have been eleven o'clock, since the shadow of Old Man Time was creeping over it. Then there was the crunch of tyres, and when Popeye rolled on his side he saw a white jeep draw up with 'Policía' on its door. The sun was reflecting off its windscreen and its windows were blacked out, making it impossible to see who was inside. It remained with its engine running.

Ramón took the initiative.

'Officers,' he shouted. 'You've arrived just in time. I've caught the dangerous criminal Jhon Velásquez. That *hijo de puta* was hiding out here all along.' Popeye guessed Ramón was pointing at him, and when he walked towards the car, he saw him tuck his Colt .45 out of view.

There was no movement in the car. Then the second vehicle arrived. This one was a flatbed pickup with a large bamboo pole strung across a metal scaffold, yet it was not the scaffold that drew

Popeye's attention – it was the man leaning on it with a rifle pointed at Ramón.

'Officers, *please*! Come and help me with this dangerous criminal. I know he's tied up, but I don't trust him.'

Popeye could hear the frustration growing in Ramón's voice, and he kept his eye on the man with the rifle. He was a gringo, there was no doubt about it. His complexion gave him away: a reddish sunburn on chalky white skin, the sort of roast-meat look that he recognised from the tourists in Medellín. He was wearing fatigues and the rifle was a hunting weapon, not a military firearm. He looked more like a big-game hunter than a police officer, and his sights were firmly trained on Ramón.

'Listen, *muchachos*,' Ramón said as he changed direction and walked towards the pickup. 'You can put that rifle down. There are no firearms here, I can—'

There was a small recoil and it stopped him in his tracks. Popeye expected Ramón to carry on walking, yet he stood rooted to the spot as though confused. Then he looked down and yanked something out of his leg. There was another recoil and he spun round. This time his body crashed to the ground, and Popeye saw a dart with a red flight in his shoulder and another gripped in his hand.

CHAPTER FORTY-FIVE

Popeye lay there and realised the joint, along with the alcohol, had scrambled his brain. What he had seen was just too good to be true. He shut his eyes and tried to break the dream. It was another trick of Luis Galán, another twist of the knife before he was dragged on his back down the highway to hell.

When he opened his eyes, Ramón was still on the ground and the gringo was bending over him. Once he had recovered the Colt. 45, he strode across to Popeye. He was still waiting for the twist, something that would turn the dream into a nightmare, but it never came. Instead, the man cut the rope from his torso and the bindings from his wrists.

Popeye sat up and untied his ankles. He rubbed them a bit before standing up gingerly, and when he looked around, the man had disappeared. Both deckchairs were back by the gas stove and it was now lit. The man had not even bothered checking if Popeye had a gun. It was as though he had expected to find him at the mercy of Ramón. The first police car turned off its engine and Popeye waited for someone to appear. Instead, the man emerged from the provisions tent with a coffee pot in one hand and two cups in the other. He seemed to be preparing the camp for an important visitor.

Popeye went to check on Ramón. He was lying motionless with a dart in his shoulder and another gripped in his hand. Popeye bent down and pressed the back of his hand against Ramón's neck to check whether he was alive or not. Then he jumped back. Ramón blinked and stared at him. He was very much alive.

'*Puta!*' Popeye swore. He had thought Ramón was most likely tranquilised . . . not paralysed.

'Motherfucker,' he shouted. 'You were going to drag me across the *salar*. A fellow Colombian . . .' It was still hard to believe that he had avoided an excruciating death. It was even harder to believe that someone from the cartel was prepared to drag him across a salt lake, to tear the flesh from his body and reduce him to a strip of meat. 'Even if I had my Beretta, *hijo de puta*, I wouldn't spare you a bullet. I don't know who these guys are, but they don't seem to like you.' He stood up. Ramón stared back and said nothing. There was a burning look in his eyes, and Popeye knew he could hear but not speak.

The doors of the pickup opened and two men got out. One of them climbed into the back and passed down the bamboo pole, and the other one carried it over to Ramón. Popeye stood back. Neither of them were local policemen; their skin gave them away, the same reddish-pink complexion as the first man. It was a gringo SWAT team led by the man with the tranquiliser gun, probably the same team that had rescued him in Peru.

A sharp whistle made Popeye turn around. He was being waved over to the camp, and it was clear that he was being invited to sit down by the gas stove. With his head pounding and his body aching, Popeye did not need any encouragement. He could hear the coffee spluttering and its aroma was drifting over. It was probably the only thing he would miss on the *altiplano*: a lower boiling point for water and a quicker coffee.

He sat down and watched the men roll Ramón onto his back then tie his legs and hands together and pass a pole between them. When they attempted to lift him, Ramón's shirt ripped and a large roll of fat spilled out of the tear. Another big effort and he was in the air, arms and legs taut and part of his belly drooping over his trousers. Strung on the bamboo pole like a huge prize, he was a big-game trophy being hauled back to the clubhouse, except this trophy was very much alive and the exact nature of the clubhouse was a complete unknown.

Popeye glanced at the broken body of his friend and felt no sympathy for Ramón. The men eventually slotted the bamboo pole onto the scaffold and Ramón hung there, trussed up with his head twisted slightly and his back sagging. He was totally at the mercy of the gringos, and it felt appropriate. Popeye poured himself a coffee and watched them bind Ramón's elbows and knees. A ratchet strap was passed between them, and one of the men cranked it up. It must have been agony, but Ramón did not make a sound.

Then someone got out of the first car and walked over.

CHAPTER FORTY-SIX

H is blond hair was thinning on top, and he walked with a slight limp. As he got closer, he held out his hand.

'Señor Velásquez, it's a pleasure to meet you again.'

Popeye recognised the voice, but it took a moment to place it. Then he remembered the same voice coming from the other side of the confessional grill. The memory of the mousetrap came back to him, and he wondered what else the fake priest had up his sleeve. Popeye got up from his deckchair and shook his hand anyway.

'Thank you,' he replied. 'That *hijo de puta* was about to drag me across the *salar*.'

The man chuckled.

'We had your back covered, *amigo*,' he replied, 'although it might not have felt that way.'

'And Martín?'

The man looked across at his crumpled body and grimaced.

'Joe, sling something over that guy, will you?' he shouted, and turned back to Popeye. 'Sit down. We've got some catching up to do.'

Popeye waited for him to pour his coffee.

'There's something I've got to ask you,' he said, taking a sip.

'Okay.'

'It might sound personal.'

'That's fine.'

'And don't take offence.'

'Go on . . .'

246

'Is Bart Simpson *actually* your favourite character, or do you prefer Homer? I mean, that sweatshirt suggests Bart, but you never know . . .'

Popeye sat back and laughed.

'You're a *hijo de puta* with a sick sense of humour, *cabrón*. There's something I've got to ask you. I know you're DEA, but where else do you perform? The confessional, that *puta* Joker outfit, the 'BANG' flag . . . you should be touring the stages of Colombia, not running around trying to catch *bandidos*.'

The man leant over, and with a magician's flick of the wrist, a playing card appeared between his fingers.

'Think of me as your guardian angel, not a comedian . . . someone with your best interests at heart.'

Popeye took the card and noticed it had the same angel rising from hell and an illustration of a pig being roasted on a spit. The reference to Ramón was all too clear.

'That's right. His card's marked,' he said, without irony. 'Your fellow Colombian tortured two of our agents and killed one of them. We'll be administering our own retribution in due course.' He leant back and chuckled. 'I don't want to spoil the surprise, and perhaps I'm speaking out of turn, but I've got to tell you, there's also a card for your boss. This time next year he'll be six feet underground. We've decided not to bother with extradition, it's just too much hassle.'

Popeye started to defend him, and the gringo raised a hand.

'No point trying to convince me. It's beyond my pay grade. Right now our focus is to restore the status quo. After that we'll reorganise the Medellín cartel. We've chosen someone to run it who's a little more amenable. You know him quite well . . .'

Piña was the obvious candidate. He seemed to be at the centre of the whole thing. The gringo read his mind.

'That's right, Piña. He's been working with us, helping us track down Ramón and Ernesto. We also had Ernesto on board as an insurance policy. He kept us up to speed on Ramón's plans and movements. The emeralds complicated things a bit as Ernesto didn't know he would be losing them . . .'

Popeye froze and glanced towards the cooler box, where the canister was lying on the ground. His ticket to redemption suddenly looked cruelly exposed on the *salar*.

'Ramón was too fat to climb the island and look for them,' Popeye said. 'He was coming back later with some men to do the hard work.'

The gringo roared with laughter.

'So you don't mind me taking that canister as a souvenir?'

Popeye felt like grinding his teeth. There was no point pleading for them, and he *had* been prepared to plead. If the DEA knew he had found them, it meant Piña also knew. And if he returned without them . . . He had lost count of the number of people the cartel had assassinated for stealing.

'We saw your friend signal to Ramón, and we knew he'd turn up once you had the emeralds. The thing is, reflecting the sun off a mirror isn't clever, unless you don't care who else is watching.' He pointed at Ramón. 'You know he can hear us?'

Popeye nodded.

'The guys at Fort Leonard have developed a smart nerve agent. It paralyses without the loss of sight and hearing, but the best bit is . . . the sense of pain remains.' He paused, and Popeye knew it was for Ramón's benefit. 'We use it for torture,' he continued. 'You know what, it's just a hell of a lot more relaxing if a person isn't screaming. We can carve off flesh, roast a person over a fire, electrocute them . . . all the usual stuff, without distraction. All the guys prefer to work with it now. They can listen to music and don't need to shout to make themselves heard. It's just a more pleasant working environment, and when the nerve agent wears off, the person talks. And if they don't talk, then it's another shot, back into the treatment room, and we start all over again.'

Popeye looked across at Ramón. He was wondering what form his torture would take, and the gringo turned to him.

'Test it out if you like,' he said, and reached for the coffee pot.

'What?'

'Test out the nerve agent. Here, stick this on the stove and brand him with it.'

Popeye shook his head, and the man waved the pot in encouragement.

'Go on, you won't hear a sound other than his skin sizzling,' he said. Still Popeye refused to take it.

'Listen, I know you're disappointed about Pablo Escobar,' the man continued, putting down the coffee pot. 'And I can see you're upset about the emeralds, but on a more positive note, you're alive, and you've got a bright future ahead.' He looked at Popeye. 'Fuck it. I'm not sure if I'm supposed to let you know, but . . . *amigo,* you've done such a good job.' He leant over and slapped Popeye's shoulder. 'There's a promotion waiting for you back in Medellín. Once Escobar's dead, you'll be number five in the new organisation. We've agreed to install Piña as the new cartel head, and in return he agreed to deliver Ramón and pay us three million dollars. It's a win-win situation from where I'm standing, and there's a lot more money to be made.'

Popeye looked down at his feet. His heart told him that El Patrón would never have colluded with the DEA, and that was probably the reason why he was being replaced with a more amenable individual. Popeye *had* been used to do the DEA's dirty work, and it was the gringos who were growing richer, not the poor in Medellín. Once more, he knew his decision to quit the life of a sicario was the right one. Piña had betrayed the very essence of what he was doing, and Popeye did not even have the emeralds as compensation.

The gringo got up and walked over to Ramón.

'Hello, Fat Toad,' he said, and delivered a crack across his head. 'Where's that emerald crown you said you'd be wearing?' Then he walked over to the canister, picked it up and gave it a shake. 'Ah . . . you didn't have time to make it? No problem. We're taking you across to Paraguay. Maybe you'll have time to take a look into it when we get there?'

CHAPTER FORTY-SEVEN

Gustavo Guzmán beamed at the camera, and ATB News transmitted his smile into the bars and living rooms of the nation. It was another newsflash that interrupted the early evening soap operas, justified on this occasion by the conclusion of the manhunt that had gripped Bolivia.

'Yes, Jorge, that's right. The hunt for the demonic killer that demolished half of Potosí has reached its end. The body of Jhon Velásquez can be seen behind me.' He pointed at some teal-green-covered legs and a beige sweatshirt. 'A blanket has been placed over his head and shoulders to protect the sensitivities of our viewers. The evil assassin was shot in the face at point-blank range, and the police have had to rely upon witness statements to identify him. Through diligent police work they managed to track down some Red Cross labels in his clothes to a small mining community near Potosí. Jhon Velásquez had been hiding there for the past week, and the community were able to identify his distinctive clothing.' The hint of a smile appeared on Gustavo's face. 'Jorge, it appears on this occasion, the old saying "he who lives by the sword dies by the sword" came true.' He gave the camera a nod of approval.

'And do we know exactly what took place, Gustavo?'

'Well, Jorge, this is where things become complicated. If we take a look behind me, you can see we are in the middle of a remote location where drug use and prostitution were widespread, and it has been confirmed to me by an unnamed source that arrests were about to be made before this unfolded.'

'And do we think Jhon Velásquez was involved in this activity?' Jorge asked.

'Undoubtedly, Jorge. He was a known human trafficker as well as a drug dealer. Another unnamed source confirmed some of the girls he brought to these events were as young as thirteen.'

'That's appalling. Do the police have any idea who killed this monster?'

'No, not at this stage. They're still making enquiries. It's believed a large number of people attended the event, and they're appealing for witnesses to come forward.'

'We've been told the police have arrested an individual who was found on the scene. Can you tell us any more about that, Gustavo?'

'Yes, Jorge. A young man, believed to be American, has been arrested on suspicion of organising the event. A large quantity of narcotics has been recovered and he's helping police with their enquiries. At this stage it's unclear whether or not he's a suspect in the murder enquiry. He was found semi-comatose in a tent, having consumed a large quantity of class-A drugs, and he may have been unable to hold a gun, never mind pull a trigger. My sources tell me he almost collapsed when he saw the body of Jhon Velásquez, and he was clearly shocked by the death.'

'But he's the man who organised these depraved parties?'

'Yes, that's right, Jorge. Although he denied all knowledge, four sets of car tracks clearly indicated up to fifteen or twenty people were at the event, including the prostitutes. It's believed he used a simple signalling system to confirm the date, twenty-four hours before it started.'

'Can you explain that to our viewers, Gustavo?'

'Sure, follow me,' he said, and beckoned the viewers to join him.

The camera followed him past the tent and up to a small rocky outcrop on the edge of the island. As they approached it, a shovel could be seen sticking up from the ground and the sun was glinting off its edge. Gustavo crouched down and the camera followed him. The shovel was lodged in a plastic pipe and a short length of rope had been tied around its handle. Gustavo gripped it.

'This is a rudimentary signalling base, Jorge. The gringo . . . er, American, couldn't risk organising his parties over the radio for fear of the authorities discovering them. This pipe had been sunk into the ground and the shovel was used to work a rudimentary Morse code. Using the rope, it was rotated to catch the sun and communicate with another post. It's ancient technology, used by the Greeks; they called it a "heliograph". My sources tell me the criminals had agreed provisional dates for the entire year and the communication posts were manned over those periods.'

'That's quite a set-up, Gustavo.'

'That's right, Jorge. It's clearly been going on for some time and has been well organised. For anyone doubting the devastating effect that drugs have on our country, I would just tell them to come to the Salar de Uyuni. Maybe the *cocaleros* and Evo Morales would think twice about—'

Jorge cut him off.

'Gustavo, sorry to interrupt you. Is there anything to explain why Jhon Velásquez was killed on the *salar*, of all places?'

'Yes, the police are confident it was a drug-related killing. A long black canister was discovered lying beside the pipe. It was empty but had clearly been used to transport drugs. Most likely, Jhon Velásquez had been selling drugs at the event and there was an argument over the price he was charging. He was a heavy drug user and well known to fund his own habit by over-charging customers.'

'And the police have confirmed the presence of drugs using the new technology now available to them, Gustavo?'

'No, Jorge, it was confirmed on the scene without the need for any further tests. There was a residue of cocaine in the canister, and a highly incriminating message was found inside it.'

Gustavo fished out a piece of paper from his pocket.

'Yes, Jorge, the police told me the following message was rolled up inside: "You found me over the rainbow, now I'm sparkling in your hand. Use me well, my friend, and enjoy your trip across foreign lands."' Gustavo shook his head. 'Jorge, this is a clear reference to hallucinogens. The level of debauchery that took place at this natural wonder can only be imagined . . .'

CHAPTER FORTY-EIGHT

R amón blinked. He was strapped to a gurney and his legs were slightly raised. The light was dim and the room had a strong smell of antiseptic. There was a slight slurping sound as though something was being sucked up a tube, and every two or three seconds, a sharp *ping* rang out from behind his head.

Although he was no longer paralysed, he could barely move his head. He was in a green surgical gown and his feet had turned purple. In alarm, he glanced at his hands and saw they were swollen. He could wiggle his left index finger, but none of the others moved, and a large clamp had been tightened around his right index finger.

A figure in a blue mask and a white surgical gown walked up to the gurney. He had thinning blond hair, and Ramón got a whiff of aftershave as he bent down and fiddled with something; then the slurping turned into a gurgle. He stood up and winked at Ramón.

'Hello, Fat Toad.'

Ramón's eyes darted around the room in panic. He was either in a clinic or laid out on an operating table. The floors were sparkling white, and the walls were covered in small ceramic tiles that stretched up to the ceiling. A huge metal sphere was directly above him. The man reached up to it and an operating theatre light burst into life. Ramón was blinded. His heart raced and the pinging went into overdrive. He went to speak and nothing came out. His throat was dry and he was sweating profusely.

'Welcome to the Body Transplant Clinic.'

The words had a chilling effect and the gurgling took on a new menace. He knew it was the DEA agent, and he was completely at his mercy. He twisted his head to avoid the dazzling light. A tall trolley with thick black wheels and a bright red finish was up against the wall. It looked like an oxygen cylinder trolley, except it was holding a long glass tube, not a hollow metal cylinder. There was a chrome band around its neck and a thick cannula was coming out of its top. Ramón's eyes followed it across the floor. It went underneath the gurney, and blobs of a yellow fluid were coursing through it. The gurgling was coming from a large diaphragm in the glass cylinder. As it rose and fell, Ramón's body fat was being vacuumed into the huge glass phial, and it was a quarter full.

'It will take ten hours to liposuction you to death, Ramón Emilio Escobar Sanchez.'

The words had a hollow ring, and when the theatre light cut out, Ramón was left in darkness with only the *ping* of the cardio machine and the gurgle of the diaphragm to mark down his time.

REDEMPTION

September – Raul's Bar

CHAPTER FORTY-NINE

It was a Saturday afternoon and Boca Juniors were playing River Plate in the match of the season. The bar was packed and there was no question which team had the men's support – each tackle made by Boca Juniors was cheered and every decision that did not go their way was booed. Almost everyone was drunk and the air was thick with cigarette smoke.

Santiago tapped a cigarette on an ashtray and craned his neck towards the television. A long ball was flying towards the Boca Juniors' star striker, Sergio Martínez, when a crunching tackle sent him to the floor and a howl of outrage rose from the bar. Santiago jumped to his feet as half the Boca Juniors' team surrounded the referee and started jostling him. The referee was having none of it, and pushed them away and sprinted across to the linesman. After a brief discussion, he ran back and pointed straight at the penalty spot, and a roar of approval filled the room. The men crowded around the television and Santiago joined them.

Martínez had just placed the ball on the spot, and he was turning round for his run-up as Popeye strolled into the bar and picked out his man. Martínez swept some hair from his forehead and ran up to the ball. Popeye let a thick metal tube slip out of his sleeve and drop into the palm of his hand. There was a slight shimmy of Martínez's hips, the goalkeeper went the wrong way and the room erupted. Popeye pressed a set of blunt prongs into Santiago's back; Santiago's body convulsed sharply and his arms went into a frenzy. The commentator shouted, 'GOOAAAL,' and the men cheered. Santiago roared in pain and his head shook wildly. Popeye delivered another burst of high-voltage electricity to see if he could take the convulsions to another level; he couldn't quite manage it, and Santiago collapsed against him.

Santiago staggered out of the bar supported by Popeye, and neither of them received the slightest glance, as Sergio Martínez was busy with his gyrating celebration and the men were toasting his wonderful talent.

Once they were outside, Popeye headed for a narrow alleyway, and Santiago slumped against its wall.

'You're lucky it was just a stun gun, *cabrón*. Tell me where you've been keeping Martín's family or you'll get another blast, this time in the temple,' said Popeye. 'If this was last month you would be dead,' he added as the man slipped to the ground. 'You've caught me in a reflective period and I'm abstaining from violence . . . for the time being, at least.'

Santiago's eyes were starting to glaze over, and Popeye wondered if he had even heard him. When he raised the stun gun to Santiago's head, his arm rose weakly, and it was clear that he had been listening.

'No, please, *señor*. You've got the wrong man,' he said, struggling with his words. 'I'm Sergio Martínez, not Santiago Flores. I play for Boca Juniors . . . I'm their top striker.'

Popeye stared at him. The man was clearly hallucinating. The high-voltage electricity and alcohol must have scrambled his brain, and there was a residue of cocaine on his upper lip.

'Okay, Sergio. Tell me where you've been keeping Martín's family and I'll send you straight back to your team in Buenos Aires.'

Santiago nodded towards his trouser pocket and whispered something.

'What?' Popeye asked.

'In my pocket . . . the key.'

Popeye pulled out a key with a large fob and an address written on it.

'And this is where they are, *cabrón*?' Popeye raised his stun gun and Santiago nodded.

The man was broken, and Popeye believed him. He had dialled the stun gun to maximum and it was enough to stop a bull, never mind a slightly overweight Bolivian. He pulled him up and led him slowly down the alley and across the scrubland to the Rio Mapiri. A large rubber balloon and a collection of yellow straps were waiting for them there, next to a tall tree.

'Shirt and trousers off, like you're going to work.'

Santiago followed the orders as though he were on automatic pilot, and his daily routine came to him easily.

'Grab the balloon and take off the screw top.'

Popeye then tied Santiago to the balloon with four sets of ratchet straps, one over each shoulder and between his legs, and the other two across his hips and waist. He looked like a man lost in another world, confused, with his arms hanging by his side and struggling to stand up.

Popeye stepped back and addressed him.

'Your actions killed my friend Martín, and I almost died in the process. In a previous life I would have responded with a bullet, and that bullet would have been justified. Right now I'm on the path to redemption, and I no longer take these matters into my own hands. I let providence decide the fate of those who I think deserve to die, not my Beretta.'

Santiago had collapsed on the balloon and bounced onto his side.

Popeye stood over him as he lay on the ground.

'If the river washes you towards the bank and the balloon comes to rest on a narrow spit, you can look on today as a lesson. If it fills with water and spins you under, then you'll meet your maker this afternoon and you can explain how it was you ended up there. Your legs are free. Use them wisely and you can paddle to safety.'

As the balloon splashed into the river it brought Santiago round, and as he bobbed away, Popeye turned back to the small town with a key in his hand and a smile on his face.

CHAPTER FIFTY

Two weeks later Popeye was in Asunción, the capital of Paraguay. Martín's family had been rescued and it was Popeye who had delivered the news of his death. He had intended to give his friend a tenth of the emeralds, worth close to three hundred thousand dollars; instead he gave his wife a third of the precious stones and made her promise to contact him should she ever be in trouble or in danger. He also warned her not to return to Rurrenabaque and to avoid Luis, as Popeye still did not know the full extent of his complicity.

There were only a few loose ends to tie up before he returned to Colombia.

A short man came into his office with slicked-back hair and an envelope. Popeye had spent the past week setting up a trust fund, opening bank accounts and selling his emeralds; now all he had to do was double-check the trust deed and sign it in a notary's office. The Velásquez Education Foundation in Antioquia (or VEFA) would fund the education of deserving children throughout the Antioquia region, where Medellín was the capital. Popeye had selected two trustees to administer VEFA, and he had retained an overriding vote; now all he had to do was check everything was okay with Piña before he got on that plane home.

Popeye thanked the man for the documents and told him to close the door on his way out. Walking over to the window, he watched him cycle down Avenida Colón towards the docks, and as the man turned the corner, part of him would have like to have followed. Were Popeye not needed in Colombia to set up the charity team then he might have been tempted to disappear on a boat down to Argentina; instead, he turned back to his desk and put the thought from his mind. He knew he could no longer put off the inevitable and picked up the phone.

Popeye had been out of contact for nearly a month and was unsure how the call to Piña would go. The phone rang several times before it was answered.

'Piña?' Popeye asked.

There was no reply, just a crackle on the other end, then a voice came through:

'Where have you been?'

Popeye had rehearsed his response.

'Recovering from my injuries, *hermano*, and finding a safe route into Paraguay. I was almost killed in Bolivia; I would be dead if it were not for the DEA.' Popeye was not sure if Piña knew that they had rescued him, and he wanted to see whether he would admit to his involvement with the agency.

'I know. They're working for me. I told them to rescue you.'

It was not the reply he had been expecting.

'What? DEA are working for *you*?'

'That's right. Think of them as paid muscle, except on a level way higher than you sicarios.'

Popeye had expected him to ask about the emeralds and *maybe* confirm his involvement with the DEA – not tell him he had won the lottery! If he had really bought off the DEA (and not just a few rogue agents) then he was unstoppable. Popeye was stunned and needed time to think it through. He turned to the subject of the emeralds as he tried to take it in.

'I found the emeralds, but the DEA took them, along with Ramón.'

'I know. Ramón's dead and the canister was full of plastic beads.'

Popeye wondered if he was about to be caught out.

'Okay. If they're still out there . . . do you want me to go back for them?'

'No, forget about them. I need you in Medellín for an important job, not scratching around in Bolivia.'

261

'I'm no longer—'

Popeye was about to tell him he was no longer working as a sicario, but Piña stopped him dead.

'Get on the first plane home, *hermano*. I need you to kill Pablo Escobar for me.'

Acknowledgements

My thanks to Christian Hayes (editing), Toby Selwyn (proofreading), Pulp Studio (cover design) and Hewer Text (typesetting) – what a thoroughly nice bunch of people. Your support and encouragement along the way made all the difference!

Finally, once more I need to thank my wife, Wendy. Had she not braved long bus journeys, tolerated the freezing *altiplano* and put up with challenging accommodation in South America then this story would never have been written.

Afterword

Paul grew up in 1970s High Wycombe when TVs
were as wooden as the sitcoms, sherbet flying saucers
cost 2½p a hundred weight and platform shoes were
both cool *and* great for toe-punting footballs.

He lays no claim to having books published in multiple languages,
but he's taught karate in Tibet and Bolivia, half built swimming
pools in Sydney and recently worked as a surveyor in Soho.

Paul lives in the Chilterns with his wife and ancient cat.

—

A big thank you for reading *The Man with the Silver
Beretta or Redemption* – I hope you enjoyed it.

If so, and you have a spare moment – please review the
novel on Amazon. Even better, subscribe to my mailing
list on *www.paulkellyauthor.com* and receive updates
on the next book in the series, plus a link to a free
download of *Plata o Plomo (A Bullet or a Bribe)*.

Of course, if you have not read the first book in the series, *The Man on the Rubber Balloon or Optimism*, you'll find it on Amazon.

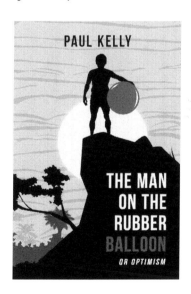

Printed in Great Britain
by Amazon